The Matchmaker's List

SONYA LALLI

BERKLEY
An imprint of Penguin Random House LLC
1745 Broadway, New York, NY 10019

Copyright © 2017 by Sonya Lalli

Previously published in the UK as *The Arrangement*.

BERKLEY and the BERKLEY & B colophon are registered trademarks of
Penguin Random House LLC.

Library of Congress Cataloging-in-Publication Data

Names: Lalli, Sonya, author.
Title: The matchmaker's list / Sonya Lalli.
Other titles: Arrangement
Description: First edition. | New York: Berkley, 2019. | Originally
published: London: Orion, 2017, under the title: The arrangement.
Identifiers: LCCN 2018009615| ISBN 9780451490940
(trade pbk.) | ISBN 9780451490957 (ebook)
Subjects: LCSH: Arranged marriage—Fiction. | Women,
East Indian—Canada—Fiction. | GSAFD: Love stories
Classification: LCC PR6112.A483 A77 2019 | DDC 823/.92—dc23
LC record available at https://lccn.loc.gov/2018009615

Orion Books trade paperback edition / August 2017
Berkley trade paperback edition / February 2019

Printed in the United States of America
1 3 5 7 9 10 8 6 4 2

Cover art and design by Vikki Chu
Book design by Kristin del Rosario

For my grandparents

ACKNOWLEDGMENTS

First and foremost, I want to thank my parents, Anita Chakravarti and Parm Lalli. You have been my rocks from day one, and I couldn't have asked for more loving and supportive people to call Mom and Dad. Thank you for showing me what it means to live with an open heart and open mind, and for encouraging me to chase after my dreams. Any achievement to my name is not mine, but ours. None of this would have been possible without you.

I am overwhelmed with gratitude for my grandparents, Maya and Aninda Chakravarti and Surjit and Bikkar Lalli, whose sacrifice and bravery brought our families to Canada. Thank you for instilling in us the values of our culture, while supporting us when we chose our own path. Thank you Nani, for your grace, love, and selflessness; Dadima, for your generosity and laughter; Papaji, for teaching us strength and kindness; and my gentle and loving Dadu, who is with me in spirit every single day.

Thank you to my brother Jay Lalli, for challenging me to be my best self; my sister Anju Sohal, for teaching me about the real world; our baby sister Georgia Lalli, for your unconditional love; my new sister Heather Lalli, for bringing so much joy into our family; my lovely Buaji, Meena Lalli, for your patience and everything you do for our family; and my uncle Baljit Lalli, for your kindhearted and free spirit.

A huge thanks to my brilliant agents Federica Leonardis and Martha Webb for your insight, perseverance, and for believing in this book as much as I did. Thank you to my fantastic editor, Kerry

Donovan, and her colleagues at Berkley for your enthusiasm and support, and also to Katie Seaman and Orion Books for publishing the UK edition of this book.

Many thanks to Kathleen Grissom for a telephone conversation that changed my life and taught me that a woman from Saskatchewan can be a writer; to my City, University of London creative writing tutors, gurus, and friends Clare Allan, Julie Wheelwright, Lesley Downer, Bea Pantoja, Stephanie Reddaway, and Lin Soekoe; and to my mentors in both life and the law, Terry Zakreski, Ken Norman, and Dwight Newman.

I am very grateful to Saskatoon's wonderful Indian community, who have been my second family, and to my earliest readers and dear friends, Annie MacDonald, Beshmi Kularatne, Sasha Kisin, Sofie Riise, Crystal Robertson, Qi Jiang, Anusha Jegadeesh, Kanika Sharma, Nick Vassos, Liz Miazga, Fafa Ahiahonu, Stephanie Hernandez, Mike Fowler—and of course Raina Upadhyay, my heroine's namesake.

Finally, I want to thank my husband, Simon Collinson, for putting up with me through all the highs and lows of this process. You have brought balance into my life and have believed in me through every twist and turn. Thank you for sharing this experience with me.

The Matchmaker's List

BOYS FOR MY RAINA

Sachin—Reetu's son in Scarborough, some kind of doctor—birthday lunch??

Jagmohan—Pinky's nephew in Jodhpur (visiting Canada this summer?)—but may be looking for immigration

Jayesh—Sharon's cousin, science professor at university . . . ~~divorced~~!!!

Rohit—Sarla's nephew, lawyer in Boston

Arjun—Sonia's son, pediatrician, probably will want to have babies soon!

Vishal—Bengali boy, also likes business things—but may be too short

Rahul—Sarla's physiotherapist, says he very good-looking boy ☺

ONE

Nani opened the front door as I was still crossing the lawn. Her nose twitching, she looked me up and down as I forced myself up the steps.

"Is *that* what you're wearing?"

I shrugged and glanced down at my weekend jeans, my favorite checked shirt. It's what I always wore home during one of my weekly visits, but I supposed today wasn't an ordinary day.

I was twenty-nine today, and walking into an ambush.

"I was hoping you would dress up, *nah*? We have guest."

A *guest*. A guest implied a cup of chai and a tray of sweets quickly defrosted from the Deepfreeze. A guest was small talk, compliments, gossip.

A *guest* was not an unannounced blind date chaperoned by your grandmother.

"What kind of guest?" I asked evenly, deciding not to tell her that my best friend, Shay, had already warned me about the blind date. Nani didn't answer the question, clucking her tongue as I bent over and brushed a kiss on the top of her head. She smelled the way she always smelled, like cocoa butter and roasted cumin. A touch of garlic. She stepped back and continued her evaluation, her tiny fingers pinching at the fleshy part of her chin as I kicked off my shoes.

"Find something more suitable." She flicked her hand up the staircase, and I bounded up the stairs to the second floor, knowing full well there was nothing nicer in my old room. Too-large T-shirts from summer camps and music festivals where my favorite band that year had headlined. Jogging pants, the type with black or white snaps running up the leg. My old trumpet.

It was odd how little of me I kept here. But of all the places I'd lived since moving out—a dumpy apartment with Shay; a shared flat in London; and now, a new condo with my name on the mortgage—it was this house that I'd always considered home. I heard Nani calling, her voice staccato and sweet, and I ran a brush through my hair and then made my way back downstairs.

She looked up at me expectantly. "Nothing?"

"All my clothes are downtown."

She arched her brows. "Anything in guest room?"

Again, I shook my head. Mom's old room. Starch white walls and a beige linen duvet, not a trace of her left in the closet. Nani sighed as I reached the bottom step, evaluating my outfit one last time. And then she shrugged, squeezed my hand, and said, "Still my pretty girl. Even in *that*."

Anywhere Nani lived would always be home.

I tucked in my shirt and followed her through the kitchen, ducking my head beneath the crossbeam as we took the eight steps down to the lower level. To the "entertaining room," as Nani called it: orange corduroy couches wrapped stiffly in plastic; the walls packed with street art bought for a few hundred lire on my grandparents' one trip abroad; Lord Ganesh presiding on the mantel, a choir of porcelain Siamese cats chiming in unison. And our *guest* stood at the room's rapturous center, awkwardly in place, his dark brown skin the same shade as the varnish on the wood paneling.

"Raina," said Nani, clutching my wrist. "Meet Sachin." She dragged me closer until the top of his forehead was square to my mouth, and I tried to ignore the dull sensation in my belly. He looked vaguely familiar. Perhaps someone I'd known as a child, or seen in the stack of pictures Nani had started leaving on the kitchen table. He was quite short, albeit symmetrical—handsome even. He smiled and brought his palms together at his chest, bowing slightly to both of us.

"Hello, Raina," he said, like my name was a word he'd invented.

"Hi."

"Sachin drove far to come for your birthday lunch."

"It's your birthday?" His face stiffened. "I didn't mean to intrude."

"No intrusion, dear." She pinched his cheek. "My Raina and I are *so* happy you joined. *Nah*, Raina?"

I nodded.

"Raina is *such* a good girl. Always coming home from her busy job to take care of her nani." She gasped and turned to me. "Sachin is a busy man, too. Raina, did you know he is doctor?"

"No, I didn't." I turned to him. "My best friend is a doc—"

"I'm a cardiologist, actually." He glanced away. "To be more precise."

I clamped down on my lower lip. *Precise, or just plain arrogant?*

"Subspecialized at Columbia," he said.

"Mhm." I tried not to roll my eyes. "Is that right?"

He nodded, fingering his wristwatch. "Diverse city. Beautiful campus. One of the top programs in the country—world, even. Some might say."

"I think I've heard of *Columbia*." I folded my arms across my chest. "Is that in Cleveland?"

"Actually, New York—"

"And you're the kind of doctor that cleans teeth, right?"

Nani jabbed me on the arm, and I tried not to laugh.

"No, no. It's—"

"*Cardio*-logist. Oh! You're a sports doctor."

He shifted from side to side. "Actually, cardiac electrophysiol-ogy is a—"

Nani clucked her tongue, waving him off. "Don't listen to her. She's a silly one, my Raina." She wrapped her arms around my waist as if she were a coconspirator in the charade.

"Oh," said Sachin.

Evidently, they didn't teach sarcasm at Columbia.

"Dear," Nani said, turning to Sachin. "Would you like chai be-fore lunch?"

"Chai sounds lovely, Auntie."

She waddled up the stairs, leaving me alone with him, and I sat down on one of the couches, the plastic screeching beneath me as I settled onto the cushion. Sachin joined me a moment later, his legs spread so wide he was nearly touching me. To my dismay, he actually smelled pretty good: the way rich men tended to smell, like Dev used to smell. An understated potency that still domi-nated the entire room.

"Your nani is very sweet," he said after a moment.

"She's the best."

"What's her name again?"

"Belinda."

"Oh."

I looked straight ahead, deadpan, trying not to look at him out of the corner of my eye.

"Is that . . . Bengali?"

"No," I sighed. "Her name is Suvali."

"But, you just said—"

"It was a joke."

"A joke, right"—he let out a stiff laugh—"good one."

Growing up, everyone just referred to family friends as "auntie" or "uncle," but I still felt mildly offended on Nani's behalf that he didn't even know her name. I reclined slightly on the couch, and stared straight ahead. Lord Ganesh—eyes, trunk, and all—stared right back.

Upstairs, I could hear Nani bustling around in the kitchen. She would be setting out her favorite teacups on the silver tray Nana had bought her as a wedding present, placing teaspoons equally spaced along the paper napkins—garish, a bold red and gold—that she'd once bought in bulk at a discount store going out of business. Fifty packages for a five-dollar bill.

"Raina, hey, listen," Sachin said after a while.

"Yes?"

He played with his rounded fingernails, picking beneath them. "I really hate to ruin your birthday, but—"

"You have to go?" I asked, a little too eagerly.

"No." He flashed me a smile, two rows of square white teeth. "Don't worry. I'll stay for lunch. But I would hate to mislead you on my intentions." He looked up at me quickly, and then back at the floor. "I'm not interested."

"That's fi—"

"You seem like a really nice girl, Raina. Really nice. And I don't mean to hurt you." He sighed again. "I'm just not in that place, you know? I'm not ready for the kind of commitment that our families—that *you*—seem to be after."

I bit my tongue. The only thing I was after was for him to *leave*.

"I know, I know." He stood up and paced in front me, his hands partially shoved into his pockets. "I'm a doctor, I get it. The biology of it all just isn't fair. It's harder for women. More pressure after they—uh—reach a certain age?"

I let out a deep, writhing sigh. "It's *so* hard."

"And your nani finding you a single doctor is—" He paused and looked me dead in the eye. "Well, it's the dream, isn't it?"

A dream? More like a nightmare.

"But really, Raina, you seem like a nice girl." He knelt down in front of me and petted my knee. "*Really* nice. And I'm sure you will find someone—soon."

I resisted the urge to tell him what I really thought of him, and studied him as he crouched at my feet. Sachin was the definition of the man Shay and I had spent so many years avoiding: the *Westernized* Indian. The one who used to be captain of the chess club or math team, and although brutalized for it in high school, now threw out the stereotypes about his culture as an anecdote to make the C-cups and hair extensions laugh as he chivalrously paid for their drinks. He was the archetype who watched sports and drank beer, had the uncanny ability to mock his father's accent, yet would still want his wife to learn how to make curry the way his mother did. He was the hybrid of east and west; the immigrant mentality distilled and harnessed, his arrogance the forgivable by-product of ambition.

Sachin looked up at me and heaved out a patronizing sigh. "Are you going to be okay?"

He was also the type of man that any nani would want her granddaughter to marry, and as I patted his shoulder reassuringly, I tried to convince myself that Sachin—that *his* type—wasn't what I was interested in, either.

There seems to be a great deal of misinformation around the modern-day arranged marriage. I am often bombarded with questions by coworkers or middle-aged women sitting next to me on long-haul flights after they've picked up on the fact that I'm half Indian. After explaining to them that I was raised by the Indian side of my family, and that whichever white guy fathered me was never in the picture, they smile and tell me that being Indian is all the rage these days. And in an exertion of worldliness, I am cited anecdotes they've picked up in the frozen food section at Costco while buying paneer, or watching twenty minutes of *Dil Chata Hai* on the Bollywood channel that comes with their deluxe cable packages. They love the bright colors and gold chains. The eccentric music. The food—oh, how they love the food. And of course, they are curious about my love life. They want to know more about this whole "arranged marriage" thing, whether soon I, too, might be enlisted.

But the protocol of today's arranged marriage in my community is less glamorous than they might anticipate. It is choosing from a roster of carefully vetted men, men whose family, religion, background, values, and sometimes even astrology match your own. It is having parents who want their children to marry into the "culture," and so they hurl them against a brick wall of blind dates until one finally sticks. It is arranged dating, really; an agreement to decide quickly whether you are in love.

I grew up with dozens of girls who went this route; women fast-tracked down the aisle, business class on a nonstop flight toward happily ever after.

And they *seemed* happy.

After all, they tell me—their mouths full of champagne and vanilla cream cake, cocooned in flowing bridal *lenghas* worth as much as a new car—what was the big deal about being set up by your family? Isn't "today's arranged marriage" equivalent to being set up by a friend, or an algorithm in your go-to dating app? Aren't their chances of having a successful marriage as high as the girl who ends up marrying her one-night stand? Or the one who met her leading man in college? I am one of the very few in my generation still unmarried in my hometown, and I never know what to say. How much to smile. And so I help myself to another drink—sometimes, another piece of cake—and reverently congratulate them on their Bollywood ending.

But I always wonder what happens after the ceremonial fire goes out and the guests go home, stuffed and slightly drunk on Johnnie Walker. Nani's marriage was arranged, and unlike today's blessed nuptials, she didn't have much of a say in the matter. Her father showed her a black-and-white photo of a lanky boy with round wire spectacles, and later, someone smeared red powder on her forehead, and just like that—well, *nearly*—she was married. It was simple. Clear-cut. A transaction performed not out of love for a would-be spouse, but for one's own family.

But wasn't an arranged marriage beneath me? I wasn't *really* Indian, after all. I was Canadian. A girl who refused to feel out of place in her mostly white, middle-class suburb in west Toronto. I had Rollerbladed and held lemonade stands, rolled my eyes on "Culture Day" at school when Shay and I were forced to wear *lenghas*, the other kids crowding around us for a chance to paw at the fake crystals sewn onto the sleeves. I only saw other Indians when I was dragged to dinner parties, and at temple every Sunday. When we went bulk grocery shopping in Scarborough because the corner Safeway didn't have the right brand of lentils or coconut milk. And even though Ravi Shankar always seemed to be playing on the radio at home, and my clothes perpetually reeked of masala, I grew up fully committed to my role in what otherwise seemed to be a white narrative. I played a girl who couldn't believe in arranged marriage—not only because of the cliché of her own family shambles, but because the cynicism of her Western world, the literary fiction on her bookshelf, barely allowed her to believe in marriage at all.

So I resisted. I resisted the idea of a planned union that might make me happy. That might make Nani happy.

"Did you like Sachin?" she asked after he had left. She stood beside me as I washed the dishes, the side of her head lightly resting on my shoulder.

Did I like him? I didn't *dislike* him. After he told me he just wasn't interested, and Nani came back with the tea, the pressure had evaporated. It wasn't a chaperoned date, a three-hour festival I'd have to immortalize in the diary I'd outgrown so I could one day tell my daughters about all the silly things their father said the first time our eyes locked.

It was just lunch.

"Will you see him again?" Nani asked.

"No." I shook my head. "I don't think so."

"Don't *think* so?"

I didn't answer, and she leaned forward on her tiptoes and turned off the tap.

"You got along with him, *nah*?"

"I don't know." I turned to face her, not quite sure how to tell her I'd already been rejected. "What did you think of him?"

"Only you know what you need in husband, Raina. What you need to be happy."

"I am happy."

She wiped a fleck of foam off my neck and stared at me, attempting to read my expression the way she attempted to read English.

"I am!"

She grimaced and glanced away, as if she'd heard it, too. The urgency. The insistence. I attacked the rice cooker, knuckles and steel wool, my palms burning red in the hot water. The suds washed off, and I held it up, set it sideways on the dish rack. Why did I sound like I was trying to convince myself? I was happy, wasn't I? I had everything, less the one thing that, to Nani, defined the rest. The boxes for college and career had been ticked; only marriage remained.

She rolled up her sleeves and handed me a frying pan. Staring at it, she said, "You agreed to this."

"I know. But I said thirty."

"You're twenty-nine now, Raina. What difference is one year?"

"Yeah, what *is* the difference?" I squirted dish soap onto the pan, and set the bottle down firmly. "What's the difference if I get married now, or in five years, or *never*—"

"Don't talk nonsense."

"Really, Nani. What's the rush? Kris isn't married."

"When he's ready, he will."

"It's because he's a man."

She didn't answer. She walked around me and inspected the rice cooker propped up on the drying rack. Tapping on a spec of white caked onto the side, she handed it back to me.

"Just because he's been married before, or just because he can have children whenever he feels like it, and his *sperm*—"

"*Beta*. Enough."

She finally met my eye. The slight scowl that had formed on her face vanished, and she reached for my cheek. "A husband, a family—it will bring you so much joy. You remember how happy your nana made me?"

I wasn't so sure I agreed, but I was too tired to argue. Her hand was soft, slightly wet from the dishes, and I let my head rest against it.

"You remember, I told you, when I was young, my father was in army and we had to move. Moving, moving constantly—and I never had anything of my own." She nodded, pressing her lips together. "And then I had your nana. I had *family* of my own."

I turned back to the sink.

"And don't you want children?"

I sighed. "I do, but—"

"*Beta*, you are getting older. Your auntie Sarla, everyone at temple—they always ask me: Why is Raina not married? Why always at that office? You cannot marry your Blueberry!"

"It's called a BlackBerry, Nani. And I'm not picky. I'm just not ready."

"You work, and work, and life is passing by. Men are passing by. Tell me, when is the right time? When will you be ready?"

I watched the pan fill with water, bits of brown bubbling in the froth. To Nani, a man unmarried in his thirties was fine—but for me, it wouldn't be. I took a deep breath, and willed myself not to fight back.

She reached for my hand, and as her slight brown fingers interlocked with my own, that's when I realized that in my silence, I was being complicit. I realized how much I truly loved this vivacious, slightly insane little woman, and what I would do to be the only person in her life never to break her heart. I would go along with it. I would live up to her expectations, and that promise I made to her two years ago—brokenhearted and desperate for my life to make sense once again—that if I wasn't married at thirty, I'd let her make the arrangements for me.

"So we will try again?" she asked. "We will find you someone else?"

"Sure, Nani." I forced out a smile. "We'll try again."

She dried her hands on her slacks and headed into the den. "Good, stay there," she called. "I am bringing the list." A few moments later, she reappeared in the kitchen, light steps on the hardwood, a piece of loose-leaf paper fluttering like she was bidding at an auction.

Was my future husband's name somewhere on that list?

She sat down at the kitchen table and pulled out the chair next to her. Dragging her thumb along the edge of the page, she muttered names under her breath.

Did I want it to be?

I abandoned the sink and sat down next to her. Looking through the list, I feigned interest as she enthusiastically explained who each of the candidates were. Going on these dates would make Nani happy, and I supposed it didn't really matter who I wanted—or who I still wanted. *This* was happening, and with only three hundred and sixty-four days to go, the arrangements had already begun.

Sachin—Rittu's son in Scarborough, some kind of doctor—birthday lunch??

TWO

It was light out now when I left; summer, it seemed, was on its way. I ran most mornings before 6 A.M., before the commuters clogged the streets and the city became a mess of traffic, delivery trucks, and the hammering from a nearby construction site. I loved the feel of bare concrete and unbreathed air, of the urban sprawl temporarily abandoned. My legs twitched, and I picked up speed, nothing but the sound of my feet beating against the pavement. I headed north past the still-closed shops, St. Michael's Cathedral, then cut through Queen's Park. The paths were damp and crusted in last season's leaves, and as the sun peeked through the branches and the sweet scent of dew filled my lungs, I exhaled and smiled into the light. Running was how I survived sitting upright in an office chair, sometimes eighteen hours a day; how, as a child, I had learned to survive.

I ran home through the university, the boundaries of four years of my life walled in brick and mortar, paper and pencil, the glare and hum of a screen. I brushed by the buildings dotting St. George Street, each of which harbored memories that became vaguer with each run: the eastern brownstone where I had a class on political economy and advanced econometrics; the building perpetually under construction where I took a seminar on microfinance in the developing world.

Had it really been over ten years since I started university? I thought back to myself in those days: slightly skinnier, commuting back and forth from Nani's house on overcrowded buses, highlighting textbooks and writing in the margins as I awkwardly stood in the aisles. There hadn't been wild frat parties with beer pong and hours of missing memories, or shots of tequila after a Monday evening lecture.

I'd studied. I'd graduated. And, exactly according to plan, I'd gotten a well-paying job.

I was soaked by the time I completed my loop. I sprinted up the stairs of my building, and each floor greeted me with a new smell. Week-old garbage and wet dog. Compost and fresh bread. I heaved my body up the last few stairs and smelled curry—like Nani's, but tangier—from the Sri Lankan family who lived across the hall. I opened my front door, and for a moment just stood in the entrance, panting as I tried to catch my breath. It never failed to strike me how, two years after moving in, my condo still smelled of absolutely nothing.

Between scenes at the office, only a shadow of me even lived here in this catalog-clean condo with two bedrooms and a view, a gallery of wicker and eggshell and midnight blue accents. Here, there were only egg whites and salsa in the fridge, vodka in the freezer, and thanks to the previous owner, everything seemed to match but me.

I'd bought it as is a month after flying home from London and hadn't changed a thing except for the handful of framed photos I'd nailed indiscriminately to the walls. Shay and our group of high school friends at graduation next to the fridge. A rare, complete family photo hanging in the front hall: Nani and Nana, me in a frilly dress sitting on their knees, Kris and Mom standing just behind. If anyone asked, I wouldn't know how to explain each of these characters in a way that made sense, or my relationships to them all. Kris is your uncle—but grew up with you like a brother? And your mom is alive, but didn't raise you?

I poured myself a glass of orange juice and, leaving the empty carton on the counter, finished it in one long swig. But no one ever asked those questions. In the two years that I'd lived here, I hadn't had anyone over who didn't already know the answers.

I showered and changed into a linen suit, and by the time I left again, the city was awake. I turned south on Yonge Street toward downtown, maneuvering through pedestrians and lampposts as I answered e-mails on my BlackBerry. Shay was already at the diner, slumped over in our usual booth, and I slid in across from her.

"Already ordered." She leaned back, her eyes half closed, and I grabbed a sticky newspaper off the seat. There were mornings when neither of us spoke—when I read, and Shay, straight from a night shift at the hospital, napped at the table. We'd been coming to the same diner since we moved out together into a shared apartment in the building above it. At the time, she was still in medical school, but tired of living with her parents, and I'd received my first big-city paycheck. I'd get home after work and find her studying her medical textbooks at a booth, and we'd nurse our free refills of coffee beneath the neon light of a decorative Hollywood sign, Shay learning how to make a differential diagnosis, while I kept her company, and stuck straws in my nose and tried to make her laugh.

Our usuals arrived: black coffee, three fried eggs and ketchup, crunchy breakfast potatoes, and four thick slices of rye; and for a while, we ate in silence. She looked exhausted, and I waited until after she'd had her first cup of coffee, and was well onto her second, to bring it up.

"Aren't you going to ask me how it went?"

"Sorry." She smiled groggily, and then nodded her head. "What was he like?"

I shrugged. "He was okay, I guess."

"Are you glad I warned you?" Shay asked, setting down her fork. She was nearly finished with her meal, and she rested her elbows on the table. "I was worried you wouldn't turn up."

Somehow, Shay's mother, Auntie Sarla, had found out Nani was inviting Sachin over—and, of course, Auntie Sarla had told Shay. Seemingly, there were no secrets in our community, and nothing Auntie Sarla wouldn't involve herself in. She was my best friend's mother, and one of Nani's closest friends, but it was hard to be in the same room with her. She judged and criticized and berated, and treated Nani and me like inferiors. She was particularly critical of her own children, even though Shay and her brother, Nikesh, had lived up to every expectation.

Sarla was a matriarch of our community, and in a way, she represented everything that was wrong with our traditions. At the same time, Nani owed so much to her—making it difficult to despise her.

After they moved to Toronto, Nani and Nana made their living as restaurant owners, running an Indian café that is now called Saffron. But the trendy, upscale establishment was nothing like it used to be: strip mall locations and empty plastic seats, Nani and Nana packing up yearly, rifling through the classified pages of the *Toronto Sun* after getting evicted. They were a homely couple, food (not business) savvy, and intent on viewing the world the way they were themselves: honest. Business parks were rezoned, neighborhoods gentrified, but more often than not, landlords took advantage. And back then, the idea of taking a slum landlord to court, asking an authority in broken English for help, was simply too foreign a concept.

It was Auntie Sarla who had turned things around for them. One of the useful features of a woman who never shut up was, well, she never shut up about their food. She and Nani became friends, and Saffron grew to be the unofficial caterer to the Indian doctors, professors, and obnoxiously rich that populated Auntie Sarla's inner and outer circles. Gradually, as Nani and Nana could afford to move the business to Roncesvalles, and brand their humble business as more grandiose, they graduated from being one of Auntie's philanthropic pursuits into full members of their community.

"Would you see him again?" Shay asked after a moment.

"Maybe. I'm not sure. But it doesn't matter, because he's not interested in *me*." I reached for my coffee. "When Nani was in the other room, he said he wasn't interested."

"In you?"

I nodded. "In me."

"Sachin, in the middle of your date, *actually* told you he—"

"Can we drop this?"

Shay bit her lip, and then nodded slowly. "Sure. Sachin doesn't matter—"

"Thank you—"

"Because I have someone else for you."

"Tell me he's not a cardiologist."

"He's one of Julien's groomsmen," she said, her mouth full again. "He spent the last ten years abroad teaching, traveling—something like that."

"You want to set me up with a drifter?"

"Asher's not a drifter. He's amazing. He's—"

"Homeless?

"Don't be bitchy."

"I'm not."

"You're being skeptical, Raina. You're *single*, it's okay, but you need to start giving guys a chance. Asher, or"—she gestured to a balding man eating alone at the counter—"that guy over there. Can't you just try and date, or do something—for once?"

I groaned at Shay's authoritative voice. Just because she had her own love life sorted, my best friend was allowed to control mine, too?

When Shay and I had lived together, I'd never taken the men that stumbled out of her room too seriously. They were disheveled, red-eyed boys who groggily waved to me as they slipped past the kitchen, Shay still sound asleep. At first, Julien seemed no different. But unlike the rest of them, he kept coming back and, recently, proposed. And so Shay got to skip the queue of suitable Indian men Auntie Sarla had been lining up for her since birth, opting for the debonair French Canadian boy in her class, the fellow pediatrician.

She didn't need an arrangement. And I couldn't help but think, then why did I?

Shay's eyes flicked back from the balding man and onto my plate, and I pushed my last piece of toast toward her. She lunged for it, watching my face as she stripped the edge off with her teeth.

"So Sachin's a no." She looked up at me hopefully. "Asher is . . ."

"A no."

She took another bite of toast. "Last week I met a few residents from South Africa. There's one who might—"

"Actually," I said, looking at my hands, "I've already decided to start dating."

"Really?" Shay nearly screamed.

"Nani gave me this . . . list. I told her I'd look it over, maybe start making a few calls."

"Can I see it?" She grabbed my purse. "Is it in here?"

I watched her rifle through my bag and dump its contents onto the table—Kleenex, pens, tampons, passport, and all. She eventually found it, and started scanning the list.

"Nani knows them through the temple, or they're friends of friends, or—"

"My cousin Rohit is on here!"

"Have I met him before?"

She shook her head. "No. He is *such* a jerk. Even Ma knows that. I don't even want him at my wedding."

"Why would Nani put him on the list then?"

"I guess because he's"—Shay shrugged—"well, *single*."

"So she'd rather have me be with some Indian guy nobody likes than be alone."

"She just wants you to be happy—and *open*. You don't only have to date Indian men"—she shook the paper—"from *this* little list."

"My birthday was *three* days ago, and do you know she's called me every day just to ask if I've met anyone from the list yet? If I've e-mailed or called any of these guys?" I shook my head. "A date I find online, or one with *Asher* or that bald guy, isn't going to be enough."

"So you're really going to do this then. Date, and"—she hesitated—"marry one of them?"

I didn't answer, and watched Shay as she deliberately crossed out Rohit's name with my pen.

"So this is . . . it," she said after a moment.

"I guess so."

"But I've never pictured you with an Indian, Raina."

I shrugged, and reached for my coffee. An Indian—one, in particular—was the only man I'd ever pictured myself with.

~~Rohit—Sarla's nephew, lawyer in Boston~~

<u>Absolutely NOT</u>

Date #1

"So here we are," Vishal said, tugging at the sleeves of his white collared shirt, which were sticking out from his navy blue suit. I looked down, wondering what kind of omen it was that I was wearing virtually the same outfit.

"Have you been here before?"

I shook my head. "It just opened, didn't it?"

"It's been two years, actually."

"Two years?" I glanced around the coffee shop, one that I could have sworn until recently used to be a take-out sushi joint. "Are you sure?"

"Positive."

A waiter brought us each a latte, and I tried to brainstorm conversation topics as I laconically stirred a packet of sugar into my cup. Had it only been one week since I turned twenty-nine? For a woman who once spent three months deciding on what handle she wanted as an e-mail address, Nani sure didn't waste any time.

Within days of receiving *the list*, I'd received a text message from Vishal—the fellow Bengali boy who also liked "business things." Unfortunately, he happened to work in the building next door to my office, and I wasn't able to find an excuse not to see him.

I thought I'd be nervous, but I wasn't. It was like having an awkward meet and greet with a client, or a job interview for a position you really didn't want. He wasn't *that* short, and sure, he was handsome—but within thirty seconds of shaking hands, I could tell we lacked chemistry. Or for that matter, failed to have anything in common. Funny how Nani thought that we could be a match made in heaven just because we both worked on Bay Street and understood how the stock market worked. The conversation was stilted, awkward, but eventually we found some things to talk about. Afterward, I insisted on paying for my own coffee, and then he walked me back to my office. Shaking my hand, he held eye contact just a bit too long. Was he also thinking about how he would spin this date to his family? I was about to joke that we should make up an excuse together for why there wouldn't be a second date, when he sighed loudly.

"Look, I'm dating someone. I have a girlfriend."

I guffawed. "Are you kidding me?"

"I'm sorry—"

"Don't say sorry to *me*," I said, crossing arms. "You should be saying that to your girlfriend!"

"I know, I know . . ."

"What on earth are you doing?"

"My mom doesn't like the fact that she's not Indian. And she's been on my case to meet you for months." He shrugged. "I just thought this would make everything easier."

"On you, maybe."

"I know." He shrugged. "This was a stupid idea."

"Stupid is an understatement, Vishal."

He smiled at me for the first the time. He didn't seem so dull when he smiled, and I half wondered whether we would have been friends had we met under different circumstances. Vishal ran his hands through his hair, and I wasn't sure what to say to him. Shay was right; Nani wouldn't care one way or the other if the guy I ended up with wasn't Indian—but that was Nani. Not everyone was lucky enough to have that.

"It sounds like you need to call your girlfriend," I said after a moment. When he smiled, I added, "And maybe stand up to your mom?"

"Perhaps." He cocked his head to the side. "But it's not like you wanted to meet *me*, either. I mean, how many times did you check your BlackBerry in the last forty-five minutes?" I hesitated, and he continued. "Sounds like *you* need to stand up to someone, too."

I nodded, even though I knew I wouldn't. What was the point of standing up to Nani? So I could let her down like the rest of her family had?

I didn't have a boyfriend, or even a prospect. The only men I met were through work—and they were all married, or single for a reason. And Dev . . . Well, Dev was nothing but a memory.

Vishal = Bengali boy, also likes business things = but maybe too short

Not single!

THREE

The humidity of early summer was starting to set in, and the air conditioners were ill prepared as the sun arched over Bay Street and streamed in through the windows. I heard the usual chatter of the break room across the hall; the slow drip of the percolator, the opening and shutting of the fridge as Emma from reception gossiped to someone in a low whisper. I sat back down at my desk, and as my wrists hovered above the keyboard, I realized I'd completely forgotten what it was I'd been working on before I'd left for coffee.

To me, *work* meant doing a lot of sinfully boring things that, regrettably, I'd once found interesting enough to get me through a minimum eighty-hour workweek without dabbling in self-mutilation. These days, I wasn't sure what kept me going. Everything had become routine. Work meant graphing variables and predicting outcomes for clients. Analyzing NASDAQ figures, Excel spreadsheets, and financial statements, and researching and sourcing investment products. It meant keeping my passport on hand and an extra pantsuit at the office just in case I needed to fly somewhere last minute to talk to or learn from people who did largely the same thing.

I'd once tried to explain to Nani the macroeconomic world and how exactly I fit into it, but she'd smiled sweetly, blankly, and then turned back to the television. She enjoyed strangers' reactions when she told them her granddaughter worked at a multinational investment bank, but that was as far as her pride went. She didn't want to understand what my job really was, or why choosing this career meant I had so little time for her, let alone anyone else.

It had been a few weeks since my date with Vishal, and I'd started texting with two other men on Nani's preapproved list. It felt wrong to have more than one guy "on the go," but Nani insisted. "Sprinkle your seeds, and see which flowers grow," as she liked to say. Arjun seemed normal, as did Jayesh—although with conflicting work schedules, I had yet to find a good time to meet either of them.

I'd overworked myself on my morning run, and my thighs and lower back throbbed. I reached up my arms and stretched, then closed my eyes. When I opened them again, Zoey's face had appeared in the doorway.

"Have a sec?" Without waiting for me to respond, she pushed through and closed the door behind her. She sat down in the chair opposite my desk, stretched out both legs, and drummed her stomach with her palms.

"You all right?"

She shrugged, and then glanced up at me slyly. "I accidentally saw Alice last night."

"Accidentally?" I laughed.

"How many weeks did I last this time?" She started counting on her fingers, and then gave up.

"Six," I said. "It's been *six* weeks since you last broke up."

"And I did really well. I didn't see her once—"

"Until last night!"

"Raina, she just showed up out of the blue. Handed me a bottle of wine, and waltzed in like nothing had happened. Like we had never broken up. And then . . ."

"And *then*?" Zoey didn't reply, and I grabbed a pen and gently lobbed it at her to get her attention.

She caught it and, blushing, set the pen down beside her. "It's fine. *I'm* fine. Really. It'll be—it'll be different this time. Won't it?"

"I may not be the best person to give you relationship advice."

"No one's perfect. You can't be worse than anyone else."

I laughed, trying to figure out what to say. Zoey was several years younger, the most junior—and intelligent—analyst on my team. I'd been assigned to train her on her first day, and by the time I'd showed her around the office and she'd laughed at one of my jokes, we were friends. Over a year later, she'd become more than that. We'd confided in each other quickly, and she'd told me about her life growing up in Canada's prairies, the difficulties she had experienced coming out as gay to her family, her on-again, off-again relationship with Alice—a law student she'd met her first week in Toronto.

I'd always considered Shay to be my best friend, but these days it was Zoey who seemed to know me best. She was the person beside whom I battled each day. These days, when Shay and I saw each other, we talked about her wedding plans, or she analyzed my text messages with Arjun and Jayesh—and then she'd lecture me about how I needed to be more "open." But Zoey and I actually *talked*.

My cell phone vibrated. It was an unknown number, and tentatively, I answered it.

"Hi, is this Raina?" The voice paused. "It's Sachin."

I covered the receiver with my palm and looked up at Zoey.

She'd heard all about the birthday ambush, and when I mouthed to her who it was, she swiped the phone from my hand and set it on the desk with a thud. She pressed the speakerphone button, and his voice, the tone now less formal, blared out.

"Hello? Hi? Is anyone there?"

"Hi," I said, slowly. "It's Raina."

"Yeah, hi! It's Sachin, the, uh—"

"Cardiologist. I remember."

He cleared his throat, his voice scratching through the room, and I tried not to laugh as Zoey gestured vulgarities at the phone.

"And how are you today, Raina?"

"I'm fine. And you?"

"Great—great, thank you. Well, no." He cleared his throat again. "Actually, I lost a patient this morning."

"I'm so sorry . . ."

"It happens." His voice trailed off, and as I caught Zoey's eye, her hands dropped slowly back to her lap.

"I had a great time with you and your nani a few weeks back," he said after a moment. "I'm sorry it's taken me so long to call."

"I didn't know you were planning to."

"Yeah . . . About that. I'm sorry I was so rude to you. My mother only told me that morning about the lunch, and I was annoyed with her. I shouldn't have taken it out on you. I'm sure you understand."

I did understand, but I didn't say anything.

"I really shouldn't have said that I wasn't interested. I hadn't even met you yet, and—well, you really are a nice girl, Raina. I am interested in getting to know you." I opened my mouth to speak, but nothing came out, and after a few seconds of static, he spoke again. "Would you like to have dinner with me?"

"Did your mother tell you to call me?" I blurted.

"No, I wanted to."

"Really."

"You're intelligent and forthright and *attractive* and—well, frankly, there's no reason why I shouldn't want to get to know you. So will you have dinner with me?" He spoke quicker, as if he had somewhere to rush off to. "Just dinner. With no pressure or anything. Just a normal date."

I listened to Sachin as he breathed heavily over the speaker, to Zoey's fingernails against her BlackBerry as she seemingly grew bored waiting for my answer.

Except for my coffee with Vishal—with whom I'd had less chemistry than my toaster—I hadn't been on a date in years, and I wasn't sure I'd ever even been on a *normal* date. My brief relationships in college had started in the library—and then there was Dev, although nothing about that date had been normal.

I could barely even remember the last time I was alone with a man. Last winter, was it? The securities seminar Zoey and I had flown to New York for last minute. Zoey had been on a break with Alice then, and she'd briefly disappeared with a woman she'd met at the hotel lobby a few hours before the flight home. Sitting there alone, I'd somehow become tipsy chatting to a broker from Atlanta. I could vaguely recall his hand grazing my waist next to the empty coat check, ignoring the longing in his glances when I refused to take a later flight home. But that was as far as it went: turning away from the kiss, forgetting the business card in an airplane seat pocket. I never let it lead to normal. I leaned forward against the desk and stared at the phone. Getting to know each other over dinner. This was what normal meant. Later, we'd go for more dinners, movies, and lunch dates—and then what? Months of sex and the superficial? A natural segue into the serious?

"Dinner," I repeated slowly, conjuring up Sachin in my mind. Indian. Intelligent. Handsome.

Nani-approved.

If I was going to do this, *really* going to do this, then it might as well be Sachin. And squinting into the glare from the window, I said, "I could do dinner."

Sachin — ~~Reetu's son in Scarborough, some kind of doctor — birthday lunch??~~

*Dinner 9:30 P.M., Tuesday @ Eldorado

FOUR

My boss, Bill, was pissed that I left work early, but Nani had insisted I come see her before my date with Sachin. After nearly an
hour battling through rush-hour traffic, I arrived home to find
that she wasn't even there yet.

She'd left all the lights on, and I walked around the house turning them off and then put the kettle on to boil. My head throbbed,
and I flopped down on Nana's side of the couch and closed my
eyes. I knew I was imagining it, but the sofa still smelled of him. I
could picture him there reading me *Little House on the Prairie*, my
head resting against his knees, impatiently tugging on the cuff of
his trousers whenever he stopped mid-sentence to sip his tea.

No one was home with Nana the morning he died, and I don't
think Nani ever forgave herself for believing him when he claimed
his chest pain was merely indigestion. Watching her lose him was
harder than dealing with my own grief. The horror of finding her
collapsed sideways on the stairs clutching his parka, her wet eyes
and nose buried in the garlicky tobacco scent of the goose down,

would never leave me. She became a widow at the age of sixty. An arranged life drastically rearranged, Nani had to start over; create a life from scratch that didn't revolve around the man to whom she'd been assigned.

It took her years, but her vivacity returned, as did the color in her cheeks. She was always practical and compassionate—most of all toward Nana and I—but these days it wasn't strange to find Nani teasing the busboys and running Saffron better than Nana ever did; driving her Mini Cooper from an afternoon tea to temple, from one charity project to another. I suppose she had to find a new balance in the equilibrium that life had imposed on her.

In a way, Nani and I grew up together. Discovered each other all over again as adults. I'd learned the way she watched the *Ellen* show, her toes wiggling in her pressure socks whenever Ellen DeGeneres and the audience danced. The way Nani showed she loved you through food—and then, through more food. The way she only called me *beta* when she was upset or irritated. How she pronounced "vegetable"—*veg-ee-table*—or invented idioms like to "take a sleep" or "open the light." English was her fourth language, she liked to remind me, after Bengali, her mother tongue, Hindi, and Punjabi. English for her came last, not until 1969 when Nana moved his new bride across the world to Canada. To the land of opportunity.

To the land of, well, *land*.

I also learned that Nani could be vain, ignorant of what didn't concern her or her own family. I'd switch on the news, or buy her a book I thought she should read, and she'd sigh like the idea of something new tired her right out. For a while, I'd tried to get her interested in politics, coming home on election night—provincial, federal, American—and she'd cluck her tongue and leave the room, annoyed that I'd disrupted her favorite Hindi soap. She thought the oil sands were polluted beaches and didn't understand why Palestine and Afghanistan, and not India, was on the news so often.

Nani had never been like the other "aunties" in the community. She wore Western clothes most of the time—Sears pantsuits and polyester sweaters—and had refused to stay home and play house. She'd worked side by side at the restaurant with Nana and kept her chin high when her teenage daughter brought home a baby. She was *modern*, generations in front of so many of her friends—small-minded women who gossiped and pettily talked about one another's children. But still, for Nani, getting married and having children was a woman's one true path.

Her daughter had become a mother too young, and now she feared I'd become one too old or not at all. But couldn't she try and understand how it worked now? Women didn't have to get married and have children anymore—and even if they did, it didn't always mean they were happy.

I was tired of arguing with her, but at the same time, maybe Nani and Shay were right: Work consumed my life, and I *was* lonely. So what reason did I have to resist?

I heard the back door open, and I leaped up. I beat Nani to the kitchen and had the tea poured into two china mugs by the time she sat down at the table. She sighed as she brought the cup to her lips, and I watched her face, the fine lines dancing and stretching as she blew on the tea.

"How was work?"

She smiled, and sank back in her chair. "I am very tired."

"I can make dinner?"

"But you will eat with Sachin, *nah*?"

"Sure, but that's hours from now."

"*Aacha*. Make some rice, and we will heat up dal I have in freezer." She took a sip of tea, and then shook her head. "But first we must discuss Sachin. I called his mother today."

"You did *what*?"

"She is in my sewing group with temple, *nah*? I had to call anyway. And then I mentioned your dinner tonight, and she grew very happy."

I groaned. "Nani, I asked you not to tell anyone."

"Reetu is his mother. She has every right to know where her son is."

"But Sachin and I said we wouldn't involve the families yet, that it wasn't any of their business until—"

"None of our business?" Nani snapped. She stared at me, and I shrunk back into my chair.

"I'm sorry, I didn't mean—"

"None of *my* business." Nani's glare tore through me, and then landed on her hands. "Your mother used to say this to me."

"I'm not like her, Nani," I said, and for several long minutes, she didn't answer.

I drove back downtown and found the door to my condo unlocked, and Shay going through my wardrobe. Nani had put me in a bad mood. Her trump card for any argument: comparing me to Mom. Telling me that I, too, wasn't good enough.

I mindlessly changed in and out of outfits Shay selected for me. Leather pants I'd bought on a lark and never wore; skinny jeans from college that, when I sucked in, still sort of fit. Work blouses paired with too-short skirts I hadn't worn since London; dresses Shay brought over, silky and static, tight or loose in all the wrong places.

"You look great," Shay said as I stood in front of my mirror, only a wisp of pale peach chiffon differentiating me from a nudist. "I'm jelly of your legs."

I whipped around. "My legs look like jelly?"

"No, it means *jealous*." She bit into an apple, crunching loudly. "It's what the kids in my ward say."

I turned away slowly, pulling down the hem of the dress. The evening before, I'd waxed and filed and moisturized and polished. Groomed and straightened. Shay, lying sideways on my bed, still in hospital scrubs, nodded or shook her head vigorously at each outfit I tried on—but still, everything felt so wrong. My clothes felt like costumes, designed to impress the guy that may or may not become my husband. I just wanted to wear one of my work suits, what I felt most comfortable in and most like myself, but I had the feeling Shay wouldn't agree.

Through the mirror, I saw Shay lean down from the bed and smirk as she felt my smooth leg.

"You're going to sleep with him."

"No, Shay." I pulled at the hem of a skirt, forcing it down past my thighs. "I'm not going to *sleep* with him."

"It's an urban myth that men won't call you after."

"And they always called you?" I saw her stick out her tongue in the mirror, and I turned around. "Sorry. I meant . . . I meant I don't even know if I like him."

"Then why do you care so much?"

"Nani's the one who cares," I grumbled.

"You did this with Dev, too." Shay got off the bed and started walking toward the bathroom. "You built everything up in your head before you even knew him."

"If you came over just to lecture me, you didn't need to bother." I turned back to the mirror, and a moment later, I heard the bathroom door shut.

I sat down on my bed. I felt the skirt digging into my stomach and the sides of my thighs. I groaned, and rolled over and grabbed my BlackBerry from where it was charging on the nightstand. I had one new text message from Zoey wishing me luck on my date, and a handful of grumpy e-mails from Bill.

I could hear Shay still in the bathroom, and so I scrolled down to Dev's last message. For more than a year after we broke up, we'd stayed in touch, e-mailing every few days or at least once a week from our work accounts. But then weeks turned into months, and that last message I'd sent him more than four months earlier had gone unanswered.

It was only a few sentences: I'd told him about Shay and Julien's engagement, a new coworker in the New York office, and then asked after his family. It was small talk; really, it was nothing. Then why was I still unable to bring myself to delete it?

I heard the toilet flush, and I stuffed my phone into my bag. A moment later, Shay appeared in the doorway. The irritation had disappeared from her face, and now she just looked tired; the dopey blue of her hospital scrubs poking out from the top of her hoodie. I wasn't sure if she'd come over straight from work, or was on her way to a night shift; I'd forgotten to ask.

"How's work?"

She flopped onto the bed beside me, and put her arm around my neck. "Okay. It's going by quickly."

"When are you done with your residency again—less than a year, isn't it?"

She nodded. "I'll be done just a few weeks before the wedding. It's perfect timing."

Her arm felt heavy, and I shifted away from her on the bed.

"Raina, my ma set the date. It's—"

"I know," I said, holding a top against me in the mirror. "Nani already told me. Don't worry about it."

Auntie Sarla had confirmed Shay's wedding date. The day Shay got married to the love of her life and fulfilled her mother's wishes would be the day I turned thirty.

Thirty.

I grabbed a cardigan from the closet, nearly tearing the sleeve as I ripped it from the hanger, and walked back to the mirror.

Perfect timing.

Date #2

I arrived early and waited outside the entrance, and at exactly 9:30 P.M., I entered the restaurant. Sachin had suggested it. It was modern looking, all burgundy and glass, and as soon as I noticed the soft smell of roasting chicken, I realized how little I'd eaten that day. I walked up to the hostess, and right behind her, to my surprise, I saw that Sachin was already there. He was seated at the end of the bar, a scotch glass nestled between his palms, watching the news on a small flat screen on the wall.

I walked slowly toward him. His suit jacket was open, a lavender tie loosened around his neck, and when I was a few feet away, he looked over and smiled.

Before I could even say "Hi," he loosely hooked his finger through my belt loop and tugged me in closer.

"Hi, beautiful."

He pulled me in for a hug. He smelled good, like whiskey and paprika, and a part of me swooned. The other part of me kicked her.

"Hi, yourself."

"What's your poison?"

"Gin and tonic?"

"Josh? Double gin and tonic." Sachin picked up his glass, drained it, and then set it back on the bar. "And another Dalmore while you're at it."

A muscular blond behind the bar threw a dishrag over his shoulder, and rolled up the sleeves of his black collared shirt. "Sure thing, Sach."

"You have a preference?" Josh asked me.

"Hmm?"

He smirked. "Of gin."

"Oh." I blushed, forcing myself to look back at Sachin. "Barman's choice."

Sachin's eyes were glossy, his smile a bit crooked, and I wondered how long he'd been sitting there; how many Dalmores he'd already drunk.

"You look amazing," he said after a moment, as if he, too, had to think about what to say. His gaze flicked between my mouth and my eyes, and I tried to think of something to say in response. *Thank you? You, too?*

A heavy silence hung in the air, and when I looked up, Josh was making our drinks less than a foot away. He smiled at me— laughed, almost—like he could feel how awkward I suddenly felt.

"Don't do that," I heard Sachin say.

"Pardon?" I looked back at him. I was playing with my bracelets, winding them rapidly around my wrist with my fingers.

"Don't be nervous." Sachin steadied my hand with his, traced his pinky finger in a circle around my palm. "Do I make you nervous?"

"Why would *you* make me nervous?"

He grinned. "Then quit acting like it."

"I'm not acting like anything."

After a few minutes of stilted conversation, Josh led us to a table at the back of the restaurant, and as we walked, I tried to ignore the weight of Sachin's hand on my lower back. It felt good, but heavy, and I wondered whether I wanted him to move it.

We were through the first bottle of wine by the time our entrées arrived. I could feel it pooling in my stomach, trickling down, and my body relaxed. The waiter brought another bottle, and as time slicked by, I tried to make a list of what I liked about Sachin; reasons that this date—that we—maybe could be something more.

Sachin was nothing like dull, distracted Vishal. Sachin was intelligent and liberal, his views extending well past the dimension of the operating room, which I hadn't expected. We had mutual friends in banking, in medicine, had spent one of our rare vacations at the same Cancún resort; even our nanis had been born in the same village. And with each course, the list of similarities and commonalities between Sachin and me grew, and I found myself again warming to the idea of being with another Indian. He, too, had been raised with a mixed bag of expectations, straddling the cusp of Western culture and Eastern values. Like most people I knew, Sachin, too, never felt good *enough*; always being compared to others.

Didn't I need an Indian man to understand that about me?

I looked down at my glass. It was full, but I didn't remember Sachin pouring more. I reached for it, and a wave of nausea shot through me. A dessert was sitting between us, thick chocolate and cream, and as I watched Sachin bring a spoonful to his lips, Dev's face flashed in front of me. And just as quickly, I made it disappear.

"I'm having a great time with you, Raina."

I had to think about the words as they came out of my mouth, and I smiled. "You—too."

"You asked me if I *cleaned teeth*. Funny stuff." Sachin pinched at a piece of stray bread on the white tablecloth until it crumbled. He looked up at me—almost past me.

Was he going to reach for my hand? I pulled my hands down to my lap and, a moment later, made myself put them back on the table. I leaned into the table, thinking maybe he might kiss me. But we were talking again—about partition? His ex? I couldn't tell. His mouth was a blur of words, and I couldn't focus on what he was saying. Just his lips. His hands. He lifted his wineglass as if to toast me, and then set it down abruptly and reached into his pocket. "Sorry." He glanced down at his phone and then set it on the table.

"You can answer it."

Dev hated it when I asked him to keep his phone off during dinner.

Sachin waved me off. "No, it's not important. Really."

"Maybe it's a patient? You should answer."

His head swayed lazily. "Raina, it's nothing." And as he leaned in toward me, the phone buzzed again. I felt the vibrations pulsate across the table and through my hands, and I didn't mean to look at the screen, but I did. *Anika.*

Sachin flipped over the phone.

"Who is that?" I whispered.

"Nobody."

"Do you have a girlfriend?"

I'd once accused Dev of having another girlfriend.

Sachin reached for my hand. I pulled it away.

"Do you?"

He pressed his hands into his thighs, looking tense, suddenly alert. "I thought we talked about this—that we're in the same boat?"

"What boat is that?"

"That we're both at that age where our parents really want us to get married, and—"

"And?"

"And Anika and I have . . . gone on a few dates. You know I'm getting set up a lot, Raina. Just like you." He shrugged. "What's the big deal?"

But Dev had never cheated. He didn't have the time. Work—always work—was his priority; above his own family; above starting his future with me.

"Do you realize Anika has probably picked out a wedding sari? And here you are playing the field?"

"Slow down—"

"A rich and handsome guy though, right, *Sach*? You can get away with it. You can get away with leading girls on—"

"Are you kidding me? This is our first date."

Our first date. He was right. I didn't know him. This—he and I—meant nothing. It would never mean anything. I could feel the tears brimming at the corners of my eyes and the sudden sensation that everything was caving in around me.

"I should have gone with my instinct on this one," I heard Sachin say. "I *knew* you'd be like this."

Vishal. Sachin. Arjun. Jayesh. They were names on a list. Names to appease Nani, to fill the page, to fill time, the gaping hole in my chest. They were nothing to me, and they would never be Dev.

I looked up, surprised suddenly to see Sachin sitting across from me. He was leaning away from me in his chair, his eyes fixated on the pepper shaker. I grabbed my purse, unsteady on my feet as I stood up. I turned around looking for the door, and flung myself forward until I felt the cool night air on my face.

Outside, Yonge Street was exactly as it was before; exactly as it was every night. Dark storefronts and eateries, dive bars giving off a sickening red glow. Clusters of kids on skateboards, bored stiff, slouching in their skinny jeans. I walked past them and took a deep breath, gulping for air.

Is this what Nani wanted?

For me to be the fool. To reduce myself to just another Indian girl desperate to get married.

I could hear myself panting, my legs like jelly as I turned onto College Street, and I waited until I was around the corner—away from the kids, their faultless youth—before I let myself cry.

~~Sachin—Reetu's son in Scarborough, some kind of doctor—birthday lunch??~~

~~*Dinner 9:30 P.M., Tuesday @ Eldorado~~

What was I THINKING!!!!

May 20, 2014

Raina turns twenty-five at 5:52 P.M. local London time. Her co-workers toast her, pints of cider and lager clinking together above the wooden pub table, the stale chips no one has yet to touch. She finishes her drink in one long swig, slapping the empty glass down in celebration. Colin's ginger hair brushes hers as he leans in and asks if she'd like another. She shakes her head and glances around the room. It's unoriginal, dank, and cold. Dark wood paneling, a brick wall boasting an oil painting of the Queen. Raina reaches for her extra cardigan, and Colin laughs at her—*with* her. She is always cold, it seems, and being from Canada, he teases her about this endlessly.

She has been living in London for several months on a shared third-floor flat just off Upper Street. It has an unfocused smell of damp laundry, burned hair extensions, Heinz beans eaten cold from the can. Raina is rarely home, but when she is, they keep the flat lively with hip-hop, Sunday roasts, and girls-nights-in. Two of

her flatmates are still students at uni—bottles and books perpetually in hand—and the third is a graphic designer with the face of a
model, and "Chatterbox Pink" lips. They are British girls, lovely
and loud, and with them, Raina feels safe.

They are a break from her sometimes sixteen-hour workdays, a
splash of color onto what would otherwise be a life walled in by the
dreary, pale demands of working in the City of London. The girls
introduce her to the real city—gigs outside Zone 1, wine bars in
repurposed churches—and also to the boys they know. Immature,
ashy brown–haired boys who find her witty when drunk, intimi-
dating when sober. To them, Raina downplays her job at the investment bank, her life among the three-thousand-pound suits
marching up and down Cheapside and Cannon Street. She was
chosen from among fifty applicants in the Toronto, New York,
and Chicago offices for a temporary transfer to the overseas office,
but these aren't the things that interest them.

Nor do *they* interest her.

His name is Dev Singh, and at present, he is a mere silhouette.

They have never spoken directly, yet two months earlier, at her
very first meeting, it was his voice she noticed first. The way he
gently commands a boardroom, she can tell he's humble. Dedi-
cated. He's a man unaware of his impact on others, and this only
affects her more.

They still haven't spoken directly, yet she's conscious of him
always. How she is slightly taller than him in heels, or the way he
crosses and uncrosses his legs when he has something to say. How
he stays at the office later than most people—even Fridays, never
joining the rest of them at the pub. Already, he is unlike any man
she has ever met. He is more than the men she talks to at clubs
through gritted teeth, her flatmates giggling nearby. The ones in
the cash-only line at Tesco. Already, he's more than either of her
college boyfriends, flings so brief, inconsequential, she often for-

gets she had them. She is startled by the way Dev affects her. She has never been attracted to an Indian man before, and this is how she knows it must be real. She knows that Dev is different.

She has already given up hope that he might turn up to the pub that evening, when she sees him. Her heart pounds. She stiffens as he walks past her, and slyly, she leans back in her chair and looks after him.

He is greeted with enthusiasm by a cluster of bankers—those more senior, sitting separate from her crowd. He leans forward against the backs of two chairs, and she struggles to hear what they are saying over the chatter, over Colin, who again asks if she'd like another pint. Dev says something she misses, and it makes the group laugh, especially the woman—Becky—who heads the fixed-income division. She throws her head back as she laughs, and the blond hairs of her ponytail catch on his suit.

Raina has never liked Becky.

After a moment, Dev turns and walks toward the bar. Raina exhales. This is it, she tells herself. Today is her birthday, and unlike any other day, she is sure that this time she will think of something to say. Witty. Original—though not overly curated. She has been waiting for a chance to approach him. To impress him. And somehow, she knows that now is the time. She counts to five before following, and as she slinks toward him, navigates through the after-work crowd, her mind once again draws a blank. Her stomach churns. She is only a few feet away, and she is considering turning back, when he looks over his shoulder and smiles.

"Ah." He leans back on the counter. "Raina Anand. Our newest import from *Ca-nada*."

She is giddy about the fact he knows her name and bites her lip to keep from smiling. She loves how he says "Canada," and her country suddenly appears elegant in her mind. She struggles not to picture him there with her, already; running to catch the streetcar on

King Street, handing Nani a bouquet of wildflowers the first time he comes for dinner.

"That's me."

"I've been meaning to swing by and chat, but—"

"But you're a busy man," she says, surprised by the evenness of her voice.

"Too busy, it would seem." He is looking at her neck. Her lips. Her hair in wisps around her shoulders. "So," he says, sliding a beer toward her. "What can you tell me then, Raina?"

She smiles coyly and reaches for the beer. As she had hoped, she knows exactly what to say.

They stand there for hours. She is dizzy from the smell of his cologne, the glasses of *hefeweizen* that keep appearing in front her. They are speaking, and at times, she has no idea what about—redemption funds and Chelsea football. The pub's fresco-style ceiling. She has never laughed so hard, been so inebriated by another human being. He is teasing her. Enveloping her. He pinches her nose, and his thumb falls slowly, parting her lips. And suddenly, they are no longer laughing.

He grabs her hand and leads her outside. Beneath the moony streets of St. Paul's, she reminds herself that she's not supposed to believe in casual sex. But the way Dev is kissing her, his fingers lightly wound through her hair, already this doesn't feel casual. Minutes pass, and then he pulls away and tilts her chin to the side. She looks up at him and cannot meet his eye, and she prepares herself to say no when he inevitably asks her to go home with him. But he doesn't ask. Instead, he thumbs the leather of her purse, wonders out loud whether she happens to have her passport.

His hand stays on her knee in the taxi as they head north on Farringdon Road toward St. Pancras station. Their wide smiles fill the back seat, and he apologizes three, four, five times, telling her that Paris would have been more romantic, more fitting for birthday spontaneity—if only the Eurostar to Paris wasn't already booked up. Brussels is perfect, she says into his shoulder. Raina has never been to Brussels, and she senses now that she'd always wanted to go.

He buys them orange juice and chicken avocado sandwiches in the cafeteria car, and as they dip beneath the English Channel, her ears pop and he tells her about growing up in West Harrow. She senses his shame as he talks about his family. She doesn't understand his resentment, but she intertwines her fingers with his and tells him that she does.

It is nearly midnight by the time they reach Gare de Bruxelles-Midi, and after hailing a taxi, Dev looks surprised when Raina begins to converse with the driver, asks him in stilted French to take them anywhere he likes. He drops them off on a lively street across from La Grand-Place. Brass lampposts and cobblestone streets, twinkle lights and fogged-in windows. Hundreds of men stripped down to their boxers parading through the square, whipping their red, sweat-drenched football shirts around like batons, chanting, "*Allez la Belgique!*"

Dev squeezes her hand as they maneuver through the crowd and onto quieter lanes. They are soon lost, and everything smells of white wine and rain. They wander past marble fountains, through alleys and impossibly green parks, and every so often, he pulls her aside—against a railing or black brick wall—and kisses her. Every time, she falls further. Becomes more convinced about the connection between them. That rushing sensation. The inability to catch her breath. And right there, on the darkened streets of Brussels, for the first time, Raina falls in love.

It's nearly dawn when they find a hotel. Dev leads her to the room, and her mind races. Her body trembles. She's twenty-five now, and a virgin. Isn't she ready?

Wasn't she waiting for *this*?

She sits on the foot of the bed, and Dev kneels down in front of her. Kisses both of her knees. And then he reaches up and kisses her, pulls down her face to his, and she's on the floor, too, pressed hard against him.

Nani's face flashes before her eyes, and then her mother's. Every time this is what has happened, and every time it's the reason she stopped.

She thinks about pushing Dev away, ending it before she becomes weak—before she becomes her mother. But he's kissing her neck, her collarbone. His tongue darts in and out of her ear, and then her mouth—and then it is consuming her. His hands around her waist, Dev lifts her to the bed, pushes her down. Raina's blouse, Dev's trousers are flung to the side, and with them her doubts. With Dev, she's alive, finally, and nothing can stop her.

Date #3

I followed Arjun's eyes, which were glued to a chubby-cheeked Asian toddler with a Spider-Man hoodie and chocolate on his face. He was perched on the shoulders of his dad, yawning and at the same time attempting to have another lick of his ice cream cone.

"Adorable." Arjun squeezed my forearm. I tried not to flinch. "Isn't he *just* the cutest?"

"Very cute," I admitted, subtly drawing my arm back. What had Nani written on that list, which was now buried somewhere at the bottom of my handbag? Arjun was a pediatrician, so he probably wanted to have kids soon? She wasn't kidding. Arjun and I had been at Canada's Wonderland for several hours, and he'd already pointed out a dozen children to me. All of them Asian. All of them spitting images of him. Gulp, or *me*.

"Do you have any nieces or nephews?" He hesitated, probably realizing I'd already told him I was an only child. "Or small cousins?"

I shook my head, as we shuffled forward in line for the park's largest roller coaster. "My experience with children is limited."

"Ah."

"But I like kids of course." I attempted a smile. "You know, my friend Shay and her fiancé are both pediatricians, too."

"Oh, Shaylee Patel? Yes, I'm *sure* I've met her." The roller coaster sped over us, and Arjun rubbed his hands together in delight. "I'm so excited! This one's my favorite."

"I've never been to Wonderland."

"No?" Arjun smiled at me, and then rested his hand gently on my shoulder. "Clearly, no one's ever spoiled you before."

The line trudged forward, and the optimism I'd embraced at the beginning of the date waned. After Shay had scolded me for overreacting with Sachin, never mind getting plain drunk on a first date, I decided I needed to try anew. Try to make an effort with the men Nani had selected. And so when both Arjun and Jayesh asked me if I had plans the following Saturday, I cleared my calendar and tossed a coin.

Heads for Arjun.

He was lovelier in person than he was via text message. Respectful. Sweet. Fun. Attractive. He'd mentioned in passing that he'd broken up with a long-term girlfriend just months before, and I knew this sort of guy wouldn't be single for long. Everything about Arjun seemed suitable, and appropriate, but as the attendants buckled us into the ride, it struck me that I was entirely bored. Not bored with him, but with myself. Who exactly was I pretending to be meeting him? A nice Indian girl devoted to her nani? A hardworking investment analyst with high-flying ambitions—that is, until she became the mother of our adorably South Asian babies?

Arjun wanted to marry a woman like the character I was playing. He wouldn't want the real me, and by the end of the dizzying ride, I was confident that I didn't want to play that role for him, either.

When we parted ways in the parking garage, I let him down gently. Afterward, I fished the list out of my purse, found a pen in the glove box, and crossed out his name. Sure, maybe there wouldn't be anybody on this list that was *more* right for me than Arjun, but I knew I was doing him a favor. There was bound to be an amazing woman on Arjun's own list who'd feel lucky to have him.

~~Arjun — Sonia's son, pediatrician, probably will want to have babies soon!~~

Has B-A-B-Y fever!

FIVE

The clear blue skies of summer continued. The bodies of Bay Street moved at a slower pace, stilled by the humidity, the souring heat coming off the Great Lakes. Summer had always meant studying and taking temp jobs at the library or as a research assistant. Coaching community basketball. Now, summer blended into the rest of the year.

My job felt stagnant, even mindless, and at least twice a day I'd find myself lying on my keyboard staring sideways at a pile of papers, eyes blurred, until one of the senior bankers' voices in the hallway startled me upright. When I was dating Dev, I'd loved my job. Or had I? He'd traveled abroad for work every few days or weeks, and when he was in London, we both spent most of our waking hours in the office. But we'd been happy. We'd made it work, although I had no idea how. London felt so long ago, and a heavy fog seemed to block me from remembering the details.

I broke up the summer monotony as best I could. There were

rooftop bars or music festivals with colleagues after work; midnight movies alone at the cheap theater near my condo; short weekends away at a cottage with Zoey and Alice—now back together "for good"—and other friends, complete with chopped logs and icy beer, sunbaked split ends and aloe vera for the drive home. And, of course, there were my morning breakfasts with Shay—although because of the wedding plans and conflicting work schedules, I saw her less and less. When we did see each other, she was distracted by the latest wedding crisis, and I'd get snappy at the mention of Auntie Sarla or Nani, and one of us would end up making an excuse to leave early. Because Nani had been a young grandmother, and Sarla had had Shay in her early thirties, the two women were close in age—and "close competitors." Seemingly, all they wanted to talk about these days was Shay's impending nuptials, and the fact that mine were still TBD.

I *thought* I was making progress on the list—although, according to Nani, two first dates that didn't turn into first husbands didn't count as progress. Sachin was a tool. Vishal wasn't single. Arjun was—well, not the one. I went to Nani's house after leaving Wonderland, and after I had made up excuses about how Arjun and I weren't a good match, she squished up her face as if she'd stuck a lemon beneath her tongue, and said, "Not him, *too*?" Nani was young enough to be my mother, but the generation between us could feel endless. Raising my mother, raising *me*, had made Nani modern quickly. Unwillingly. But she still couldn't understand that women no longer needed to get married.

Was that unfair of me? Hadn't I wanted to get married? Fulfill every fantasy and stereotype? How many hours had I wasted wondering when Dev would propose, envisioning garlands of marigolds and traditional saris, silk drapery and bhangra music. Dev in a kurta pajama, and everyone in my family—for the first time—sitting peacefully in the same room.

One Sunday in late August, the first day in over a month where I had the option to sleep in, Nani insisted I come home and spend the day with her. I relinquished my plans of sleeping off my hangover, of spending the day on the balcony with a tub of ice cream and the book I'd been meaning to read for over a year, and instead, Nani and I made paratha.

It had been years since I'd helped her in the kitchen, and I was proud of the result. Parathas, gold and flaky, smothered in butter, stuffed with spicy *aloo*. After, we ate them beneath the backyard awning, cooling ourselves down in the lazy summer breeze. Nani had slipped a disk in her back the summer before, and I'd hired a neighbor's son to mow the lawn, to trim the hedges and plant, while Nani pointed and prodded, sat on a stool as she instructed him on how she wanted the beds arranged.

"Andy's doing a good job with the yard," I said, yawning, admiring the lawn, almost a forest green.

"What is *that*?" She reached forward and pulled at my ear, and then squinted at the blue paint that rubbed off onto her fingers. "Paint?"

"Um, yes?"

"*Vhy*? Are you renovating your apartment? This is not a good color."

"No. I went to a—uh—pride party last night." I thought back to the evening before—Zoey, Alice, me, and some of our other friends bodysurfing, drunk off electronica music at a warehouse in the Gay Village—and decided to leave out the details.

"Pride?" she asked after a moment.

"Like, you know"—I hesitated—"a celebration for LGBTQ—"

"Huh?"

"For gay people, Nani. It was a party celebrating gay people," I said, trying to rack my brain for the most straightforward way of explaining the term. "I went with my friends. With Zoey—you remember her, right?"

"Oh. Was Ellen there?"

"Ellen DeGeneres lives in Los Angeles."

"But I thought you said you were too busy this weekend to see Jayesh. His mother is calling me *many* times."

"I was busy," I grumbled, refusing to feel guilty about the fact I kept postponing my date with Jayesh. "I was at the party."

"Raina . . ." She clucked her tongue. "You are pushing luck—just like your mother used to. Please *try*. Jayesh comes from very good Hindu family."

"So he's automatically perfect for me?"

"I am not a silly woman." Nani sighed, and turned to face the lawn. "His family is very educated, very stable. These things become important in raising children. *Values* are important."

"Being Hindu. Being . . . Indian." I buried my toes into the dirt in front of me, twisted them in the damp earth. "Is that what's important to you?"

"*Nah*, Raina. Julien is Catholic, he is white—and look, your Auntie Sarla is fine with it. Please just stop looking for things that are wrong. They are men. White, brown, yellow, blue; they all have *something* wrong with them." Nani guffawed. "Just pick one!"

I knew she was trying to be funny, and so I laughed. But I had picked one—and in the end, Dev wasn't ready to get married. Did that mean I should just pick another now? One that I liked well enough, and one day could maybe fall in love with?

I watched the geraniums shudder as the sun grew fierce. I checked my watch. It was nearly noon, and our temple's Sunday service usually went until 1 P.M.

"Nani, you want to go to the *mandir*?"

"*Aacha?*" Nani smiled, and sitting forward on the lawn chair, she squeezed my chin. "Okay, let us go."

Our temple, all limestone and Mughal-influenced architecture, was only a ten-minute drive away. It sat at the edge of a public park, its grounds clean lines of lawn and concrete. The puja was already under way as Nani and I walked in. The front altar was decorated with tin bells and displays of fruit and sweets, rose petals, shiny jewelry, and garlands strung of marigolds. Nani maneuvered her way through the crowd toward the front where she always sat with Auntie Sarla, and I lingered near the back searching for space on the crowded floor.

I was surprised to find Shay sitting against the back wall. Both of us went to temple so rarely these days that I figured she would have texted me about it beforehand to see if I wanted to go, too. She made room for me, and I sat down and closed my eyes. The priest continued chanting, the room echoing in unison. I had never had the patience to meditate, to practice yoga like Nani— but this time I didn't mind. His deep voice soothed something in me. The long, reverberating vowels. I breathed in and out, and a few minutes later when I came to, the sharp lights lifting me back to the present, Shay was looking at me.

"Ma is making us go to India," she said, a little too loud. An auntie in front of us coughed loudly, her doughy back rippling out of her blouse as she whipped her neck around to glare at us.

I leaned closer to Shay after the woman turned back around. "When?"

"In January," Shay whispered. "To shop for outfits and gifts. Stuff for the wedding. Julien's actually excited about the whole thing. He cannot *wait* to see the Taj Mahal."

"That's exciting."

"Is it?" Shay argued. "No sleeping in the same room. No meat or alcohol. Having to dress like a monk. It sounds *terribly* exciting."

I'd only been to India once—a two-week trip with Nani and Nana as a child: a quick collage of coddling distant relatives and rich goat curry; the smell of putrefied garbage and endless compliments about my fair skin, my light hair; pails of sliced mangoes and having to rinse my toothbrush with boiled water. And the memory, as vague as it was, polluted by the smog that seemed to settle into eyes and chests, still felt like home. The sprawling courtyard and the mango tree in my grandmother's village an hour outside of New Delhi. Her talcum powder scent as I fell asleep on a bed beneath the stars. It was Nani's history. Nani's home. In its grounds, built of baked bricks and timber, it was my home, too.

But Shay hated India. It repulsed her. The people, the country, the heritage, the politics. The dichotomies of injustice: excess and poverty; humility and greed; men and, much further down—women. Growing up, Shay and her brother, Nikesh, had been dragged "home" yearly to their family's estate in Rajasthan, a fortress of over thirty relatives. An extended family, an entire culture, which Shay grew to despise. She'd come over after every trip, throw both herself and a bag of gaudy souvenirs down onto my bed, and moan. Moan about her three weeks locked in a metaphorical interrogation room. The way they soaked her twine-like hair in coconut milk, stuffed her with sweet *rasmalai* and then faulted her for gaining weight. How she was rarely let outside for fear of a suntan or, slightly worse, being accosted by the local men.

Shay said the men there leered at her, smacked their lips, and tried to pull down her skirt. They would drive back and forth on scooters calling her names until she'd yell at the top of her lungs for them to screw off. They didn't treat their own Indian women like that, Shay said to me, her smile limp; even though she spoke both Hindi and Rajasthani fluently, to them, she wasn't really Indian.

I suppose neither was I.

The priest resumed chanting, and I spun Nani's heavy gold bracelets around my wrists. I looked toward the front. Auntie Sarla was hovering beside the priest, assisting him as he poured holy water out of a silver tin. Shay's engagement party was less than a week away, an elaborate affair in its own right, and over the past few weeks, I'd spent hours on the phone with Auntie Sarla helping her organize the party—answering her calls and running errands whenever she couldn't get a hold of Shay.

"How did the fitting go?" I asked her.

"The *lengha* fit, but Ma said 'not well enough.'" Shay shook her head. "I have to go back again tomorrow."

"Do you want me to come with you?"

She looked over, as if surprised. "Yes, oh my God—*yeah*. I need a buffer between me and Ma." She smiled, and then leaned over and kissed me on the arm. "I wish I was getting married next week. Get it over and done with, you know?"

I nodded.

"Who needs an engagement party anyway?" Shay glanced at me. "But at least the 'drifter' will be there."

"Who?"

"Asher. The guy I told you about, remember?" She sounded irritated. "Julien is picking him up from the airport right now. He just flew back from Bangkok . . ."

The auntie sitting in front of us turned around again, her glare forcing Shay's voice down to a whisper as she nattered on about Asher. The photos he posted online of the lychee orchards on a trek near Chiang Mai. How she and Julien might now honeymoon there on his recommendation. I refrained from rolling my eyes as Shay spoke. Mom had gone to Thailand when I was in high school, and none of us had known she'd been gone until she was home again, arriving at the house in the middle of the night needing a place to sleep. Tanned skin and bleached hair, a backpack the size of a small child clamped onto her shoulders. A tattoo on her calf— a Hindi phrase inked in pitch black—one that was supposed to mean *peace*, but, Nani had claimed, meant nothing at all.

"—so is that okay?" Shay nudged me again. "I'll introduce you guys."

"No," I whispered, turning to Shay. "I've been meeting enough men."

"How was your date with Jayesh?"

"I didn't go in the end." I shrugged. "Maybe next week . . ."

"Oh." Her voice conveyed her annoyance, like I should have already told her that detail. "Well, have you met anyone else— anyone I should know about?"

I hadn't told Shay about Arjun. I knew she would harass me for a play-by-play if I did, and force me to explain in detail how I could be so sure after one date that Arjun and I wouldn't work out. That I wasn't ready—or maybe didn't want—what he had to offer. She'd accuse me of comparing him to my ex, or self-sabotage, or say a dozen other go-to phrases she'd probably picked up from a hand- book on "how to manage lonely best friends"—and I didn't feel like another sermon when I'd had plenty from Nani.

So I shook my head, pressed my lips together for a moment, and turned back to face the priest. "Nope. There's no one else."

SIX

Nani and Shay left right after the puja, but I stayed behind to help the volunteer caretakers water the flower beds and trees lining the temple grounds. When I arrived home, I found the driveway full of cars I didn't recognize, and when I opened the front door, I could hear Nani and her friends downstairs in the entertaining room.

I lingered in the foyer, evesdropping on Nani, Auntie Sarla, and the others speaking together in Hindi; Auntie Sarla's shrill exclamations steadied by Nani's voice, low murmurs of what I sensed to be assent. I'd never learned to speak Hindi properly, and only knew the most basic nouns, verbs, and phrases, but it was everything else that made the language so identifiable to me; it was a language of pitch and tone, emotive cadence and expression. As their voices ricocheted up the stairs from the entertaining room, even though they weren't saying my name, I could tell they were talking about me.

I leaned against the wall and slid down onto the floor. I flattened my legs and felt the cold linoleum on my bare calves. I leaned back, and my hair caught onto the fibers of the wallboard, the way it always had when I'd sat in this spot as a girl.

What exactly was Auntie Sarla saying about me?

That every day I was letting another potential husband slip through my fingers, and not getting married like her Shaylee? That I was twenty-nine, and with each breath, each step, inching closer to thirty?

Without saying hello, I went upstairs and stretched out on my bed. Soon after, I heard that someone had started playing on the harmonium, and the disharmony of singsong voices blared upstairs through the vents. I focused on the glow-in-the-dark stickers I'd stamped onto the ceiling as a child, now just flecks of mild green.

Except for the dirty laundry on the floor, Nani had left everything exactly as it had looked the day I moved out. The vintage tea-stained map I had framed. My bookshelf, an antique maple hutch well stocked with Puffin Classics and novels from garage sales and the clearance shelves of supermarkets. The mash-up of throw pillows and raw silk curtains that we'd sewn together. I had been a hopeless student of basic domestics and slammed my foot on the treadle like I was race car driver, and she'd had to undo every stitch I made with her Hobbycraft sewing machine.

I thought about going back downtown. I had client meetings to prep for, recycling to take out, groceries to buy. But I knew I wouldn't do any of that. I knew that if I went back downtown, I would just sit on the chaise lounge by the window and close my eyes in the sun. Listen to the faint noises of families walking their dogs and buying gelato. The teenagers shuffling aboard the streetcar with H&M bags and neon headphones. I yawned, and before I could decide one way or another, the doorbell woke me up.

"Nani?"

I could still hear the harmonium's music, Auntie Sarla's voice shrieking over the rest of the voices. The doorbell rang again, and I pulled myself off the bed and down the stairs. I opened the front door, and squinting into the afternoon light, it took me a moment to realize who it was.

"Depesh?"

"Raina, hey." Depesh was at least six inches taller than the last time I'd seen him, and not nearly as scrawny. His muscles were more defined now and filled out his shirt, his dark wash jeans. The black, wayward curls I remembered on him as a kid were flattened and slicked behind his ears.

"Wow." I crossed my arms. "I haven't seen you in forever! You grew up nice."

He rolled his eyes.

"How old are you now—sixteen, seventeen?"

"Eighteen."

"Eighteen. God, you make me feel old."

"Well, you look exactly the same, Raina."

I led him into the family room, and sank into the couch. He looked around the room, his hands on his hips, and then tentatively took a seat in Nana's armchair.

Depesh had once been like a brother to me. His mother had been diagnosed with MS when he was ten, and I'd spent the summer after my junior year of college babysitting him. His parents—a rotund lady I called Sharon Auntie, and her husband, whose name I still hadn't figured out—had spent long days at the hospitals, at clinics for drug trials, three-day trips to Boston or San Jose for experimental procedures. So Depesh and I baked cookies and played Monopoly, went to the park and watched television until our eyes hurt. At the end of the summer, his parents moved him to New Jersey to be closer to a specialized facility, and I hadn't seen him since.

Depesh's hands were perfectly still and straight on his lap, and he stared at them.

"Do you want some tea?"

He shook his head, and looked up. "Just picking up Ma."

"Oh, I didn't know she was over."

He nodded. "Your nani is like the only one who's been able to get her to leave the house."

"Wait." I sat up. "You moved back?"

He nodded. "We've been back a month already."

"Nani didn't tell me"—I racked my brain, trying to remember—"or maybe she did, shit. I can't remember."

"It's okay."

"She calls me a lot. Sometimes at work I put her on speaker and drift off . . . God, am I a terrible person?"

"No, you're not." He laughed nervously. "But what do I know? I haven't heard from you in, like, a decade."

I knew he didn't mean to make me feel guilty, but I did. Depesh had been a kind, genuine kid—and I could still see that about him; in his eyes, his smile—it was impossible to miss. But he was different, too. He had been playful and silly when I'd known him. Exuberant. Brave enough to climb to the tops of the jungle gyms, face the tallest slides while I trailed behind.

Now he seemed awkward in his own skin. Nervous, unsure of himself. I realized that I didn't know him anymore, either. For the past eight years, I'd basically forgotten all about him.

"Do you want to go get some ice cream?"

He rolled his eyes. "Raina, I'm not a kid anymore."

"Maybe *I* want ice cream."

He glanced over at me nervously. "Well, you could buy me beer."

Nani rarely kept alcohol in the house, and the bottle of whiskey Kris stored beneath the sink was missing. So we slipped out the front door and walked a few blocks north on the wide suburban streets toward the strip mall nearby. He waited outside while

I went in and bought two large bottles of beer, and on the walk home, we stopped at the park beside my old high school. A few other people were around—kids about Depesh's age smoking weed by the basketball courts—and we picked a spot to sit a fair distance away in the grassy field.

I opened my bag, and then reluctantly handed him the beer. "I'm a bad influence on you. Don't tell your mother."

He laughed. "I'll be legal in a few months."

He twisted off the cap of the beer, and brought the bottle to his lips. He stared at it for a second before taking a sip, and I saw him wince.

"Do you like beer?"

He wiped his mouth with his hand, smiling. "Not really. I never really drank in high school. I wasn't invited to the parties."

"Me neither. But my best friend was, so sometimes I tagged along."

"I didn't really have a best friend . . ." Depesh looked down at his beer, and with one hand started to peel back the label. "Actually, down there I had trouble making friends."

I put my hand on his shoulder.

He continued. "Jersey was . . . hard. And now I don't know anybody here anymore, you know?" His fingers shook, and the label—partway off—split in two. "I'm starting university in a few days. That will be good."

"It will be, Depo." I smiled at him, and then took a quick sip from my own beer. It was already warm, tasted stale, and I set it down beside me. "And until then, you know you have me, right?"

"I don't need your pity or anything."

"It's not pity." I stared at him until he looked me in the eye. "I promise. I'm really glad you're back."

He nodded, and looked back at his beer.

"So, what classes are you taking?"

"Bio, chemistry, math"—he sighed—"you know, the usual pre-med stuff."

"You want to be a doctor?"

"Doesn't everybody?"

"So what if everybody else does? You should be what you want to be."

He grew quiet, and stretched back on his elbows. It was hot, and the sun was in my eyes, scorching my face.

"I heard you're getting married."

My stomach dropped, and I turned to face him. "Who told you that?"

"My mom did." He paused. "Is it that British guy? I heard something a while back about a British guy."

So that's what Nani and her friends were talking about in the entertaining room: that I was about to get married? How many in our community were preparing to shove me down the aisle, had picked out a punch bowl for a wedding gift, when I—when *Nani*—had yet to find me a husband?

I grabbed the beer and swigged it, drank until it was nearly half gone.

"So you're not getting married?"

Slowly, I set the beer back down. The aftertaste was disgusting. "No. I'm not."

"But there was a British guy? I'm not making that up?"

I pressed my lips together. "There was. We broke up when I left London."

"I'm sorry. That sucks. But London—that must have been *amazing*, hey?" Depesh's smiled brightened. "I would love to live in Europe—or *go* to Europe even."

"Yeah, it was wonderful . . ." I trailed off. A moment later, I realized Depesh was still looking at me.

"What's London like?"

"Busy. Diverse. In some ways, entirely overwhelming." I shrugged. "Lonely, in other ways. Like any big city."

"Lonely? But you had a boyfriend."

I cleared my throat. "So you've never been?"

"No"—he shook his head—"I really want to, but we could never travel because Ma's treatments cost too much." He paused. "That's actually why we moved back. Tuition to a good school down there was *expensive*."

"Oh . . ."

"It's a lot here, too, though," he said. "I took out a loan, and I'm working part-time at Star Labs to save up."

"Star Labs is across the road from my company. You can drop by sometime." I picked up my bottle. "Like if you need beer, or something."

He laughed.

"Or you can borrow my car if you want to take a girl out, or whatnot."

He smiled at me vaguely, and put his hand out in front of his face. The sun cast a shadow across his eyes, his nose, and I couldn't tell what he was looking at. After a while, he fished his phone out of his pocket and looked at the screen.

"Ma is wondering where I am." He pushed himself up onto his knees, and wiped his hands together, grass and dirt falling from his palms. "We should probably go back."

I nodded, and we walked back together in silence, my mind racing. In Nani's eyes, my marriage was a done deal. But what if it wasn't?

I stopped short at the foot of the driveway, breathing through the tightness in my chest.

What if I already knew that what Nani wanted for me wouldn't be enough?

DATE #4

"So you're Auntie Suvali's granddaughter," he said, without standing up to greet me.

"And you must be Rahul." I shuffled into the seat across from him. He was reading the *Paris Review*, and bookmarked his page with a peacock feather. Then, as if on purpose, he set the magazine down on the table between us facing toward me.

I was exhausted, and as I made introductory chitchat with Rahul, I realized I was not prepared for yet another blind date. I'd worked crazy hours all week, all the while fielding panicked calls from Shay and Auntie Sarla about the engagement party—which was tonight.

I'd stayed up late the evening before with Shay's younger brother, Nikesh, designing, printing, and manually cutting out place cards for the table settings. Afterward, I'd thought seriously about canceling on Rahul, but Nani had called me excitedly at the crack of dawn asking me what I was wearing and where Rahul was taking me—and I didn't want to let her down again.

To Nani's dismay, Jayesh had given up on me. I guess postponing a first date for an entire summer does that to a guy. To make matters worse, earlier in the week I'd bailed on a Skype date with Jagmohan in India, something Nani had organized so I could check whether he was still coming to visit.

"Absolutely not. Nani, he just wants a marriage visa," I'd said, pointing at the list. "You wrote it down yourself."

"Even nice boys can have ulterior motives, *nah*?"

Rahul was the very last name on her list. So when she asked me to call him, I didn't know how to say no.

A server with gray-blue hair dropped off two jam jars full of water and a wicker basket full of what appeared to be—and nearly smelled like—dog shit.

Rahul lunged for the dung, and popped one in his mouth.

"What is it?"

"Gluten-free vegan raw bread," he said, his mouth full.

"Can bread *be* raw?"

He scowled at me as he swallowed. "Don't you have a dehydrator?"

I shook my head.

"Wow, okay." He looked alarmed. "Well, it's a must-have when you're on a gluten-free vegan raw diet. It's as indispensable to me as my NutriBullet."

I snuck a look at my watch. I'd been at the restaurant for *four* minutes, and already I wanted to leave. Rahul seemed insufferable, but maybe we had gotten off on the wrong foot? Maybe I was judging him too quickly.

I forced out a smile, trying to make an effort. I picked up a piece of the "bread" and nibbled on the corner. It tasted like mildew.

"Mmm," I purred, nodding heavily. "What's in it?"

"Vegetables, mostly. Onions, tomatoes, peppers, broccoli. Sunflower seeds, too, I think." He chewed loudly. "Whatever it is, it's ethically sourced. Everything here is farm-to-table fresh."

"My nani owns a restaurant."

"Oh yeah? Which one?"

"Saffron. It's in Roncesvalles—"

He waved me off. "Oh, I know it. It's quite . . . popular, isn't it? I imagine a lot of tourists go there. Must be in the guidebooks or something."

"What's wrong with tourists?"

"Where you should really go is to this place I know on Keele Street." He grabbed another turd, and I thought about telling him that he still had pieces of the last one all over his teeth. "It's less overplayed. You walk in, and you think it's a run-of-the-mill ciggys and gum convenience store, right?"

"Right," I deadpanned.

"And then the guy takes you through the back door and . . . BANG!"

"He shoots you?"

"Best Vietnamese food in the city. And *decent* virgin cocktails."

"Naturally."

"All in all, the evening will cost you around fifty bucks." He eyed my handbag, which I'd hung off of my chair's armrest. "I'm guessing that's less than that purse you have there. That isn't real leather, is it?"

I glanced at it, suddenly recalling that the ebony black tote was Shay's. I'd borrowed it the year before, swearing to give it back, but never had.

"I'm not sure . . ."

"Consumer culture. Am I right?"

I laughed, and it sounded about as awkward as I felt. "I sure could consume a *drink* right about now—"

"Raina, this place is alcohol free."

"Oh, I was kidding . . ."

He rolled his eyes, and after handing me a menu, I resisted the temptation to hit him with it.

Rahul suggested we try the five-course lunch tasting menu, and I obliged. He ordered an aloe vera smoothie, and despite his rave reviews of the birch juice, I wasn't quite in the mood for tree. I settled on an organic root beer, and while it tasted nothing like root beer, it was actually pretty good.

We discussed the weather—hot, but not sticky hot—and then took turns commenting on the restaurant's decor. The twinkly lights and green-brown ferns. Persian rugs and throws in piles, as if to enforce a sense of coziness.

Rahul had strong opinions, even on things that you wouldn't think warranted such fervor—such as the choice between wood flooring and carpet. Everything was right or wrong, authentic or "trying too hard." I glanced at the hemp necklace dipping between the V of his distressed T-shirt, the twisted tuft on the top of his head that very nearly fell into man-bun territory, and wondered which category Rahul fell into.

My favorite Drake song came on, and Rahul groaned. "Really? *Drake?*" He glanced around accusingly, as if prepared to prosecute whomever it was who had dared to play popular music.

"What's wrong with Drake?"

"Nothing, I suppose." Rahul rolled his eyes. "He's just so passé."

I suppressed a smile. Authentic. Rahul certainly was authentic.

"We should have met up tonight," he said after a moment. "I

know this hole-in-the-wall club around the corner. Great vibes, low-key—and like, you know—*fresh* beats."

"I thought I mentioned already; it's my best friend's engagement party tonight."

"Oh. Right."

"And it's been a bit stressful I suppose, with the planning and—"

"Ah," he said, blinking at me. "*Stress.*"

"What about it?"

"I feel sorry for you."

Mister pays-fifty-dollars-for-noodles-in-a-broom-cupboard felt sorry for *me*?

"I just don't get worked up about that kind of stuff."

I sat up in my chair. "What kind of stuff?"

"You know. Logistics. Details. Everyday . . . *stressors* that wig everybody out—and to be honest—make life unpleasant for those around them."

I nodded earnestly, thinking that maybe if I was unpleasant enough, he'd leave, and take all the organic shit-bread with him.

"Stress. The mental, physical, sometimes even spiritual reaction to the world outside of us. Aren't they all just feelings we can control?"

"You're kind of a superhero then, if you have the power not to feel. How do you do it?"

He smiled at me coolly. "Meditation. Yoga. Eating clean. It's all about bringing balance to the everyday."

"Like a Jedi."

"Huh?"

"They bring balance to the force? *Star Wars*?" The muscles around his lips twitched, and I sat back in my chair. "Oh, let me guess. *Star Wars* is also *passé*."

"I really don't get what all the fuss is about."

Our food arrived, if you could call it that. A vegan cheese board. A course of dandelion salad and eggplant bacon. A bowl of bloodlike broth that claimed to be pureed avocado, beets, and tigernut milk. (Note to self: It's not from a tiger, or a nut.)

No matter how hard I tried, Rahul shot down every topic of conversation I attempted. The Toronto Blue Jays? *Too pedestrian.* His favorite band? *You wouldn't have heard of them.*

What school did he go to? *What does it matter? We live in the present.*

I let the conversation dry up, much like the prunes, figs, and apricots that had gone into making our next course: a granola bar. At least I had chia and oat pudding to look forward to, and then, a cross-examination by Nani about how the date went.

I knew she would laugh when I told her about Rahul's raw, meat-, bread-, and milk-free diet, and how definitively incompatible we were. But then again, Rahul was the last name on her list . . .

"You're not enjoying the food," Rahul said, as I poked at a loose fig with my fork.

"Sure, I am," I lied.

"Raina, one must always be true to oneself."

Was he being serious? Did he think of himself as some kind of wise, Gandhi-like pundit? "I'm just not used to it," I said finally, wracking my brain for something nice to say. "But I admire your discipline."

Smugly, he laughed, shaking out the elastic in his hair. His man bun parted into an inverted pyramid at the top of his head.

"It's not discipline, Raina. It's being informed." He held out his hand, as if signaling an oncoming vehicle to stop. "Do you know how many pesticides you have in your body? How many you've accumulated"—he pointed at my stomach, which was still growling for food—"that are compounding in you right *now*?"

I was about to ask him to enlighten me, but then he did anyway.

"Let me guess, for breakfast you drank coffee, which is an addictive stimulant, and had some sugar-and-gluten-based cereal?"

"Are you sure you're not a Jedi? Because you just read my mind!"

He smiled. Had I been too rude? I was about to apologize, but then realized he'd taken it as a compliment.

"I had Special K for breakfast today, yes."

"See? What did I say? And I bet that when you're home with your nani, she makes you paratha in the morning, which is made from white flour, white potatoes, and butter—which, by the way, was *stolen* from a helpless cow imprisoned in some industrial farm outside the city. A cow that, as a Hindu, you should be honoring."

"Hindus honor cows because they help sustain life, and provide sustenance like *milk*."

"Whatever, Raina. My *point* is that all you need is three dates with me. Eat three of *these* meals, and you'll see how much better you feel, and realize how much crap you've been putting in your body. You'll be happier, sleep better, might even be able to lose some weight—"

I guffawed. Audibly. Did he just tell a girl to lose weight?

His cheeks reddened. "No, I didn't mean it like that. You look great—"

"How can I look great?" I grabbed my handbag, wondering what the hell I was still doing there. "I had coffee for breakfast!"

"I've really put my foot in my mouth, haven't I?"

"Rahul, it was really . . . *interesting* to meet you, but I have an engagement party to get to, where I'll be poisoning myself with tandoori chicken and cowy paneer." I stood up. "Lots of alcohol, too."

"No, don't go." He stood up after me, and reached for my arm. "I'm sorry. I'm just being defensive. My whole family thinks my lifestyle is ridiculous. Most Indian people do, and—"

"Your lifestyle isn't ridiculous," I snapped, turning to leave. "Your manners are."

Rahul—Sarla's physiotherapist, says he very good-looking boy ☺

OMG UGHHHHH!!!

SEVEN

"Holy. Shit. I am *so* underdressed." Zoey hesitated at the entrance and glanced down at her beige suit. I'd offered to let her borrow a sari, but she'd claimed to be allergic to sparkles.

"Don't worry. It's just an engagement party."

Zoey turned to face me, eyes wide. "*Just?*"

The mezzanine level of the hotel had been transformed. I had tagged along for an inspection the week before, nodding mechanically as Auntie Sarla waddled about with a measuring tape, the back of her chubby arms swaying as she visualized her masterpiece. And it was. It practically wilted in decadence; an eruption of crystal and light turquoise. At its center was Shay, gilded like a Christmas tree, eight hundred people—mostly Auntie Sarla's own friends—milling by the open bar.

I led Zoey through the foyer, past the twenty-foot fountain of peach punch, through the clusters of families, mothers and daughters in matching *lenghas*; men in stiff suits, their white girlfriends gowned in spandex dresses, blissfully unaware that in *this* crowd, showing that much leg was the equivalent to being stark naked.

In the main hall, the tables were clothed in satin, a monstrous cake and head table at the front. At Indian celebrations, the families sat at the front, I explained.

"I guess that makes sense," said Zoey, darting into the queue for the bar. "They're the ones paying for it."

"*Wooow.*"

I turned around and looked down toward the voice. Nani and a few of the aunties had found us. Nani was dressed up—pink lips and shawl, a gin and tonic in hand—and when I leaned down for a hug, I could smell the perfume she rarely had the courage to wear. Chanel No. 5. The last gift Nana had ever bought her.

"You look wonderful, Nani."

"Me?" she exclaimed, her accent thickened with gin. "No one is looking at me next to *this* beauty model." She squeezed my chin and tugged until my face was level to hers, plopped kisses over my cheeks. After a moment, she leaned back, and then started picking imaginary lint off of me like a chimp.

"Nani, stop."

"The boys here will be lining up for you." She winked. "And about time, too."

"Nani, you remember Zoey?"

As if she hadn't noticed her before, Nani turned slowly to look at Zoey. She studied her oddly, and looked her up and down.

"How have you been, Mrs. Anand?"

"Oh, fine"—she looked between Zoey and me, and then down at the floor—"and yourself?"

"I'm well, thank you." Zoey touched my arm. "Work has been surprisingly busy this summer, plus we had those weekends away—"

"We rented a cottage with friends, remember?" I looked at Nani. "I told you, didn't I?"

She nodded slowly.

"I love your sari." Zoey smiled eagerly. "I'm regretting my outfit choice, now that I see how beautiful they look on you and Raina."

"Thank you, dear." Nani smiled at us faintly, and then snapped her head toward me. In a loud whisper, she said, "You met Rahul today, *nah*?"

"Yes . . ."

"Tell us"—Nani winked—"was he a *dish*?"

I laughed. "Yes, Nani. He was handsome, but it's *not* going to happen. First off, Rahul took me to a *vegan*—"

"Enough," she snapped, cutting me off. "I cannot hear another of your stories. It is too much now."

I could feel myself shrinking. I looked down at the ground. "But Nani . . ."

"And here I thought . . . soon, I would also have engagement to celebrate."

I heard her sigh, and then felt her beside me as she brushed a kiss on my cheek.

"Zoey, maybe you have boy for her? She is so hard to please, *nah*? No one I suggest is good enough for her."

By the time I looked up again, Nani had disappeared, and I felt Zoey squeeze my hand. "Are you okay?"

I nodded, without meeting her eye. "Yeah. Come on. Let's go find our seats."

Our table was disguised in a garden of gerbera daisies, cream wax candles, and chiffon seat covers. Zoey and I were seated across from Shay's older cousins and their husbands—women who as girls used to bully Shay and me. They arrived with smiles and hellos, and then seemed content to ignore us. Soon Kris arrived with

Serena—Shay's good friend and bridesmaid. I hadn't seen Kris in months, and wondered whose idea it was to seat us together.

Kris was thirty-eight, halfway in age between Mom and me, and I'd never really known what to make of him. He'd moved out for university when I was still a kid, and it wasn't that we weren't close; I'd just never really gotten to know him.

It was strange seeing him a suit, and not in gym clothes, or his uniform of khakis and ill-fitted T-shirts that he wore as an engineering consultant. He pulled out Serena's chair, and she folded into it suppressing a smile, tucked her hair and sari perfectly into place.

Ever since his divorce, Kris avoided going to temple, Indian weddings, or parties—anywhere he said the aunties and uncles would stare at him judgingly. But as I watched Kris and Serena effortlessly interact, pour each other water, eat each other's appetizers, I realized that already they seemed to be the community's next "it" couple.

Serena was the golden girl of my generation, so as her date, the community must have pardoned him.

I helped myself to another glass of wine as the main course was brought out, and then another. Serena and Zoey became engrossed in a discussion about politics, and Kris and I sat together in silence. I had nothing to say. I glanced behind me, and saw Nani in fervent conversation at her table with Auntie Sarla and a few other aunties.

Had news gone around already that I'd walked out on Rahul in the middle of our date? Was this evening's gossip that Raina, yet again, was being too picky—and not that Rahul was just a complete dick? My wineglass emptied again, and I reached over and poured more in.

"Quite the fish tonight, aren't you?" I heard Kris say, and I didn't answer. "I saw you talking to Ma earlier. She must be thrilled to see you all dressed up. You actually look nice, Raindrop."

"Please don't call me that."

He leaned in. "Are any of them here?"

"Any of who—" I stopped, seeing his smirk.

"She's even asking me if I have single friends for you." He laughed. "That would be strange, hey? My little *niece* marrying—"

"Kris, can we please not talk about this tonight?"

He brought his wineglass to his lips, and winked. "Come on. Lighten up."

I gestured toward Serena. "Why don't we talk about you two, then?"

"What do you want to know?"

"You two seem pretty cozy."

"So?"

"So when are you getting married?"

"Funny, Raina." His eyes glinted. "That's what everyone here wants to know about you."

At the front of the hall, Shay and Julien stood up in front of their audience, waving and holding hands—the most public display of affection they were allowed in front of this sort of crowd. It was the first time I'd seen them that evening. She was wearing a harvest gold sari. Her eyes were painted, her black hair winding into a bow at the back of her neck, and Julien, dressed up in an embroidered kurta pajama, smiled down at her.

"She looks wonderful, doesn't she, Raina?" Serena asked me.

"Yes," I said, wineglass in hand. I surveyed the room: everyone paired off and smiling. "Absolutely wonderful."

An hour later, the speeches continued as the backlog of Shay's extended family were still toasting her and Julien at the podium. I was restless, my feet vibrating, and finally, I couldn't take it. With a quick excuse to Zoey, I found my heels beneath the table and then snuck outside of the main hall.

My throat was parched, and outside in the foyer I grabbed another drink and wandered around. Others had gathered outside, too, perhaps sick of the frills and gimmicks, the insincere congratulations and tears from everyone fighting over a chance at the microphone. The wedding was still eight months away, yet everyone inside was acting like they were already married, as if something was about to change. Everyone thought that Shay and I still lived together—that she rented my spare room, but the only thing in there was a rack of my winter coats, a few boxes of junk, and a treadmill. Shay and Julien already lived together. They had a mortgage together. They had stupid things like a butter dish and a garlic press. Matching bureaus they'd picked out together and bought on their joint credit card.

And what did I have? Dates with men who told me to *lose weight*. A Nani who acted like she was disappointed in me because I refused to settle for a partner she'd arranged for me.

I wanted to fall in love; who didn't? But I wanted it on my terms. With a guy *I* got to choose. A man who accepted me for me, and wouldn't expect me to raise our children on my own, or have a three-course Indian dinner prepared for him when he waltzed through the door.

I wanted something real. A *real* partner. Not some random Indian guy who would look handsome standing next to me in a wedding photo. Was that too much to ask?

From inside the main hall, I could hear Auntie Sarla speaking into the microphone, making a rambling speech about family and community and marriage. What gave her the right to stand up and tell people what was right and what was wrong?

I moved farther away from earshot and examined the desserts. Carts of fruit, meringue and lemon pie; custards and salted caramel cheesecakes. Another cart full of Indian sweets. Lassi and *gulab jamun* and *rasmalaii*. My stomach felt unsettled just looking at all of it, and I grabbed a fistful of green grapes and walked onward. Just behind the dessert spread, I saw three long tables full of small sandalwood boxes, each hand carved with the name of a guest. Auntie Sarla had spent months organizing the shipment from India—delaying the engagement party for their arrival, even though surely everyone would be too drunk to remember to take one home, or would throw it in the trash as soon as it started to collect dust.

I weaved through the tables, looking for my box, and just as I found it, something fierce blew in like a foghorn. She was singing. Auntie Sarla's voice crescendoed, a throaty hum traversing the scales of a traditional Indian *bhajan*, and I couldn't help myself. I snorted, needing to reach up to wipe my nose, as I tried to stifle my laughter.

"I saw that."

I covered my face and whipped around. He was tall, much taller than me, his honey brown hair clumped behind his ears, a thick beard dripping down like moss. He smirked at me and rocked back and forth on his heels.

"What? I sneezed."

"You *sneezed*."

"Yes, I sneezed."

"Well," he said, rubbing his large hands together. "Then bless you."

Auntie Sarla was still singing, her voice blaring through the speakers. I pressed my lips together and started to turn away.

"Wait," he said. "You're Raina. Shaylee's best friend."

"I might be. And who are you?"

He chuckled.

"What?"

"Nothing?"

"*What?*"

"Nothing." His eyebrows arched high. "Although I wouldn't have thought you were that kind of bridesmaid."

"What is that supposed to mean?"

"It just makes sense. Laughing at Sarla's singing"—he motioned around the room with his hand—"pretending that this entire thing is funny."

I crossed my arms, my cheeks flushing. "What are you trying to say?"

"I'm *saying* that while that sari looks beautiful on you, Raina, envy does not."

"I am incredibly happy for Shay, okay?"

"Jealousy and being happy for a friend aren't mutually exclusive."

"What are you, a bumper sticker?" I moved to brush past him, and as I did, I caught hold of his scent. Like pepper and musk. Blackened greens and burned aluminum. Like Mom's winter coat, or the sixth-floor fire escape in my and Shay's old apartment.

I stopped. "What's that smell?"

"What smell?"

"Are you *high*?"

His idiot grin gave him away.

"You can't just come to an engagement party high, okay? Have you no respect?"

"I wasn't the one 'sneezing' at my best friend's mom."

"Who the hell do you think you are?"

He turned away from me, eyes laughing, and picked a box up off the table. *Klein*. Asher Klein.

"Oh. Well *that* makes sense."

"Seems like you've heard of me."

I uncrossed my arms.

"Come on now. What have you heard?"

That he was Julien's oldest friend from Montreal and, after

years abroad, had just moved to Toronto. That he'd dropped out of teachers' college a semester away from graduation. That he'd just gotten back from Southeast Asia after ten years of traveling and doing whatever it was that his type—the *drifter*—seemed to do.

"That you existed," I said flatly.

"And does my existence"—he paused—"interest you?"

"I'll buy your story when it comes out in paperback."

"And in this story—am I the hero?" He smiled. "Do I get the girl in the end?"

"You wrote it. You tell me."

"I think I do." He nodded to himself. "Adventure. Thriller. Romance. It'll be a bestseller."

"A regular Jack Kerouac."

"I'm handsome like Jack, aren't I?"

"You know he died from alcoholism?"

He knocked his glass against mine. "He died a happy man."

I crossed my arms again. "So—Jack—what did you do while *on the road*? Bit of a drifter, were you? Bounced from hostel to hooker?" I touched his elbow. "Tell me. Have you gotten yourself checked lately?"

"Gossip is a powerful thing, Raina."

I leaned up on my tiptoes, and whispered close to his ear, "So is herpes."

Asher laughed, and the creases around his eyes deepened. I could feel him looking at me, and my cheeks burned. Seconds passed, and he was still laughing, like I was the funniest thing in the world.

"Done?" I asked after a moment.

He nodded. "You're—"

"Hilarious, I know. But it's so easy to be funny around you," I said, gritting my teeth. "A thirtysomething with nothing to show for himself—"

"Better than being a thirtysomething drunk bridesmaid, don't you think?"

"I'm twenty-*nine*—"

"Always the bridesmaid, never the—"

But then I shoved him. Hard. He wobbled, nearly regaining his balance before toppling behind him and straight into a dessert cart. The metal trays clanged together as they spilled onto the ground and all over Asher. A few people standing nearby turned to look, and he picked himself up off the floor, his shirt a soppy swell of mango lassi and graham cracker crust.

"Shit." I covered my hands with my mouth. Had I just pushed him? I wasn't sure I'd ever pushed anyone in my life. Asher slowly pulled himself onto his knees, and I stretched out my hand toward him. He took it, pulling on me lightly as he stood back up. I had to concentrate not to fall over, too, and I realized that Asher was right. I *was* drunk.

I ran toward the restroom. It was all too much. Everything—Nani and Auntie Sarla, Shay's preoccupation with the wedding, work—it was boiling up and out, and I didn't want any of it. I locked myself in a stall, the seafoam green walls spinning, and I flicked down the toilet seat lid. Sitting down, I took three deep breaths, and then opened my eyes.

What was happening to me? What was I *letting* happen?

I thought I might cry, but the tears refused to form. I wanted, I needed *something*—but I didn't know what. I reached into my purse and found my BlackBerry. It was dead, and I resigned myself to the fact that I'd have to leave without telling Zoey. I couldn't face going back inside that hall again. I would make it up to her.

Outside, I slipped away from the main area and found a service staircase. I took off my heels, and toed my way down step-by-step, trying not to trip on my sari, my hand dragging behind me on the banister. I got to the last step and was about to push my way through the fire exit door when I heard a rustling behind me. I whipped around, thinking Asher had followed me. But instead, I saw a young, muscular blond, who I found vaguely familiar, rolling a cigarette on the landing behind me.

He held my eyes as he licked the rolling paper. Then he slid the cigarette through his fingers, and stashed it behind his left ear.

"It's Raina, right?" he said, still holding my gaze. "I remember you."

I pressed my lips together, and shook my head.

"I used to bartend at Eldorado. You came in a few months back with that jerk. *Sachin.*"

Slowly, it came to me. The bartender who had given me the eyes and made me a stiff gin and tonic. I nodded in recognition. "What's your name again?"

"Josh."

I nodded. "Sorry."

"You should be. You ran away before I could steal you away." He took a few more steps toward me, and suddenly, I felt self-conscious. Woozy. I put my arm back on the rail.

"I just got off my shift. You leaving already?" Josh opened his jacket, and motioned to a bottle of gin wedged into his inside pocket. "I nicked this from the bar upstairs."

"Don't worry. I won't rat you out."

He smirked. "Looked like a great party."

I shrugged. "It wasn't so great."

"Oh?" He took another step down. He was inches away, and I could smell the cigarettes, the stench of beer and wine and detergent, his breath from whatever he'd had for dinner. "Then maybe we should start another one."

He seemed like such a cliché, but then again, wasn't I? I held his gaze as he moved toward me, as he touched my neck with the very tips of his fingers. "Come home with me."

Josh up close was surreal. He was beyond attractive: blond, with a cheeky boyish grin and sculpted arms. He could have been a model. I would never be able to trust a man that handsome, but what he was suggesting wouldn't require that kind of trust.

My head pounded at the thought that, after only a few months of dating, I'd just crossed off the last name on Nani's stupid list. Now what would happen? Now what would she make me do? I didn't want to date. I didn't want to get married. And right then, exhausted and overwhelmed, I wanted something else. I hadn't ever been with anyone except Dev, and just looking at Josh, I thought about letting that change.

Josh leaned forward and brushed his lips against mine. For a moment, I just watched him kiss me. Hungrily, the muscles expanding and contracting on his cheeks and forehead as he moved his mouth—and I, in turn, moved mine. He put his hands on my waist, and a second later, I felt them slide down to my ass as he pinned me against the rail. His stubble ground coarsely against me, his tongue prodded and his hands pulled, and eventually, I closed my eyes and surrendered.

Josh—hotter than Nani's chicken vindaloo (BUT ONLY 23!)

I was already standing by the door when he woke up. He lifted his face an inch off the pillow and squinted at me.

"You're leaving?"

I nodded, and his head fell back on the pillow. I was sober now, filled with heavy guilt at having left Zoey at the party, and I noticed how his bedroom smelled like the inside of a hockey bag—how the walls were covered in creased *Lord of the Rings* posters. I vaguely remembered seeing them from just hours before—dim lighting, the bottle of expensive gin—teasing him for being a dork, while admitting that I, too, used to have those same posters. Later, falling back onto the bed, laughing so hard that one of his roommates banged on the wall and told us to shut up. Josh had smothered our faces beneath a thin pillow, and in a muffled voice, told me I was the most entertaining girl he'd ever had over.

Most entertaining *woman*, I'd reminded him.

He made a sleepy noise—a yawn, whimpering like a hungry puppy—and I sat back down on the bed. The flannel sheet crunched beneath my weight, and I wondered how long it'd been since its last wash. He rubbed his eyes, and then looked up at me smiling.

"My phone's dead. Could you call me a cab?"

He propped himself up on one elbow, and I resisted the urge to rub the sleep out of his eyes. "I can drive you," he said, kissing me on the lips. His mouth had crusted white overnight, and when I pulled away, I could still taste his morning breath.

He drove me home, the late summer wind blowing in through the windows, a strange voice singing at me through the dashboard, a random wool sock hanging from the rearview mirror. The passenger seat belt was missing, and I tried not to grip the seat as we sped east on Queen Street. Outside my building, he asked me for my phone number, and I gave it to him, knowing he'd never use it—and surely, Josh knew I didn't want him to. After one more dry kiss, he left.

I took the elevator up, and sighed as I unlocked the door. My sari stuck to me, and I felt the grime on my teeth, my hair in greased pieces behind my ears. I found an extra charger in the kitchen and plugged in my BlackBerry, left a trail of clothing down the hall, and stepped into the shower. Standing beneath the pressure, I opened my mouth and drank until my stomach hurt.

I closed my eyes, and tried to decide how I felt about what just had, and hadn't, happened. Damp sheets. Josh's eyelashes. Falling asleep with my head on his shoulder, both of his hands secured around my waist. The heat of a body at rest next to mine.

I lathered, and then rinsed it all away. I stepped out of the shower and wrapped a fresh towel around my body, walked around the apartment and opened all of the curtains. The light flooded in. My phone had powered on, and it lit up in beeps and flashes. I grabbed it and scrolled through the alerts. I had missed calls from Zoey, Shay, and Nani—surely, each of them wondering where I'd disappeared to the evening before. I made a mental note to call them all back and then kept scrolling. Surprisingly, Depesh had texted, wondering if I was also at the engagement party. Feeling bad that I'd missed seeing him, I texted him back asking if he enjoyed his first week at university, and then opened my work e-mails.

I'd received seventeen since my phone had died the evening before. Not bad for a Saturday night. Two were from Bill, another six from other analysts on my team. Five were from clients. Another three were spam. And then, I saw it.

My Raina,

It's been too long. There's so much to say, but I suppose now isn't the right time to say it. I'm not sure London is right for me anymore . . . if it ever was. There's been some rearranging, and the transfer paperwork was filed today . . . Will start shortly at the Toronto office. I'll see you then, darling.

Dev xo

EIGHT

Autumn set in, but Nani's hot stove kept out the cold. The countertops overflowed with baking sheets of raw chicken cut into cubes marinating in the masala she had taught me how to make. Onions, ginger, cumin, turmeric. Just the right amount of fresh coriander. Standing beside me, she guided me as I stirred the biryani and marinated the chicken, fried two vegetable *subjis* side by side on the back burners. It had been over a month since Dev told me he was moving to Toronto, and every weekend since, I'd come home to watch movies with Nani, or get cooking lessons to keep myself preoccupied.

I still hadn't figured out what it might mean. In the e-mail, he'd called me *darling*, and he hadn't called me that since the weekend before I left London—while we made spinach and goat cheese omelets, and he'd said, sipping his espresso, "Darling, you take the one that hasn't flopped over."

That morning had only just reappeared in my mind. Others,

too—the ones I had been pushing away for two years. Mere flashes of our life in London. Kissing after hours at the office with the curtains drawn. Brunch with his friends in Covent Garden, his hand sliding up my thigh beneath the table. After months of begging, going on an afternoon date to the Victoria and Albert Museum because I'd never been; licking scoops of gelato and rolling our eyes at wedding dresses from the Renaissance. Standing next to him in a crowded elevator; Dev leaning into my neck, and whispering, "You know that I love you, right?"

October crawled by. I jumped whenever I heard a British accent in the corridor at work, and checked my e-mail fifty thousand times a day. I trolled through the bulletins posted by HR checking to see if his start date had been announced, needing to confirm that he really was transferring. In his e-mail, Dev hadn't mentioned what day he was coming, or how long he might be staying—and I didn't know how to ask.

Was it his choice to move to Toronto?

Then there was that other question that I always typed out, and always deleted.

Are you moving here for me?

I hadn't seen him in two years, but the more I thought about it, the more it made sense. Of course he was supposed to move here. I hadn't spent the happiest years of my life with a man just so we could break up. And relationships like that—like the one Dev and I had—were never just a relationship. It was a love affair with a screen of its own on the Central Park lawn. The heartbreak had to be worth it, and suddenly, I knew that Dev was going to be my happy ending.

A sputter of oil escaped the pan, and I noticed that Nani was watching my face.

"Do you want to watch a movie after this?" I asked her. "Shah Rukh Khan has a new one out, doesn't he?"

"Do you not have other plans tonight?"

Other plans. Nani's code words that suggested I should be out on another date, trolling the streets, bars, and temple for another suitable Indian.

I thought maybe she'd lay off after I'd exhausted the list. Stupidly, I'd assumed that it would be over—and that I could wait for Dev in peace—once I'd met up with (or ruled out) everyone on her list, and she'd realized her arrangement just didn't work. But she continued to push, pulling eligible Indian bachelors out of some sort of magical hat. A new list she hadn't given me access to. I wasn't even sure where she was finding them—and whose sons, nephews, or cousins they were—but they wouldn't leave me alone. She'd started to give out my phone number, and now I couldn't go more than twelve hours without receiving weird texts from guys named Billy or Harpreet, voice mails from mouth breathers who'd forget to leave their name.

Each time my BlackBerry lit up, I'd hope it was Dev, and get that sinking feeling in my stomach when it wasn't. He'd be here soon, wouldn't he? Surely, all of this would be over *soon.*

"No, I don't have plans," I said to Nani after a moment, trying to sound firm.

"Did Neil not call? He sounds very promising—"

"Please. Not today?" I gave her a pleading look. "Work has been really busy, and right now I just want to cook and hang out with you."

Nani nodded slowly, and then kissed me on the cheek. "Well, you are natural cook. I am very proud. Your mother was never good like this."

"She liked to cook?"

Nani sneered. "Manu liked to do a lot of things."

"It's so relaxing," I said after a moment. "I never realized that before."

"*Aacha*. When you have time, yes. But when cooking for hungry customers, hungry children—it is not so relaxing."

Nani rarely spoke about the past, and I thought about pressing her. How had she felt about leaving her parents, one day suddenly packing her things and moving in with a husband she barely knew? What was it like getting on a plane for the first time in her life, crossing into a new country—cold, barren, and raising children in a land you knew nothing about?

I reached up to the spice rack and grabbed a small glass jar full of *methi*. I pinched some between my fingers, and then carefully sprinkled it over the pan. With a wooden spoon, I folded it in, another rich wave of aromas escaping.

"Was it hard?" I finally asked.

"Do you know I still am not sure the English word for *methi*?" I felt her beside me, watching me as I cooked. "Yes, Raina. It was very hard."

"Zoey said her grandparents were immigrants, too," I said. "From the Ukraine, but still."

"You spend a lot of time with Zoey, *nah*?" She paused. "Is she—"

I heard the front door open and, a moment later, slam shut. My eyes locked with Nani's as we heard a jingling of keys, the rustling of the hall closet. Nani's lips were pursed as she watched the kitchen door.

"Mom?" I called out.

Footsteps dragged across the hardwood in the other room, and a moment later, a deep voice. "It's me."

Nani's shoulders relaxed as Kris opened the kitchen door. His hair was wet, and he had at least a week's worth of stubble on his face. He sat down heavily at the kitchen table, tossing his gym bag in the corner.

"I didn't know you were coming," she said without turning around. "Not with Serena today?"

"No." He sat down at the table. "We broke up."

Nani leaned forward against the counter, and massaged her temples. Eyes closed, she inhaled deeply, and then exhaled like she did while meditating. It was only the week before that I'd overheard Nani and Auntie Sarla gossiping in the living room—calloused feet on the coffee table, plates of sweets on their stomachs—speculating on who, after Shay, would be the next in the community to get married. *Kris.* They'd been confident. Kris and Serena were the right age, and had established careers. *What was he waiting for?* Auntie Sarla had wondered aloud.

"Sorry to hear that," I said finally. Beside me, Nani was still crouched over, slowly shaking her head. "Nani, do you want to sit down?"

She whimpered.

"Ma, stop being so dramatic. We weren't even together that long."

"But *why*, Krishna?"

He winced. He hated it when Nani called him by his full name.

"Serena was *nice* girl—"

"All my girlfriends were nice. Maybe it's not—"

"Your auntie Sarla has practically planned your wedding. And now?"

"And now you tell your beloved Sarla to cancel it."

"What will I say? That you—again—have broken up with a girl for no reason? This time with that lovely Serena? That my Krishna is refusing to settle down? Just like Manu, never considering others—"

"That right there," yelled Kris, staring at me. He stood up from the table and reached for his gym bag. "That's why I never fucking come home."

Nani didn't say another word after Kris walked out. She went upstairs, and after a few minutes, I realized she wasn't coming back
down. I tried to finish cooking alone, but I was frazzled, uneven,
and ended up burning half the dishes.

I scraped the tray of blackened chicken into the garbage, trying
not to focus on the way Kris had just left like that. I managed to
salvage the biryani and one of the *subjis*, but I didn't feel like eating
any of it. I put the food away in Tupperware containers, washed
and dried the dishes, and scrubbed down the stove top and kitchen
surfaces I'd splattered.

When I was done, I found my way into the living room and
slumped into the couch. I glanced up at the cuckoo clock. It was
early evening, and it was already getting dark. I had a lot of catch-up
work to do before the end of the weekend, but I didn't want to leave
Nani alone. Not yet.

Her tablet was on the coffee table, and I grabbed it. I'd discovered the year earlier that she didn't like using the desktop computer I'd bought her because the den was too cold, so I'd given her
my tablet. She'd been an infuriating student, wanting to play with
it like she had with my old Nintendo before I'd even taught her
what meant what, but eventually, she'd learned. Now she used it to
Skype her sister in India, and send e-mails to her friends about
temple gatherings and her charity projects. I'd even seen her playing games on it, which she'd taught herself to do.

I keyed in her password—1 2 3 4—and spotted in the bottom
right-hand corner that the e-mail icon displayed thirty-eight unread
messages. I clicked on it, determined to set up a spam filter for her.

But when the e-mails appeared, all of them—every single
one—was from IndianSingles.com.

My mouth dropped.

I stared at the screen; was I imagining this? I blinked hard, but the words didn't change. Hesitantly, I clicked on one of the e-mails, and I could feel the blood pumping through my stomach, my throat, my ears.

A welcome message appeared that was addressed to me, and it said I had another "suitor" interested. I scrolled down, and a profile appeared.

> **Pradeep. 35. Accountant. Toronto. Hindu, olive skin, 5′9.5″. 80k salary per year, looking for educated, fair-skinned <30.**

I exited the e-mail, and without thinking, clicked on another.

> **Neil. 32. Dentist living in Oakville. Jet-setter and avid reader. Open to meeting the love of my life.**

And then another.

> **Nish. 27. Computer science geek, Taurus, 5′8″, searching for grl w/ good values + vegetarian chef.**

I clicked through each of the e-mails. One after another. *Jeetu. Vinod. Baljit. Ajay. Gopal. Amar.*

Nani had made a new list, given out my number to men on the Internet, and hadn't even told me. Had I exhausted all the single men she knew? Now she had to go online to pawn me off? All this effort to make sure I found a husband before I turned thirty?

I clicked through the link in the final e-mail, and the web browser flashed to life. IndianSingles.com, it read: "An online destination for Indian singles living abroad searching for that special someone."

I scrolled down, and there I was. My very own profile. My entire life summarized. Everything a man would ever need to know.

Raina. 29. Works at investment bank in Toronto. Nice Hindu girl in search of husband.

I felt the bile rising in my throat. *In search of husband.* Is that all that mattered about me?

And what about after I'd found a husband? Who was I then: A wife? A mother? Eventually a grandmother? Is that all an Indian woman would ever be? *Could* ever be? Someone defined by her relationship to others?

I stared at the photo Nani had used in my profile. She had taken the picture when I wasn't looking, at a café in Southwark during her one visit to London. I was wearing a leather jacket, a cream and poppy red scarf we'd bought that morning on Portobello Road. My hair was combed back into a ponytail, and I'd worn makeup that day. Mascara, black-blue liner. Even lipstick. The canvas tote bag on my shoulder was full of honey-cinnamon cashews and a piece of German chocolate cake that we'd bought at Borough Market for Dev, before we realized that he wasn't coming to meet us.

He'd been called away to Zurich. A merger on the brink of collapsing. I didn't see him for three weeks, and Nani never saw him at all.

I found Nani upstairs meditating by the foot of her bed. She sat cross-legged, her eyes closed on the grape-jam purple yoga mat I'd bought her for her last birthday. Her glasses were off, and there were clumps of balled-up tissues on the floor beside her.

After a moment, she opened her eyes. They were red. "There's my sweet." With her left hand, she tapped on the floor next to her, and I obliged.

I lay down on the mat and rested my head in her lap. She stroked my forehead, brushing the hair out of my face, as I looked up at her. From that angle, I could make out the faint lines in her neck and at the corner of her lips. Her broad cheekbones, the roundness of her small, delicate nose.

"How is chicken? I smell burning."

"That's because it's burned," I said curtly. Her face fell, and I was immediately filled with regret.

Nani playfully pinched my nose, looking down at me. "Well, I would have eaten anyway. I will eat anything my Raina makes for me."

I could feel the tears forming. The lump in my throat. A heaviness in my chest. I wanted to reply, but what was there to say?

Your son is angry with you, just like Mom is, but maybe you deserve it? Maybe it was you who pushed them away?

I thought about the list of men in her inbox waiting for a response. My marriage ad she'd posted online without telling me.

Nani loved me. I was her whole life. But why couldn't she see that she was pushing me away, too?

I rolled toward her, closing my eyes, breathing in her scent. Baby powder. Ginger. Paprika. I started shaking, the tears forming, and I felt her arms wrap around me.

"Don't cry, my Raina," she whispered. "We have each other."

Nani and I would always have each other. But as I buried myself against her, I'd never felt so alone.

Pradeep. Neil. Nish. Jeetu. Vinod. Baljit. Ajay. Gopal. Amar.

Not in a million years.

MAY 20, 2016

Twenty-seven and alone. Twenty-seven, and starting over. She watches marathons of *Degrassi* and *James Bond*. *Golden Girls* and *Star Trek*. She cries most of the day, and then again as she lies in bed trying to fall asleep. She stares at the fading star stickers taped to the ceiling of her old bedroom, thinking how, at twenty-seven, her nani ran both a business and a household in a country that wasn't hers.

How at twenty-seven her mother had had an eleven-year-old daughter and the vivid life of a flight attendant. How even Shay, not quite twenty-seven, is a doctor—and has just moved in with her boyfriend.

And what do I have? Raina thinks to herself.

She has a new condo that she'll get the keys to the following week. She has her old job at the Toronto office, one that they are anxious for her to resume. She has Nani. Shay and her other friends. But the thing she wants most of all—what she must relearn to live without—she has lost. And she has no idea what to do. Raina has no memory of the woman she was before she met Dev, or how that woman managed to function. She barely eats, and moves listlessly from bed to couch. Couch to bed. She is heartbroken and unkempt. She is carelessly adrift.

Nani bakes a cake for her birthday, and in the evening Shay arrives, still gowned in her mint green scrubs. Raina can hear them talking about her in the kitchen.

"This is not depression," she hears her nani say. "This is a breakup. She will be fine."

"She's stopped running." Shay's voice lowers. "I've never seen her like this before."

"Time will heal her. It heals all of us . . ."

Raina rolls her eyes and turns up the sound on the television. She is tired of them. Tired of hearing how that much passion was unhealthy, about their rage for the "asshole" who hurt her. But Dev was not an asshole; it was Raina who walked away, and as she stares blankly at the television, she thinks maybe she shouldn't have.

Was she asking for too much?

Marriage. Kids. Love. A *life* with Dev. She had grown tired of the bits and scraps he left for her to gather up, scavenge for between work hours and out-of-town meetings, between 12 and 6 A.M. when they lay in his bed, half undressed, beaten down from exhaustion. But did she need him to propose? They weren't that old, and it's Nani that wanted to see her married, was it not? It was Nani who *really* wanted the lavish Indian wedding; the weeklong celebrations and the showing off. The expense and traditions. Raina didn't need it, and as she feels acid spark in her stomach, she regrets having asked Dev for it.

Had it only been three weeks since she left? One day they had been lying next to each other, their ankles intercrossed, deciding whether to make Earl Grey or honey lemon tea. And the next?

She plays their breakup scene over and over again in her mind, rewinding and fast-forwarding. Agonizing over every word, every look, every pause.

She had surprised him with plane tickets and a hotel reservation: a two-night stay at a resort in Tuscany for their anniversary.

"You didn't even ask," he had said, not looking at her.

"That was the point." She sat down next to him at the kitchen table. His head was on his hands, and she watched him stare at the surface—shiny, varnished—that neither of them ever ate on.

"I told your assistant not to book any meetings, and even Raymond was—"

"You asked my boss?" He scoffed. "Jesus, Raina, don't you know how unprofessional that is? This is my career—sometimes I don't get a choice about when I have to work."

"It's always a choice—"

"It makes me look bad enough I'm dating a coworker."

She stood up, tears threatening to spill, and slammed the bedroom door behind her. He came into the room seconds later and cradled her, held her until he made her believe he didn't mean it.

Then she had asked him, for the first and last time, the questions that were—and still are—constantly on her mind. Was she ever going to come first? Would he ever meet her nani?

Would he ever ask her to marry him?

When she thinks of what came next, she feels the entire world buckle around her. She was the one to make unreasonable demands, force him to talk about the future, their plans. She had triggered everything, pushed and pulled, molded their relationship, their unhappiness, until there was nothing left to do but leave.

And even though he didn't stop her, she knows it was all her fault.

She reaches for her laptop. With trepidation, she begins typing on the keyboard, drafting an e-mail without knowing what she wants to say, or what purpose it would serve. She is clicking at the keyboard, more furiously now. The pads of her fingers type and clack, and then she hears a floorboard creak.

"What the hell are you doing?"

Raina snaps the computer shut. She turns around, and Nani and Shay are standing behind her, trays of tea and cake in hand. They are glaring at her.

"Were you e-mailing him?" Shay shoves a cup into Raina's hand, and hot tea spills onto their fingers.

Raina sets down the cup, wipes her hands on her shirt. "No."

"Don't lie to me." Shay turns to Nani. "They've been talking still. They text all the time, and *e-mail*, and—"

"Shay!"

Nani gasps. "Why, *beta*?"

"We love each other," says Raina, looking down at her hands. "I don't know if it's really . . . over."

"Oh, it's *over*, all right." Shay shakes her head. "After how he's treated you? You can't stay in contact with him. I refuse. It's masochism."

"*You* refuse?"

"Yes, I refuse. This isn't your call anymore. You have no judgment right now."

Raina turns to Nani. "She's being ridiculous. Are you listening to her?"

"Yes," says Nani. "I am listening, and Shaylee is right. It is time to move on."

Shay has crouched down in front of Raina. She opens the laptop, and skims the screen. Dramatically, slowly, she presses the delete key. "Absolutely not."

"Shay!"

"Don't *Shay* me." She tugs on Raina's ankle. "What's it going to take to get through to you?"

With birthday cake and tea comes another sermon. How Dev is now a lesson learned. How the years she gave him are not a waste; they will make her stronger. She tunes them out, still thinking of Dev. Minutes pass, and when her mind reenters the room, she realizes that Nani and Shay are discussing arranged marriages—*her* arranged marriage. They are discussing how Raina is not ready to start dating again, but how—in a few months, maybe a year—she would be.

Raina starts to resist, but Nani is adamant. She says she does not want to see Raina hurt any longer. She wants to find her a match. See her happy and settled. She wants to make an arrangement and help Raina find the right partner.

As much as Raina wants to please her nani, as much as she's always wanted to, she doesn't want *this*. She wants Dev. She will always want Dev.

"A couple years from now, Raina," says Shay. "If you're single at—thirty, let's say. Why not consider it?"

Nani smiles, rubs Raina's forearm until the fine brown hairs stick upright. *Thirty* feels infinitely far away, the destination elusive. She cannot imagine not yet being married by then, not having Dev in her life.

Nani and Shay are talking on either side of her about what type of man Raina might like—or rather, *should* like. Someone who is tall and handsome, says her nani, but will provide a stable home. Shay disagrees, and says that above all else, he must be humorous and kind; that Raina doesn't need a good match—but someone who can match *her*.

Raina tunes in and out of the chatter. She doesn't bother telling them to settle down, stop planning something that, surely, will never come to fruition. Instead, she nods her head and agrees to the plan. She is suddenly famished, and cutting herself another piece of cake, she glances at the computer. Already, she is crafting another e-mail; just the thought of Dev—the mere suggestion that it's not yet over—has revived her.

NINE

It was well into November already, and I woke up one morning unable to get warm. It hurt to move, to swallow, to think. Still, I was restless, and I almost wished Dev would e-mail me and tell me that he wasn't coming, and my life—however small it was—could get back to normal. But what did normal even mean these days? Tackling Nani's new *online* list, the one with seemingly an infinite number of men? It had been weeks since I discovered her online escapades, and still she hadn't confessed to taking out an ad on IndianSingles.com. She pretended that the men who were calling me—men who I told her I was simply too busy to see—were potential suitors she'd somehow found through her friends.

I abandoned my suit jacket for a thick wool sweater, and swaddled myself in my heaviest parka for the walk to work; still, the late autumn wind tore right through me. Chilled me to the bone. Most of my colleagues' offices were empty when I arrived. My brain felt like a block of ice, and I shut my door, rolled my coat into a thick pillow, and put my head down on the desk. Still, with my eyes closed, I felt queasy, and a sickening dread washed over me.

Did I have the flu? I wanted to call Nani, but I felt too weak to reach for the phone. I kept my eyes closed, thinking I would try in a moment, but the next thing I knew, Zoey's face had appeared in front of me.

She was squatted down next to my desk. A dull sunlight filled the room, and instinctively, I glanced over at the clock.

"Shit!" I tried to lift up my body, but I couldn't.

Zoey touched my forehead, and I wasn't sure if it was my skin that was wet—or hers. "Raina, you're super hot."

I closed my eyes. "A babe, I know."

"I'm being serious . . ."

I noted the tone of concern in Zoey's voice. I felt her tuck my hair behind my ears, and I opened my eyes again. "How was the meeting?"

"Fine . . ." Her eyes hit the floor. "Don't worry. I don't think Bill noticed you weren't there."

"Liar."

"Raina, you're sick." She cushioned me as I tried to sit up again. "You should go home."

Once I sat up, the room spun, and I blinked until it stopped. "I'm fine."

"You look like shit."

"Really, I'm fine." I fumbled for the keyboard, for the button to switch on my PC. "So how was the meeting?"

She stood up and sat on the edge of my desk, her legs waving in and out, knocking against each other. She wouldn't look up from the floor.

"What is it?"

She looked away.

"Zoey, what? Am I fired or something?"

Her eyes darted up and around, out the window, and by the time they finally landed on me, I already knew.

"Boardroom D," she whispered.

I tried not to sprint, to walk at a normal pace, but I kept stumbling. My shoes refused to keep up with my feet, catching on the carpet. I let my hand drag against the wall for balance. A right. Another sharp right. The hallway seemed longer, endless, a mirage of doors and suits, impractical art and sharp edges.

Then finally, I was there. And so was he.

Dev. Exactly as I'd left him. The way he still looked in my mind. The same Dev I knew—and now here—not thousands of miles away, but sitting right in front of me. Handsome and angular, a few sprigs of gray feathered into his sideburns. He was so close, only a glass wall between us; thin, angular lines of fog. He was facing away from me, toward Bill and a few other senior bankers lined up on the opposite side of the table. Dev reclined into his chair. Crossed his right ankle over his left knee, and from where I stood, I could only just see him thumbing the silk of his tie. I knew he would turn around before he did, and sure enough, a moment later, my palm resting on the glass between us, his neck craned slowly around. He looked right at me.

It was only a moment—but that one moment dragged on and on, frozen between heartbeats. Then he waved. A small wave. His hand traveling no more than a couple of degrees. A second later, he turned back around.

Was that it?

I turned and ran. My senses boiled up to the point I couldn't breathe. I felt the weight of it all rising. Tipping. I barely made it to the restroom before it all came retching out.

Dev . . . ?

TEN

Later that week, I saw him through the glass door before he opened it. He hesitated, surveying everyone in the fifty-fourth-floor conference room before slowly pushing through the door. A waiter standing just inside the entrance offered him a mimosa, and Dev, startled, almost dropped it as he picked it up off the tray.

I maneuvered myself farther behind the bar, so he couldn't see me. Watching him, I felt numb, and I didn't know what to say. Or how to feel. I'd been waiting to see him—waiting for *this* moment for so long, and now it felt too sudden. Sprung on me before I was ready. I'd been off sick for two days and had kept my BlackBerry off the whole time, unable to face whether a message from Dev awaited me—or didn't.

"Are you hiding?" I heard Zoey say.

I didn't answer, my eyes glued to Dev. Was I ready to face him? Ready to just walk up like our reunion was the most normal thing in the world? The truth is, I wasn't. I hadn't even fully recovered from the flu, but it was Bill's sixtieth birthday, and his assistant had organized a reception for his division. I had to come in.

A woman I didn't recognize clustered with some of the junior analysts waved Dev over. He smiled, and then walked in their direction.

"Who's that?"

Zoey looked up from her phone, and followed my eyes across the room. "Bridget," she said after a moment, and then looked back down. Zoey had been cool with me ever since I'd left her alone at Shay's engagement party. I'd apologized profusely, and she said she'd forgiven me, but I wasn't so sure she had.

"Are we okay?" I said after a moment.

"Yes, we're fine."

"You're still mad—"

"I'm *not*." Zoey looked up, and sighed. "I'm not mad. It's just hard to see you pine after him like that."

I looked back in his direction. He was talking to the group, and I watched Bridget flick her long, shiny black hair. She was very pretty, and young, with a healthy glow like she was vegetarian and never ate junk food.

"Raina, stop staring. She's just sucking up to him—she's like that." Zoey touched my elbow, holding it until I turned to face her. "Let's go eat."

"Do you like him?"

"Who—Dev?" Zoey scrunched up her mouth, then took a sip of her drink. "Yeah, I do. We had a training seminar with him yesterday. All the juniors like him." She nodded again. "Very experienced—"

I nodded, and looked back toward Dev. He was still talking to Bridget, and I wondered if Zoey was right. Was she really just trying to make a good impression? Or was she flirting—trying something with him? I shuddered. I'd looked at him like that once, too.

"What does Shay think?"

"About Dev being back?"

"Yeah."

"I don't know. Haven't told her." I turned back to Zoey. "Don't look so surprised. She hates him."

"Raina, she's your best friend. I understand your nani not knowing . . . but Shay?"

A waiter passed by with a tray of mimosas, and I wished I could reach for one. But Nani had called, again, saying that I needed to drive home after the party and help her move old boxes out of the garage.

"She doesn't need to know." I glared back at her. "She's busy with work. With Julien, and planning her wedding. Plus, she'd probably kill him before I . . ."

Before I what?

I started to walk over to the buffet, ignoring Zoey's glances as she trailed behind me, knowing she wanted to ask me the same question. What was I doing?

I reached for two plates and handed one to Zoey. We waited in line behind a few bankers I recognized from Chicago. They hovered over the olives, debating the greens and blacks, chili and salty, oiled and preserved.

I felt Zoey's hand on my wrist. "I think you should tell Shay," I heard her say. "I can't help you the way she can, Raina. You're going crazy in there, I can tell. This isn't you. You need some perspective."

"I have perspective," I said coolly. "It's been two years, and I"—I lowered my voice—"truthfully, I am still in love with him, Zoey. What am I supposed to do?"

"You're supposed to tell your best friend—"

"I can't." I grabbed the spoon, dished olives onto her plate, and then another spoonful onto mine. "I won't. I *can*—but I won't."

We inched forward in line, stopping again in front of the salads.

"Your nani. She seems modern—"

"Zoey, please try and understand." I turned to face her. "I'm not telling anyone he's back. I need time to figure this out on my own. So either you help me *deal* with that, or leave me to deal with it my own way."

"Fine," she said, evenly. "I'll help."

"Thank you."

"What do you need help with?" She reached over me for the bread. "Besides all your work Bill keeps sending *me*."

"I need Nani to stop pressuring me to find a husband. That's what I need." We reached the end of the line, and I glanced around, looking for a free spot at the tables. "I need her to stop forcing me on so many dates until I figure out everything with Dev."

"You mean the guy who didn't bother to tell you when he *moved* here?"

"Let's change the subject," I said, looking at her. "How are you? How's Alice?"

"She dyed her hair blond. Raina, it's terrible."

I laughed, which surprised me, because I wasn't sure I'd laughed in weeks.

"Do you think I should tell her?" She followed me to a nearby table and, sitting down next to me, said, "I don't know the protocol."

"Well, does *she* like it?"

"She thinks she looks like Beyoncé. I mean, I think my girlfriend is *hot*, but brown skin and blond hair only works on the queen."

"Do you have a pic—? What is it?" I followed Zoey's eyes to the opposite corner of the room, to Dev and Bridget. They were standing near the entrance, away from everyone else. He was leaning against the wall, her hand on his shoulder, and he was laughing.

He was fucking laughing.

And I was the butt of the joke.

I could feel myself shaking, and I pushed my plate toward Zoey.

"Raina, where are you going?"

"Home," I said, without turning around. I pushed my way through the crowd, trying to keep cool, trying to keep from crying. I had to pass them to leave. I kept my face down as I walked by, but he saw me.

"Raina, hi. How are you? It's been . . . It's been so long."

I had to stop. I forced my feet to slow down, come to a deliberate halt. I looked up, tensed the muscles in my cheeks. "Hello, Dev." I nodded, and then glanced briefly at Bridget. "Hi, there."

"Hello." She had a slight Chinese accent, and perfect teeth.

"I tried ringing you a few times . . . after . . ."

After you turned up to my office without any warning?

"Did you get my messages? How are you feeling? Unwell, still?"

"Oh? I'm just fine." I tried to sound nonchalant, and I avoided his gaze. "Actually, I'm just heading out."

"You're leaving already?" he asked softly.

Why was Bridget staring at me? Why did I feel like I had interrupted something? As if it were Bridget who knew Dev, the one who had the right to stand there speaking with him, and not me? My heart was beating fast, too fast, and I took a deep breath. And then another. "Yes. I have to go. I . . . have a date."

I pushed through the glass door without replying. My feet sped up, and I maneuvered down the hall, trying not to run. I pressed the elevator button, two, three, four times—praying it would hurry. I pushed again, and finally, it arrived. I could sense him running behind me, and I flung myself into the elevator, and a second later, as the doors were closing, he wedged his leg in and the doors stopped short.

"What was *that*?"

He was angry, his jaw tense, and I pushed the close button again, and again, but it wouldn't shut with him there.

"Dev, I'm late. I have to go."

"Raina, stop it." He fought his way into the elevator as a bell started to ring. He put his hands on my arms as the doors closed, and we started drifting downward. "What was that all about?"

"What was *what*, Dev?"

"Please—" He pulled me closer as I tried to move back, as I tried to distance myself for my own good.

"I—"

But then his mouth was on mine; his body, his heat, pressed up against me. My back to the wall, he kissed me—his hands through my hair, on my neck, my waist. I was burning, my senses on overload; and I wanted to push him away, and bring him closer at the same time.

Another bell chimed, and he pulled himself off me just as the door opened. I was out of breath, and I pushed myself off the wall and forward through the door. I walked slowly through the lobby. I could feel him a few steps behind me, and right before I reached the door, I turned around to face him.

"I don't know . . ." I breathed out. "I can't—"

"I didn't mean to make you jealous," he said. He inched closer toward me. "She's on my team. She's just young and ambitious. That's it."

I nodded, looking at my hands, wondering how he managed to make me feel so small and like I was his entire world in the exact same breath. "Why did you move here, Dev?"

"It's not exactly clear. It's been decided I'll go back and forth between here and the New York office for a while—others, too, perhaps."

"So it's temporary that you're here."

"Maybe. Well, I'm not sure." He drew closer to me. "But, now that I'm here, Raina. Now that I see you . . ."

"What?"

"I don't know. But I know I need you in my life. You've always been so good for me."

I *was* good for him. Before me, he'd go weeks without eating green food. Forget to eat, to sleep, obsessed by a file, a problem he couldn't figure out. I'd bought him vitamins and baby aspirin, towels that didn't reek of mildew. Outside, he was tailored suits and the brick walls of a flat he could afford to buy outright, but inside, he was cavernous. Undiscoverable. A boy who played with his power like a small child played house.

"Do you really have a date?"

His voice weak, I knew he still cared. After what we'd shared together, how could he not?

"It's okay if you do." Dev crossed his arms, and I could see on his face he was struggling, putting up a fight.

But for what? When, still, after all this time, he couldn't give in—give in to *us*?

I thought about how Nani had instructed me to come home to move boxes that evening at precisely 7 P.M., but how we didn't have anything in the garage she'd want to throw away or donate. I did have a date. By now, she was fed up with me refusing to meet the new men she'd been suggesting, so tonight, there'd be another ambush. There would be an Ajit or Sheev or Raj waiting for me at home, and there was nothing I could do about it.

"I wouldn't like it." He put his hand gently on my face, on my neck. "But you need to do what makes you happy, love."

Dev made me happy. He *would* make me happy.

"You're off on a date, then?"

And even though I hated myself for it, I knew that I would keep waiting. All I wanted was this second chance.

"No, Dev." I shook my head. "I don't have a date. I'm . . . still under the weather. And I need to go."

I walked home in a trance. Two years later, Dev was back in my life, exactly how I had left him. Still threaded in ambition. Still a man who wanted me. Still a man who needed time.

Date #5

"Raina, did you hear that?"

I looked up from my food. "Sorry?" I looked between Nani and . . . I'd already forgotten his name. I shook my head.

Nani touched her napkin to her lips, as if embarrassed on my behalf. "Neil was telling us about—"

"Auntie, it's nothing—"

"What is this *nothing* business?" She sat up proudly in her chair. "You protected this country—like in the movies, like that man with brown hair—"

"You were in the army?" I asked him, trying to make an effort.

"Just so they would pay for dental school."

"Clever."

Nani pressed another naan into his hand. "More?"

"I'm good, Auntie."

"Please. Eat *more*." She lunged for the raita, ladled it onto his plate. "You're too skinny."

"Let me finish this, and then I'll have more." Neil wiped his hands on a napkin and touched her hand. "Auntie, please sit down and join us. I can't eat until you eat."

"Nonsense—"

"I insist." He stood up and guided her to her own chair. "Don't tell my ma," he said, leaning in close to her as he helped her sit, "but this—*Auntie*—it's incredible. Much better than her cooking."

Nani arched her eyebrows at me. "So cute, Raina. And *so* sweet."

I zoned out again. I'd been remembering that time that Dev almost proposed. Or could have. Two months before I'd left London, when we took a Sunday morning off from work, caught the 55 to Chinatown for dim sum. The sun was out, and in the February chill, we walked back, wound our way through Soho, Holborn, and then right through Hatton Garden. The Jewelery Quarter. Where men like Dev came to buy a ring.

We walked by one shop, and then another—endless windows of round cuts and princess cuts, gold and platinum. In the reflection of one of the windows, I caught him staring, and I looked down at my shoes.

"What if—"

"Do you reckon—"

"You first." He pulled me out of the sidewalk traffic and against a shop wall. The wind had blown a strand of hair into my mouth, and he gently brushed it aside.

"No. You go."

Was this it? I remembered thinking—hoping—as he looked at the sky, the brick walls, anywhere but me. He leaned in. He opened his mouth. And then, just when it could have happened—when, in a million times replayed over in my head, it *should* have happened— I felt a vibration through his touch, and he reached into his pocket.

It wasn't it.

"I should take this," he'd said, darting briskly across the street, his BlackBerry wedged against his shoulder, me half a stride behind him the whole walk home. And by the time we got back to his flat, and he set down his keys on the coffee table with a tired clang, the moment had passed. Our laptops were back open. And our lives resumed their usual course.

Nani's voice roused me. "The one with Tom Hanks?" she asked. She reached over the table and spooned more dal onto my plate. Eyeing me, she knocked the spoon hard on the ceramic. "Raina, what do you think?"

"Huh?"

"*Saving Private Ryan*," said Neil. "Great movie."

"I haven't seen it," I said.

He clutched his chest. "You haven't seen it?"

"No."

"It is on the movie channel all the time," said Nani.

"I'll have to check it out."

"You should." Neil pinched off a piece of naan and dunked it in the *saag*. "Maybe we should watch it sometime . . ."

"Raina loves reading, too," I heard Nani say. "Not just movies."

I winced, and I felt Nani and Neil looking at me.

"Don't you, Raina?"

I nodded, avoiding their glances. Did Nani see Neil as the picture-perfect son-in-law and father of my children? A man who would rouse me from my own limp life and, magically, make everything okay? Nani wanted me to fall in love with him, leap after him. Skip over Mom's generation and turn right into her. She wanted this kitchen table full, full of hungry, smiling people—a fantasy no one in her family had ever been able to fulfill. Neil was exactly what she wanted. But wasn't I finally ready to admit to myself I didn't want her to choose for me?

"What do you like to read?" Neil asked.

I moved my food around with my fork. "You know. Whatever's around."

"And who's that written by?"

I looked up. He was smiling at me. His perfect, genuine smile. Straight teeth—unlike Dev's, pale white and splintered—hidden beneath a smirk. Was Dev still at the party? I wondered. Why wasn't *he* at our kitchen table?

"Well," I said finally, looking at Neil. "I have a lot of favorite books."

"Pick one." Neil leaned toward me.

"My friend Zoey just lent me *The Catcher in the Rye*." I shrugged. "I never read it when I was young. I liked it."

"That's one of my favorites."

"Yeah, well, a lot of people like it."

Neil grinned, and I caught him looking at my neck. I saw that familiar flaring of heat, and I winced.

"Neil," said Nani. "I can make you chai?"

Was it only that afternoon that Dev had finally pressed his lips against mine the way he used to? A moment of blinding exhilaration, and then the metal doors parting, the fluorescent light pouring in. I squeezed my eyes shut. But what about Nani? I loved them both so much. *Too much*, as Shay liked to say. Loved them more than I knew how to understand. Why couldn't they fit together somehow?

"Sure, Auntie. Would you like some help?"

"You sit. I will make."

Nani stood up from the table, and the moment she turned around, I grabbed my phone from my back pocket. I checked the screen, and there it was. A message from Dev—from thirty-eight minutes ago.

Raina—I need to know you're all right. Are you feeling
better? The party is shit without you here.

Just then, another e-mail popped up.

I can't stop thinking about that kiss.

Dev wanted me. I knew he still wanted me.

Why had I run—*again*? Why hadn't I stood there, face-to-face,
and told him that he had to choose? That it was time for him to
pick me—this time *really* love me—or let me go?

"Are you okay?" I heard Neil's voice. "Raina?"

What was I doing here? With Neil? I needed more time.
My breath came uneven. Jagged. I felt my body flashing hot and
cold.

Nani's voice, drawing closer. "Ill again?"

"I'm sorry." I stood up so hard my chair flung backward. "I
can't do this now."

I could hear her saying good-bye to what's-his-name at the door.
Making excuses for me—that I was still ill, overburdened at work.
After a moment, the front door thudded shut, and when I heard
her start to climb the stairs, I shoved her list back into my purse
where I'd kept it all these months. I heard the door creak open, the
hum of the light as she switched it on.

"I made ginger tea."

I felt her sit down on the edge of my bed; the shifting of her
body weight as she released a sigh. "You should have told me you
were still feeling ill. I would have postponed."

Postponed something I hadn't even agreed to? That she and

Auntie Sarla, and probably even Shay, had concocted together? So there was no more single Raina to worry over?

"Tell me, where are you feeling ill?"

"I'm not *ill*." I tugged at the covers and wrapped myself tighter. "I'm a lot better today."

"You didn't eat much." I felt Nani's hand on my back, and I resisted the urge to pull away. "I wrapped your plate and put it in fridge."

I didn't answer.

"Okay, so you didn't like Neil. Maybe he is a bit boring, *nah*?" She laughed. "I have found another. His name is Chirag. He—"

"Will you just cut it out?" I barked into the pillow, because I couldn't look at her. "I saw my profile on IndianSingles.com. I know where you're finding them now. Did you really have to put up a marriage ad for me?"

I heard Nani sigh again. "I am sorry, my sweet."

"Well, you should be."

"I should have asked first. I can take it down, *nah*? It was silly idea your Auntie Sarla gave me. We can look elsewhere. Not online, then. I'll find others."

It suddenly occurred to me that she wasn't going to stop. This was it. Until I got married, this would be my life.

If only I could marry *Dev*. He was Indian. He would understand that I was almost thirty, and that there'd be pressure on us to get married quickly. We were two years older, and we were still in love after living an ocean apart. Now, wouldn't he be willing to meet Nani? I had to trust that he would be ready for our future.

"Sarla says she knows a nice boy in—"

"Nani. *Please*." I was choking. I couldn't breathe. "Please, *please*, stop." I was crying now. "Just stop. I know I agreed, but I can't—can't take this anymore."

She didn't reply, and my face burning with shame, I buried my face deeper in the pillow. How could I tell her? Would she understand why I was waiting for Dev?

"Raina," I heard Nani say after a moment, her voice wavering. "I must ask you something."

"What's that?" I grumbled.

"Again, at dinner you mentioned this Zoey girl. You mention her often." Nani paused. "Is she more than friend to you?"

I opened my mouth to answer, and then realized what she meant. Was she asking me if I was in a relationship with Zoey?

"I have seen things in movies, you know. And on *Ellen*." Her hand, momentarily frozen, had resumed its comforting massage on my back. "And I was thinking it is so common now, *nah*? It is very *normal*. And I thought that maybe, maybe this is why you are resisting marriage. Maybe I am not finding you the right match because . . ."

She trailed off, and the silence hung thick in the air. I could hear her breathing, the hum of the lights. The sound of a car driving by. The distant tick of the cuckoo clock echoing in the kitchen. Seconds passed, and it occurred to me that Nani didn't just think I was gay: She was okay with it.

"Is this why you've been unhappy with me, my sweet?" Her voice came out tentatively, and I felt her lean down and kiss me on the back of the head, her other hand brushing stray hairs away from my cheek.

What had just happened? Was it really possible that the idea of me being gay didn't upset her? When she was so traditional about other things in her life? My breath was trapped in my lungs, and my heart pounded. I knew I should say something. Letting her believe I was gay couldn't be right. But for some reason, already it made more sense than the truth. If I were gay—just for a while— there'd be no more dates. No more pressure or ambushes. There'd be time. There'd be Dev.

I should have told Nani the truth. I wanted to—everything, all of it—but I couldn't.

I didn't know how. So I didn't say anything.

IndianSingles.com guy w/ Tom Hanks obsession
(Ned? Neil? Nigel?)

ELEVEN

Within days of Nani offering me an excuse for my behavior, strangely, I was beginning to feel like my old self. I'd started sleeping through the night. Running. Eating normal meals, and not bags of chips for dinner. It was as if all the pressure was off my chest and I could finally breathe. No forced dates and looming marriage deadline. No worrying about Nani, or whether Dev would be ready before Nani shoved me down the aisle toward some guy whose name I could barely pronounce. Finally, I had time.

"I don't see how this is a good idea," Zoey had said, when I finally worked up the courage to tell her.

"You think this is a bad idea?"

"No. Not necessarily." She scratched her head. "But it's not a good one. Letting your nani believe you're gay to get out of a few bad dates? It's actually the stupidest thing I have *ever* heard."

"A few? I was practically getting an e-mail every morning with her top ten matches. Organized by height, weight, income tax bracket—"

"All right. I get it. There was a lot of pressure." She bit her lower lip. "Does anyone else know?"

"About Dev?" I shook my head. "No—"

"Raina, no." Zoey rolled her eyes and, her voice lowered, said, "Does anyone else know that you're a 'lesbian'?"

"Kris does. He came over that evening, and I kind of had to tell him."

"And what did he say?"

"Called me a brat and then poured us both a whiskey." I shrugged. "He's never been that interested in my life."

Zoey nodded slowly. "So the damage is minimal. Good. It's not too late to undo it."

I looked at the floor.

"But you don't want to undo it, do you." She paused. "Raina, why are you doing this? I want you to admit it to me."

"I . . ."

"If you have to lie about him to the people you love—can he really be worth it?"

Was she right? Zoey knew me well, and I usually trusted her judgment.

Dev had taken me for lunch only the hour before—a full forty-five minutes between meetings with our BlackBerrys on silent. Reminiscing at the corner table over pesto and chardonnay, it was as if nothing had changed. He was the man that I had fallen for—and I was still the woman in love with him. Every time he e-mailed, whenever I heard his voice passing by in the hall, my mouth curled into a smile. Dev was back in my life—and I was happy again. Couldn't it be as simple as that?

Now that Nani's matchmaking arrangement was off the table, every morning there was that same flutter in my stomach. A feeling of delight, rather than the weight of constantly disappointing the person who meant the most to me.

Sure, Dev traveled constantly, and was just as likely to be in New York, Chicago, or Los Angeles, but he was part of my life again—and I was in his. In every passing moment, I grew more and more sure that this was it. I knew that the last two years would only be one chapter of our story. Dev needed time to fully commit—and finally, we had it. The Bollywood struggle behind us, it was time for the third act.

"He's worth it," I said. He had to be.

The moment I hadn't denied to Nani that I was gay, everything changed. Harder than her questions I didn't know the answers to, more disconcerting than a fresh list of potential husbands, was her concern. Her empathy. Accepting who she thought I was seemingly defied everything she had grown up to stand for. It was as if ten years of the *Ellen* show had changed her into a woman I hadn't realized she'd become. And while it impressed me, it was downright baffling.

Shouldn't she have been angry? No one in our community was gay, or at least publicly out of the closet. It just wasn't something Indian people did. No matter how progressive she'd become in recent years, how was this acceptable to her?

The idea of me with another woman did not upset her; rather, she couldn't wrap her head around why Zoey and I were just friends. Didn't I care about her? Wouldn't Zoey make a great partner for me? Nani wouldn't let up, and I started to avoid her, and visited her less and less often.

It was harder to put on the act face-to-face, and until Dev was ready for a real commitment—until I could face her with the truth—I didn't want to see her. I didn't know how I would "come out" again, or how she would respond. But as I wrestled with my relationship status with Dev, the few hours we spent together every time he was in town never culminating in more than a hug, sometimes a kiss, I couldn't bring myself to think about what would happen next. I couldn't even imagine what I would say, or how long—another week, or month—I would have to keep up the charade.

But surely, after he'd settled into his new job, he and I would meet Nani as a united front.

"Just a few months now! Can you believe?" Auntie Sarla's voice boomed from the back seat of my Jeep.

"Coming quickly, Shaylee!" said Nani, reaching forward and patting Shay on the shoulder. Shay glanced over at me, grinning, shaking her head from side to side in mock excitement.

I turned up the heat, and wrapped my scarf tighter around my neck as we waited at a red light. The four of us had spent the day running wedding errands together. Shay, who it felt like I hadn't seen in months, and I barely had time to catch up as Nani and Auntie Sarla remained fixated from the back seat on discussions of tiered cakes and Hindu priests, chiffon lining and perfectly timed flower deliveries. The whole time, Shay listened to Auntie Sarla plan her wedding with glazed disinterest, piping in only to change the radio station during the drive from one vendor to another, or to mock Auntie Sarla's accent.

After our last appointment with a ribbon vendor, we drove back toward home. It was only late afternoon, and already it looked like dusk, night slowly falling over the icy roads. While Nani and Auntie Sarla were speaking in Hindi about the guest list, Shay leaned in toward me.

"Are we okay?" she whispered.

I concentrated on the road, carefully steered around a patch of ice. "Not really. I still haven't put on my winter tires."

"You know what I mean, Raina."

From the side, I could see Shay still looking at me, and then she looked back at the road.

"Yeah, Shay. We're fine."

"How's the dating—have you met anyone you liked?"

Mid-sentence, Auntie Sarla stopped talking, and her face appeared between us. "You live together—and you don't *know*, Shaylee?"

Shay looked at me, and then back at Auntie Sarla. "Raina and I work different hours. Remember, Ma? I don't see her a lot."

She nodded, and then slid a stubby finger across the armrest. "Raina, do you ever clean your car?"

"Sarla," I heard Nani say. "Don't interfere. We're going to have accident."

Auntie Sarla's face disappeared. "Well. *Someone* should interfere with that girl."

"Ma," said Shay. "Don't start."

"Speak to this child, Suvali. She will never get married this way."

I pressed my foot hard against the brake pedal, wishing I could kick it.

"There is nothing to speak of, Sarla," I heard Nani say after a moment. "Who Raina marries is *Raina's* decision."

"What marriage? There won't be a marriage if she keeps on like this. Not like my Shaylee—"

"Ma, don't bring me into this."

"Raina is being selfish—"

"Sarla, enough!" Nani's voice prickled my skin, and the car fell silent. "Do not lecture us like this. I will handle my own girl." I turned back to face the front, slowly lifted my foot off the brake as the light turned green.

"I have confidence in whatever she decides," said Nani.

I saw Nani glancing at me in the rearview mirror, and as I accelerated through the intersection, a wave of guilt tore through me.

I'd decided to create a mess, one that Nani and I might not be able to get out of easily.

MAY 20, 2015

"You're getting old, love."

Raina giggles, and rolls over to face him. "How sweet of you to remind me."

It is still dark outside on the Clerkenwell Green, and the only light comes from the touch lamp on Dev's nightstand. In its warm, buttery glow, Raina can vaguely see the outline of his body nestled next to hers, the profile of his nose and eyelashes as he moves his head on the pillow.

"You're properly over the hill now."

"Oh, *shush*."

"Let me think," he says, moving his face closer to hers. "When I turned twenty-six, I—"

"Bawled like a baby?"

"Got promoted."

"Well then," whispers Raina, as he kisses her nose. "Why don't you promote me."

They hit the snooze button three, four times—and on the fifth push, Dev declares he will forgo his morning routine at the gym. Raina kisses him, sleepily, and smiles. They both work long hours, but despite the demands on their time, their health—even, at times, their relationship—Raina has never been this happy. It is her birthday, the one-year anniversary with the man she loves— and she lives in *London*, a thriving, humming city that fiercely loves her back. She works in the very heart, the very center of the world, and sometimes, lying there in a dreamlike state, Dev curled around her, it's hard to believe this is her life.

It is nothing like her nani's; a limb of her husband's journey into a new world, working hard with little respect for a community to which Raina never even felt she belonged. It is nothing like her mother's, either: a life disjointed and misunderstood, carelessly formed at the fringe of others'.

For the first time, Raina is finding her own way. She is doing things on her own terms, without anyone telling her who and why, how and where; she is living a life that is completely her own.

With him, Raina feels like a different kind of Indian.

Together, they are modern Indians. Ones who don't go to temple just to prove to others they believe in God, who can try a non-Indian cuisine—blander, with less spice—and enjoy it. Together, they command power and respect; dine, drink, and travel without worrying about money the way their families did. And, Raina often muses, they will raise their children differently, too. They will teach them that they don't need to be a doctor to succeed in life; they will teach them to believe that they are good enough exactly as they are.

Raina and Dev are kissing and his hand is up her shirt when a phone buzzes on the bedside table. Dev removes his hand and reaches for it.

"Oh, it's yours."

Raina grabs it, and a moment later, frowns. "It's Nani."

"Go on, then."

Raina takes a deep breath, and accepts the call. "Hi, Nani."

"Haaaaappy bird-*day*," she sings, almost screams, into the phone. She is loud, so loud that Raina uses her hand to cover Dev's mouth, muffle the laughter. Raina has tried many times to teach her nani that cell phones these days are better than landlines; that she needn't yell into the phone just because Raina is overseas.

"Are you having a happy bird-day?" Nani asks. "Did I wake?"

"No, no. I'm up. Just getting ready for work."

"*Aacha.*"

Raina glances at the clock. It is past midnight in Toronto. "Why are you up so late?"

"Oh, just missing my Raina," says Nani. "You are twenty-*six*, now, *nah*?"

Dev mouths "so old," and Raina lightly pushes him away. He smiles and closes his eyes, rests on his back beside her.

"How is Dev?" Nani asks.

"Good."

"He will have a nice birthday for you? If you were home, I'd make you your favorite—"

"Yes, Nani. I'll see him at work, and then we're having dinner with friends."

"What are you eating?"

"Turkish, I think."

"It is not Thanksgiving—"

Raina laughs. "No, Nani. Turkish—from Turkey, the country. Middle Eastern food. Like couscous?"

"Huh?"

"It's kind of like rice."

"Are you eating enough? Are you being healthy?"

"Yes, Nani."

There is a pause—long, palpable—and Raina wonders if her nani is still there.

"I'd like to meet Dev," she says finally.

Raina turns to look at him. His eyes are discernably closed, and Raina pokes him until he opens them.

"He wants to meet you, too."

"When?"

"I don't know." Raina leans back in bed, stares at her toes poking out from the covers. "You know you can come visit anytime."

"He can come here?"

Raina nods into the phone, and a moment later says, "Yeah. Maybe."

She had asked Dev to come with her on her last trip home, but he said he was too busy with work. Lately, she has been thinking about asking again for him to come home and meet Nani and Shay, to see a glimpse of her old life, but she is afraid to bring it up; afraid he'll say no again.

"*Beta*, it has been long time now. It is time for Dev to visit—"

"Nani, please, not today."

"You are planning to marry him, and I don't know if he's nice boy. I don't know his family—"

Nani continues, her voice growing louder, and Dev rolls over on his side.

"He cannot come and meet us? He is Indian, *nah*? He does not understand how things should be—"

"*Please*, not now," Raina says firmly. She looks over at Dev, and sees that he's crawling out of bed. Without looking at her, in only his pajama shorts, he walks out of the bedroom.

". . . Dev cannot at least *call* and tell me his intentions? His parents cannot call me—"

A panic boils up inside of Raina, the warmth beside her suddenly gone.

"—and you will stay in that country for *him*? You—"

This is what she fears: Dev walking away. Dev leaving her, taking everything—her whole life—away with him.

"Nani," she says sweetly, placating. Her hand on her chest, she forces herself to calm down; forces out the words that her nani needs to hear—that, right now, Raina herself needs to say.

Dev and Raina will get married.

Dev and Raina are in love, and there is absolutely nothing to worry about.

After a few moments, she hangs up and sets her phone back on the nightstand. The bedroom door has closed behind him, and she can't hear anything—just a garbage truck outside the window, beeping, rumbling back and forth along the Clerkenwell Green.

"Dev?"

She is cold, and pulls the blanket around her. Has he already hopped into the shower, started his day without her?

Is she—is her nani—scaring him away?

They are together, committed, in love—but marriage, a life in permanency, is still far away. Together, Raina and Dev decided they wouldn't be *Indian* about their relationship: Their families wouldn't be involved, and they would date and take their time. They would enjoy life, and only talk about the future in an abstract way that didn't tie them down, didn't tie them together.

They decided it *together*, didn't they?

Raina sits up. She is about to get out of bed, when Dev pushes the door open. He stands in the doorway with a sleepy smile, and holds out two cups of tea.

Raina's mind releases, her muscles thaw. He walks to the edge of the bed, and sets the tea on the nightstand.

She smiles at him. "Come back to bed."

He drops to his knees on the mattress, and crawls over to her. "Anything you say, love."

"Sorry about that," Raina says after a moment.

He laughs. "I have a nani, too."

His family lives only a forty-five-minute tube journey from the city. She thinks about asking when she'll meet them, but decides against it.

Raina hears the metal gates opening from the shop across the road, and she glances at the clock. "Wait, what time is it?"

He groans, rolls more fully on top of her.

"What time is your meeting?"

He opens one eye, and then shuts it again.

"Honey, you really need to get up." With half strength, she tries to shift him, but he is deadweight on top of her.

"Dev?"

Sleepily, he kisses her chest. "Five more minutes?" He rolls onto his other cheek. "I can't make it through the day without this, Raina."

TWELVE

No one said much on the drive back to the suburbs. We dropped off Shay and Auntie Sarla, and then I drove Nani home. She insisted I come inside for dinner and wouldn't accept my excuse about work deadlines, my wet laundry still in the machine. After almost five minutes of bickering in the driveway, her voice crawling an octave higher with each breath, I turned off the ignition and agreed to come in.

Dread washed over me as I walked into the house. I knew what was coming, and I wasn't ready to deal with it. I'd skirted around the truth before—small lies about my blind dates, and in high school, about missed curfews or why my hair smelled like cigarette smoke—but never like this. I followed her into the kitchen, and I sat down at the table as she washed her hands and started to dice an onion. Halfway through, she set down the knife and looked at me.

"Why have you not told Shaylee?"

"Nani . . ."

"I am *proud* of you, Raina. She will be too, *nah*?"

"Not now, okay?"

"And you won't bring Zoey here for dinner? So I can get to know her properly?"

"I've told you a hundred times we're not together. Zoey is just a friend."

She wiped her hands on a dishrag. "You know, I read a blogger today. Do you know an Edith Windsor? She married a woman, and changed the American constitution."

"That's not exactly how it happened."

"This *Edith*—very strange name for a woman, but—"

"I really appreciate you trying to support me, but I just don't want"—I struggled for words—"I don't need—"

"Yes." Nani's voice cracked. "You do *need*. I refuse to be one of those mothers who say it's okay for everyone else to be gay, but not their own child." She bit down on her lips, and looked away. She always looked away when she cried, even when I was young. Even when the worst had just happened.

I walked toward her, wrapped my arms around her, and gave her a hug, and she turned around and pressed against me. She was so tiny in my arms, frail yet plump, her head resting beneath my shoulders. After a few moments, she pulled away, and wiping her face with the backs of her hands, she looked up at me.

Why was I putting up this wall between us? She loved me. She *supported* me—even with something like this that was foreign to her. Why wouldn't she approve of me getting back together with my ex-boyfriend?

Except I wasn't with Dev. Not yet. And if I told her that two years later I was still waiting for him, what would she say? Would she look at me the way she looked at Mom?

The daughter who had a child at sixteen. The daughter who

wanted nothing to do with her family, culture, or traditions. The daughter who seemingly lived with a new man every time she called home.

"What do you need, Raina, *nah*?" Nani brushed my face with her hand. "Tell me."

"I . . ."

It was the first time we'd spoken alone and in person since that evening, and I couldn't look at her. What the hell was I doing lying to her about something like this? I opened my mouth, keeping my eyes on the floor.

"I . . ."

Where did I even begin?

"You are seeming very tense." Nani touched my chin, tilting it upward until we were face-to-face. "I have idea. I know what always makes you feel better . . ."

"Vodka?"

She tutted at me.

"*Fine*. Gin then."

"Oh, *beta*." She pointed up the stairs. "Do you still have running shoes here?"

I nodded, suddenly grateful for the escape.

"Then *jao*. I will have hot dal *makhani* waiting for you!"

I dug through my closet and found my old pair of bright pink sneakers and ratty sweatpants. Nani had chopped off the frays around the ankles, and my winter-themed socks peeked out. She stopped me at the door, and tucked one of Nana's old newsboy caps on my head, a vomit brown fleece around my arms.

I stepped outside the door, immediately thankful for Nana's coat, which, surprisingly, fit me perfectly. I slammed the door behind me and picked up speed as I hopped down the front steps.

The air had chilled, and I took a sharp breath—concentrating on breathing in and out—while closing my eyes briefly as I hopped off the sidewalk, over a partially frozen puddle, and ran toward the park. I focused on my breath, on the feel of the road. Anything but Nani, but Dev, trying to will myself to once again feel light.

As I ran faster, my nose and mouth grew numb. I darted off the road and onto the dirt path toward the school, and the faster I ran, the lighter I felt. I ignored the sharp feeling in my lungs and pushed on. I started to sprint, the wind shrieking into my ears as I crossed onto the football field. It was close to dark, the streetlights faint behind the old brick of the school. My legs were tired, but I pressed on, forcing myself to go faster, and faster, my fingers clenched as I swung my arms back and forth.

I ran the long way around the field, and on the final side of the square block, it struck me that it had been fifteen years since the first day I had walked through the doors of a school where so much of consequence seemed to have happened. It was where Shay and I had gone from being the offspring of two friends to being best friends ourselves. Where I'd thrown the winning basket in the city basketball championship. It was where Mom, crying and bloated in the nurse's office, had found out she was pregnant.

I was less than fifty meters from the school, and again, I picked up speed. In the distance, I could see a lone silhouette shooting a basketball in the courts beside the parking lot. I drew closer. He looked too old to be a student, too tall, and I watched him arc the ball effortlessly through the hoop again and again. Even in the dark, I could almost see the creases on his face, the square of his jaw. I rubbed the sweat from my eyelids with the back of my hand, and just as he went up to take another shot, right when I passed him, our eyes met. He missed the shot, and the ball ricocheted loudly off the rim.

"Well," he called out to me, his arms still poised in the air. "Look who it is."

"Asher?" I panted, walking up to the fence. I barely recognized him without his beard. "What are you doing here?"

"Me?" The ball bounced back to him and he grabbed it. "What are you doing here?"

"This is"—I breathed—"my school."

"This is *my* school."

"What, you never graduated?"

He ducked the ball between his legs and caught it on the other side. "I teach here—thank you very much. The university let me re-enroll, so this year I'm going to finish up my teacher training."

"I see. Well, I used to go here. My grandmother's house is right over there," I said, gesturing across the field.

"You lived with her growing up?"

I nodded. "Mom's in Philadelphia. But Nani is here."

"A family saga?"

"It's not important."

"I imagine it's quite important."

I'd caught my breath, and I ducked through a tear in the metal fence and walked onto the court. Up close, in the shadows of the streetlights nearby, I noticed again how different Asher looked. His wide nose and lips. The slate gray of his eyes. And even though his beard was gone, there was still something wild about him.

He caught my eye, and I looked away. I bent down and tucked my laces into my red and white socks. "What happened to your face?" I mumbled, standing back up. "It was quite the ecosystem."

He smirked. "I decided to shave it. Thought the kids would take me more seriously."

"They certainly won't take your ball skills seriously. That last shot there." I shook my head. "Just brutal."

"I was frightened. Thought I had a stalker."

I lunged forward and tipped the ball out of his arm, catching it with one hand. "I used to play, you know. Varsity."

"Really? I coach the girls' team here."

"Oh yeah?" I dribbled the ball between my knees in wide figure eights. "And how are they?"

"They play like a bunch of girls."

"So they're *much* better than you." I shot the ball. It arced too high and bounced off the backboard.

"Someone's out of practice."

I ran for the loose ball, turned back to him, and then sliced it into his chest. "At least I'm not out of shape."

"Is that smack talk?" He dribbled the ball toward me, and I crouched down, preparing to swat it from his hands. At the last moment, he jutted out to the left, and then right again, dribbling the ball around me and up to the hoop for a layup. He caught the ball after it swished through the net, planted it slowly on his hip, and winked.

"Game on."

Asher won—by a long shot. For every point I managed—a fluke toss from the top of the key, a blind hook shot from beneath the basket—Asher scored five. He had at least fifty pounds on me, and a good six inches. I had forgotten how much I loved the game when challenged.

After I'd graduated high school, Nana hadn't wanted me to try out for the university team; he wanted me to focus on studying. So instead, I joined rec leagues when it fit into my class schedule. Played pickup games on the weekend when the girls from the team—who'd gone off to play college ball all over Canada—were home for Thanksgiving or summer vacation. My skills stalled while theirs got better. And even though those games reminded me of what I could have been, or not been, I loved that feeling of having to work for something. Work *at* something, and having the motivation, the passion, to be better.

After over half an hour of mocking each other, Asher overpowering me, effortlessly swatting the ball down whenever I tried to shoot, I was laughing too hard to keep playing. Panting, I lay down in the middle of the court and sprawled into a starfish.

"That's it?" In the shadows, I saw his smirk hovering above me. "Did I *beat* the infamous Raina?"

After I nodded, he disappeared from my view, and a few seconds later reappeared. He sat down next to me and handed me a water bottle. I took a long sip, some of it spilling down my chin, and handed it back.

"Good game."

I smiled. "Shut up."

"What?"

"You're being smug."

"I'm not being smug. I'm being *civil*." He knocked his knee lightly against mine. "I think someone just isn't used to losing."

"I let you win."

"Really? And here I thought I was teaching you a lesson."

"And what lesson is that, Mr. Klein?"

"It's not over yet—I don't want to spoil it."

"Is there going to be an exam?"

He grinned at me. Crooked, almost naughty, and I blushed. I could feel Asher's eyes still on me as I sat up. I reached over him and grabbed his water bottle, and before taking a sip, aimed it at him like a sword. "Don't think this means we're friends."

"Of course not," he said. "You and I are enemies."

"Sworn enemies."

"And besides." He leaned in close, and I could smell him—like pepper and laundry detergent, and the sticky way boys smell after being outside. "I don't think I can be friends with you. I don't have any sparring equipment."

I rolled my eyes. "I see you're still whining about that."

"I was attacked! Pushed into some desserts—*delicious* desserts, mind you."

"You were bruised for weeks, I'm sure."

"Me?" Asher smiled. "Or your ego?"

I shoved him.

"Ow!"

"As if."

"You're so *physical*." He massaged his shoulder. "What did I ever do to you?"

"Besides embarrass me at my best friend's engagement party?" He didn't answer, and I glanced toward him. He was looking at me, a plain expression on his face. The muscles in his cheeks and around his eyes were relaxed. Genuine.

"I shouldn't have pushed you," I said after a moment, looking back at the pavement between my feet. "I'm sorry."

"Me, too."

"I'm under a lot of pressure from my nani right now." I shrugged. "I'm not—I *wasn't* in the greatest place."

"It's okay. I could tell." He smiled. "I can read you like a book."

"I didn't know you could read."

He grinned, and then a second later, added, "Could that bartender read?"

"Who?"

"He looked a bit young." Asher pressed his lips together, as if thinking hard. "Pass along my number if he needs a tutor, would you?"

"Wait, what?"

Asher's mouth scrunched tight as if he was trying not to laugh, and when I caught his eye, something flickered. Then it hit me.

Josh. The bartender I'd gone home with. Asher had seen us.

"Oh. My. God."

"Please tell me you didn't wear *that*," he said, glancing down at my socks. "Kids these days don't understand fashion."

I hid my face in my knees, and I felt Asher's hand brushing the back of my head. "I like your hat. My dad had one just like it."

"Please. Stop talking."

"Oh, quit worrying so much. It's really not a big deal."

My face was red-hot, and I was sure my entire body flushed. "I'm so embarrassed. I'm never talking to you again."

"What?" He laughed, moving his hand to my back.

"Asher, I can't believe you saw that. I never—"

"Raina," he said loudly. "Look at me." Slowly, I peeled my face up from my knees. He straightened out my shoulders with his hands, waited until I was looking him in the eye. "I was just teasing you," he said gently. "Seriously. Who cares?"

"I care."

"Why?"

I turned away from him, not able to say it out loud: *Because Nani would care. She expects more from me.*

Asher dropped his hands to the pavement and leaned back, his legs outstretched in front of him. The sweat was starting to cool on my skin, and I shivered.

"You know, I dated an Indian girl once. We were like—twenty-one, twenty-two, maybe?" He dug the heel of his sneaker into the pavement. "Her family was very traditional. And they put a lot of pressure on her . . ."

"Is this an analogy?" I asked drily.

"Anyways"—he patted his finger against his lip, shushing

me—"even though she wasn't 'allowed' to date, I convinced her to go out with me. As you can imagine, she was conflicted about—you know—*sex*. Hugely conflicted. But then one afternoon after class she came over, and I thought maybe she finally liked me enough to—"

"Get it on?"

Asher laughed. "Yeah."

"And did she?"

"Not even close. The moment I came near her she started crying—*bawling*, actually—and then left. She refused to speak to me for the rest of the term. And as I'm sure you know, I left university early and—uh, well, I never saw her again."

"You think my problems are about *sex*?"

"No, Raina, my point is that she hated herself. I see so many kids raised to feel shame about who they are, what they want, who they love. And whether it's about sex or identity—or even just making mistakes—when people grow up, sometimes, they screw up. Isn't that the point?"

I looked back at the ground.

"This girl I dated—she was under so much pressure to do the right thing, she didn't even know what it felt like to make a mistake. She didn't have the courage to go out and try something new, something different, and know that she'd still be okay."

I could feel him looking at me, waiting for me to say something. His eyes bore into the side of my neck, and after a minute, I couldn't handle his scrutiny. I jumped up and grabbed the ball.

"Another game?" I turned to face him and dribbled the ball, hard, down and through my legs.

He was biting his lower lip, and I turned back around. I lined up the shot and took it, and it swished through the net.

"You see that?" I ran a lap around the court, pumping my fists in the air, and then ran back toward Asher. "Did you see that?"

"Yeah. I saw it."

I extended my hand. He grabbed it, and I leaned back from his weight as he used my support to pull himself off the ground.

"You know what we should do?" I asked.

"What's that?"

I glanced around the empty field. "Smoke," I whispered.

"You're a smoker?" He winced. "That would explain how easily I beat—"

"No. I mean a *joint*," I mouthed. "Let's smoke up."

"You want to smoke up."

"Yeah, I haven't in years." I grinned.

"You're kidding, right? Shaylee mentioned you liked to joke around."

"No, I'm not joking." I shook my head. "I'm kind of in the mood."

"Being here with *me* . . . puts you in the mood."

"Yeah." I laughed, touched his arm. "So do you have any?"

"You know what, Raina . . . No. I don't have any on me right now." He grabbed the ball from my hand. "Not today."

"Oh. Okay—"

"Must have used it all up at work this week," he said frowning. "Teaching *children*."

"Asher—"

"Look. I've got to run. Dealers to meet. Things to blow up. Irresponsible stuff—you wouldn't understand." He grabbed a tuque from his pocket and shoved it on his head, and without looking at me, turned away. "I'll see you around."

"Asher, wait, I didn't mean—"

But he was gone, already jogging toward the parking lot, his basketball tucked beneath his arm.

MAY 20, 2007

Raina turns eighteen and smokes her first joint. Before this day, she has never thought seriously about smoking marijuana. Even as it billows at the edges of the school parking lot, on back decks, and in the basements of parties, she has never considered it. Her coaches tell her to stay away, threats of slowness and sluggishness, and Raina listens. But on her eighteenth birthday, the season is already over. Basketball, volleyball, track and field—all the games are over. The scores tallied. In the muddy spring schoolyard, the one around which she has jogged thousands of times, there is no one left to race. In a way she is relieved, allows her body to slacken, but knowing graduation is less than a month away, she is also terrified.

The final bell rings, and Raina rushes out of sixth period ahead of her friends. Shay told everyone it was her birthday, and they decorated her locker with dollar-store stickers and ribbons, tacked-on messages penned on hot pink construction paper. Raina tears it all down as she throws her textbooks into her locker, and then races outside the front door. She is greeted by the heat of a May afternoon, the air still fresh with spring. She can smell nothing but the green of the lawn, the clipped hedges running along the sidewalk, and she smiles as she takes a deep breath. She is about to walk home, and she is still smiling when, right in front of the school, she sees Manavi.

Raina hasn't seen her mother in over a year. Her hair is different than the last time she visited. It is now cropped short, light blond and browns like a patchwork quilt. She sits cross-legged on the hood of a cherry red convertible parked in front of the school, and as Raina approaches, she looks up from the magazine open on her lap.

"Happy birthday, Raindrop."

Raina smiles. Now that she is older, she doesn't know what to call her. Manavi. Manu. Ma. Raina has always just avoided addressing her directly, but this time, when she says hello, calls her "Mom," she notes how natural it feels.

Manavi slides off the hood and wraps her arms around Raina. She is a few inches shorter, slightly wider, and she beams as she pulls back. "Shit, when did you grow up?"

"What are you doing here?"

"It's your birthday. Where else would I be?"

She has missed Raina's last three—maybe four—birthdays, but Raina doesn't remind her of this. Raina throws her backpack into the trunk next to her mother's worn-out duffel bag, and they get into the car. Manavi slides on a pair of cat-eye sunglasses and smiles at herself in the rearview mirror, pursing her lips together. Then, she opens her purse and hands Raina an identical pair.

"Really?" Raina can tell they are expensive. She recognizes the brand from airport billboards. Department stores that don't accept cash. She slides them onto her face. "Thanks, Mom. I love them." Their eyes hidden, their noses partially obscured, Raina notes how similar their mouths are. Rosebud lips that bloom into wide, slightly crooked smiles, just a hair too close to their equally soft chins. Manavi starts the car, and Raina turns to face her. "Where are we going?"

"*C'est une surprise.*"

They snack on Dr Pepper and cheese fries Manavi buys at a truck stop outside Belleville, racing down the highway with the windows down, Top 40 music blasting through the speakers. It is dusk by the time they reach Montreal, and they drive to an apartment in Laval that belongs to a friend of Manavi's. He isn't home, and she lets them in with a key. The rooms are tattered—peeling wallpaper, blue carpets with zebra patches of brown. Slits for windows that peer into a back alley. Manavi drops her bag in the middle of the hallway, steps over it as she searches for a radio. They listen to French Canadian pop and get ready for the evening squeezed side by side in the tiny bathroom. Raina is wearing Manavi's dress, sleek red and short, while Manavi has put on emerald green pleather pants, a black top that drips beneath her rib cage. Raina realizes with some surprise that her mother is thirty-four. *Only* thirty-four. Yet, as they stand next to each other, the same light brown foundation highlighting their faces, Raina can barely see the age difference; she can barely see a difference at all.

"You always look tired, kiddo," Manavi says, sorting through her makeup kit. Raina glances sideways in the mirror as Manavi applies black paint to her lids and lashes, erases the faint circles beneath Raina's eyes with a beige pencil.

"I stayed up late last night." Raina notes Manavi's bemused expression, and then shakes her head. "No, not that. I had a math test today."

Manavi rolls her eyes, and Raina, momentarily, feels embarrassed. She tries to think of something to say, wonders why it's so hard, and then it occurs to her that she can't remember the last time she was alone with Manavi. No Nani hovering in the background, disapproving of whatever it was they decided to watch on television, or ordered for dinner. No Nana and Kris making sarcastic comments, sucking the air out of the room. No Shay, filling the void, whenever the silence became too much.

While waiting for a taxi, Manavi sends Raina across the street to a liquor store. She is nervous when she slides her driver's license across the counter, prepared to confirm out loud that she is eighteen and, in Quebec, finally legal. The man slides it back without looking, and Raina smiles to herself. She stuffs the bottle of vodka into her purse, the expensive brand with gold glitter floating in it like a snow globe, and with her chin up, she walks back across the road to Manavi.

Raina is drunk by the time they stumble out of the cab in Montreal. Over half of the glitter floats in her empty stomach, and Manavi buys them both a hot dog from a street vendor on St. Catherine's. Now, Raina feels like talking, and she natters pointlessly to Manavi as they eat—about the lights, the churches, the strip clubs they pass—and when a group of boys stop to talk to them, Manavi slyly wipes the crumbs off Raina's lips, and winks.

The boys take them to club, and once they are standing in line, Raina begins to waver, a flood of nausea passing through her every time she blinks, and she grabs on to the black metal bars stretched across the window for support. Manavi pulls her hands away, and a moment later, the boys are leading them to the front of the line, and Raina sees one of them shove a fistful of bills into the bouncer's hand.

Raina can barely walk. Electronica pounds through her ears. With her eyes closed, she stumbles around aimlessly, guided by hands, people's breath like wet fog on her face. She can smell mold, the sweat on everyone around her, and soon she finds herself leaning on Manavi. She hands her a shot. Mindlessly, Raina drinks it, and then another—shiny blue liquid burning the back of her mouth, trickling down. Every time she opens her eyes, Raina thinks she might be sick, epileptic flashes of light, emerald green pleather, and clusters of faces she keeps pushing away. Raina is disoriented, and every time she hears her mother's laugh, the blinking lights that blister her eyes, she thinks of her nani.

She wants to go home.

The taste of blue rises in her throat, and then she smells Manavi's perfume, and feels her tuck a stray hair behind her ear. She catches Manavi's eye and points to the door. Manavi glances at her watch, rolls her eyes, and without saying good-bye to the others, they leave.

They don't speak as they turn off of St. Catherine's, as Manavi leads her to the Latin Quarter. They wind loosely through cobblestoned streets—some pitch black between the crossroads. The sound of traffic grows more distant, and in the hollow silence, Raina can hear nothing but the even click of Manavi's heels. It strikes her that her mother knows exactly where she's going, her footsteps assured and direct, as if, without Raina ever having known, Manavi has lived in Montreal before.

Ahead, Raina sees a group of men standing on the stoop of an old apartment building, and the men stop talking as they approach. Raina glances behind her. No one else is around, and she slows her feet. She feels hesitant, but Manavi's heels keep pace.

"*Mademoiselle*," says the one with a goatee. His mouth is open, and Raina can make out his tongue as it slices across his front teeth. He is looking at Manavi. "*Vous êtes belle ce soir.*"

"*Merci. Toi aussi.*" Manavi smiles. Flashes him her white teeth. He beckons her, and to Raina's surprise, she walks up the stairs. They speak French to each other, quickly, effortlessly. She tries to catch what they are saying, but Raina has never been good at

French, and until tonight, she has always assumed Manavi wasn't, either. Every so often, one of the other men, his eyes black, glances down at Raina and gestures for her to join him. Raina shakes her head. She still feels nauseous, light-headed, and she wants to go home.

"*La soeur?*"

Manavi laughs, and then glances down the stairs. "He thinks we're sisters."

Raina inches up the steps. She stands at the edge, watching them converse. After a few minutes, the man with the goatee—the one whose hand is now tucked around Manavi's waist—pulls out a joint. He sets it on Manavi's bottom lip, lights it, and she inhales until the end glows amber. She breathes out, smoke billowing, and then offers it to Raina.

"No, thanks," Raina mumbles.

Manavi turns to her. "Just take it." She looks irritated, and when Raina hesitates again, she pushes it into her hand. "Be chill, Raina. Stop worrying about everything." She glances back at the men, mumbles something in French, and everyone laughs. And they keep laughing until Raina takes a long, thick puff, and her lungs start to burn.

Raina doesn't remember the rest of the night. Bits and pieces. Faint smells and feelings. Coughing so hard she thinks she just might die; her cheek, cold against a toilet seat reeking of shit. The night—and well into the morning—is a trance. An unfamiliar room spinning above, her eyelashes batting to a beat she makes up in her head. Vaguer memories, still, of how she falls asleep on a couch next to the man with the black eyes, the one who, as she dips in and out of sleep, smells like pot roast and keeps trying to touch her.

Manavi shakes Raina awake, smiles down at her weakly. It is

light outside, and Raina notices that Manavi's top is inside out. Without saying a word to each other, they slip out and take a taxi back to the apartment—and ten minutes later, they climb back into Manavi's rental convertible. Raina's head pounds the whole way home, made worse by the music—brash and loud—that Manavi insists on listening to. Finally, hours later, they are home. Raina swings open the door, and she is surprised that no sounds or smells are there to greet her. Nothing is cooking, and Nani's voice does not bubble out beneath the crack of the kitchen door, ushering her into the kitchen for a cup of chai or a taste of whatever is simmering on the back burner.

Manavi throws down her bag. "Anyone home?"

Nana appears at the top of the stairs, the cordless phone pressed into his chest with both hands. His hands slowly drop to his sides.

"Is Ma home?"

He glances between Raina and Manavi, and without saying anything, he turns around. Raina hears his door upstairs click, the lock slide into place, and she is overwhelmed with a sense of dread. She glances at Manavi, who is seemingly unchanged, and follows her into the kitchen. Nani is sitting at the kitchen table. She is motionless, her hands clenched white into two fists resting in front of her. She doesn't look up to greet them, and when Raina leans in to hug her, she shudders.

"Nani, what's wrong?" Raina steps back. She remembers that she hasn't washed off the makeup or brushed her teeth, and she wonders if her hair smells of smoke. "Nani?"

Still, Nani won't speak. Her hands unclench, slowly, and she sets her palms lightly on the table. They are shaking.

"Yeah. About that." Manavi has propped herself on top of the counter. She opens a bag of chips, and stuffs a handful into her mouth. Crunching loudly, she says, "I took Raina to Montreal last night. For her birthday."

Raina stiffens. She feels as if she's been punched, and she squats down beside her nani. She searches her eyes, only to find they have chilled. "Nani, I'm so sorry. I didn't realize you didn't know—"

"You are *both* adults." Nani looks different. Her voice is changed, and Raina feels as if she is speaking to someone who has emerged from the past—a woman of whom she heard rumors and, until now, never had the misfortune of meeting. Nani stands up suddenly, walks out of the kitchen, and Raina resists the urge to follow. She can hear Manavi crunching chips behind her, the plastic crackling, and she turns around. Manavi swings her legs in small circles, and when Raina finally meets her eye, Manavi is grinning.

"Raindrop, pass me a bowl—would you?"

THIRTEEN

"So he's gone."

"Until the spring."

"That's that, then." Zoey stood up from the chair facing my desk. I thought she was going to leave, but instead she shut the door and sat back down. "Are you okay?"

"What do you think?" She handed me the box of tissues next to her, and I pulled out three. My nose was running, but surprisingly, I had no tears left. Was I surprised that Dev, after being based in Toronto for merely five weeks, was being carted off to Singapore to temporarily oversee an emerging markets division—and that he wouldn't be back in town for months?

Did it surprise me that he'd dropped the news on me during dinner the day before he left, so casually that I felt tempted to laugh?

I always tried not to care about his lack of work/life balance, or his constant need to travel or push harder than any other banker we knew. Hadn't I been inspired? There was a certain nobility about a self-made man—the work ethic, the passion, the devotion it took to become one of the few people in the world who—rightly or wrongly so—had influence on the economy; on how the world worked. He was bright and powerful, and this man, the one who left and returned on a moment's notice, the one who had so few moments to spare—but wanted to spend them with me—was the *real* Dev.

I'd learned quickly that the man I fell for in Brussels had been on holiday. A chance glimpse, really, because he rarely took vacations. The Dev who had the inclination to read in bed with me, whisper secrets between the hotel sheets, was as rare as the London sun. And I was fine with it. It had always been clear what life would be like holding Dev's hand. Sleeping beside his furrowed brow. Cajoling him to cheer up during dinner, his mood soured by a deal gone bad.

Our life would be Dev hunting for a Wi-Fi connection, leaving me to sun myself on the beaches of Corfu alone while our complimentary bottle of champagne chilled in the honeymoon suite. Dev e-mailing a client during our child's Christmas concert, leaving during his solo to take a call. Dev having to keep a flat near the office for all the late nights and last-minute meetings; the rest of us in our town house in Totteridge or Haywards Heath—a light therapy lamp beside the davenport desk where I'd watch the clock and try and figure out my life's passion.

Life would be Dev growing older and even more powerful. Meeting him for a quick bite near his office in Westminster. His hand on my waist as he avoided eye contact with the waitress our daughter's age and I massaged my wrinkles, convinced he didn't have time for an affair. Life with Dev would be fast and slow at the same time; a waiting game between moments of bliss—between trips to Brussels. It hadn't bothered me. It had all been fine back then, but now I didn't feel so certain.

Why was I misleading my nani—and for what? What if I was waiting for nothing?

"How did you guys leave it?"

I leaned back on my chair. Zoey's patience with me was waning, but I appreciated so much that at least she was trying. "He said he would call me as often as he could—"

"Uh-huh. *Sure*—"

"And that we would figure 'us' out when he got back."

"Is that what you want?"

I nodded, but I wasn't sure which one of us I was trying to convince anymore. I was so busy with work, and went home so rarely these days, that surely I could maintain the lie to Nani for a short while longer? Surely, when Dev got back, we *would* figure it out.

"Just do me a favor, would you?" Zoey leaned forward and gave my forearm a squeeze. "It's almost Christmas. Try and enjoy the holidays, and do your best to forget about him. For now, at least?"

I promised her I would try, and surprisingly, it kind of worked. I took off the week before Christmas, and from the moment I arrived home, I felt better. Just being home and away from downtown, I felt ready for the holidays without Dev.

I established a new routine—a suburban, more relaxed life away from the city. In the morning, I'd wake up early and bring Nani her tea, two digestive biscuits resting on the saucer. I'd help her with housework, and at Saffron if she needed it. In the evenings, we cooked dinner, and Nani and I watched TV huddled together on the couch, and after she fell asleep, I'd go on a run, sometimes past the school's basketball courts. Once, I saw the girls' team practicing—running drills, shuttles, and layups. Asher was standing in the corner with a clipboard, and I'd slowed down and waved as I jogged past. But he didn't see me—that, or he purposely turned and looked in another direction.

The only downside of staying home with Nani was having to deal with her questions—questions it was becoming harder and harder to avoid.

Why were Zoey and I not together?

Did I have a different girlfriend?

Would I have natural children or adopt?

How did I define my sexual orientation, and was that different from my gender identity?

It wasn't until Christmas Eve, while surfing on Nani's tablet after she'd gone to bed, that I found out where those questions were coming from.

Her browser history was littered with LGBTQ websites. Organizations, support groups, blogs, and chat forums. Terminologies, ideologies—tips on *how to set aside your feelings on homosexuality* and *how to redefine your relationship with your gay child*. There was even a link to some gay porn (which, I gathered, she'd stumbled across by mistake). I laughed out loud at first, as I made my way through the websites—the new *list*—feeling rather proud of my progressive nani.

But then I imagined her on the couch, her wrinkled brow mouthing along with the words, and I realized that maybe it wasn't so funny. I kept scrolling, and more websites appeared. Ones outlining in layman's terms same-sex civil marriages, how Canada had been the fourth country in the world to legalize gay marriage. Sites with advice on raising kids of gay parents—for *grandparents* of kids raised by gay parents. Sites on adoption. Donor insemination. IVF treatment. Another on adoption. Then it hit me like a frying pan to the skull. Nani didn't just support me being interested in women.

She wanted me to marry one.

Nani and I both pretended not to notice that Kris didn't come home on Christmas morning, or that Mom hadn't even called. We spent the day cooking together and watching old movies, and then got ready for Auntie Sarla's party. She had first invited us over for Christmas dinner after Nana had died. It had started out of sympathy and included just our family and Shay's, but over the years the numbers had grown, and these days, Christmas dinner felt like just another one of Auntie Sarla's famous parties. Her two dining tables became a hodgepodge of salads, curries and dals, shrimp fried rice and oversalted stuffing. And in true potluck style, sometimes there were six turkeys—and other years there were none.

Their marble foyer was already littered with winter boots by the time we arrived for dinner. The house was all extravagance and no taste, a house of oversaturated colors. Rosewater pink carpets and blindingly gold walls; an indoor swimming pool only the dog used; a six-foot statue in the middle of the living room—just because.

Since their engagement, Shay and Julien had decided to alternate holidays with their families, and this year was Shay's first Christmas away from home. It felt odd being in her house without her; usually, we'd sneak upstairs away from the party, hide in her old bedroom with a plate of stolen desserts, ignoring everyone until Auntie Sarla found us and insisted we come back down and socialize. I thought about going up to her room alone, but it felt too strange. I wasn't sure how it happened—or when—but these days, Shay and I barely spoke.

Sure, I'd become more distant since Dev moved to Toronto, and avoided seeing her for fear of letting the lie slip, but I wondered whether it had started before then. Things hadn't been right since she got engaged, and started pressuring me to settle down, too. Maybe there'd be time over the New Year to talk things out, at her bachelorette party in New York City. Julien and his grooms-men would be there, too. Ironically, they'd both be spending their last "singles' trip" together—a group holiday I'd had planned for months. But ever since my misunderstanding with Asher, I wasn't sure I looked forward to it.

Shay's house was packed with some familiar faces and a lot of new ones. Most of the girls Shay and I had grown up with had moved away—Los Angeles, Vancouver, Calgary—or were away on vacation with families of their own. The few I did know sat in clumps in one of the living rooms, holding hands with their hus-bands or boyfriends, chasing after toddlers dressed up like rein-deer, in tiny novelty onesies bought specifically for the occasion. I quickly said my hellos, my congratulations, and then moved to-ward the kitchen.

I peered around the corner and saw Nani and Auntie Sarla arguing in front of the stainless steel oven, their faces flushed. Quietly, I drew closer, coming within earshot.

"This is not right, *ji*."

"Suvali. I am helping her. I am helping *you*. Raina needs a husband."

"Raina doesn't need—"

"You know what everyone is saying? They are saying none of the men she meets like her, that she is too difficult to please—"

"Why are you making up lies?"

"Suvali, why would I lie?"

"Raina doesn't need a husband, and—and—"

Nani's voice dropped off, and they both turned to look at me.

"What's going on?" I asked slowly.

"Nothing." Auntie Sarla turned back to the stove. "Have you eaten?"

"Not yet."

"*Jao*. Go make a plate." She nodded at me, and then threw Nani a glare. "Take your nani with you. She is looking pale."

I led Nani into an empty hallway. She was perspiring, fanning her face with a folded piece of paper towel. I found a table nearby with fresh glasses of champagne, and I thrust one into her hand.

"What's going on?" I asked.

"That woman is going on and on—always talking, talking." Nani tapped her fingers together. "She knows nothing—and still? Always talking. Who is that woman to talk like that about my Raina? We need to tell them. Band-Aid"—she flicked her hand like a musical conductor—"off."

I set my hands on Nani's shoulders and took a deep breath, trying not to imagine what would happen if everyone found out about the lie I'd told. Another scandal in the Anand family. Another daughter who didn't live up to expectations. What would Nani have to endure if everyone thought I was a lesbian? Most of Nani's friends couldn't even pronounce "homosexuality"—let alone support it.

"Should we tell them?" Nani reached up and stroked the side of my cheek. "I am *okay*."

I shook my head.

"Raina, please—"

"No, Nani." I looked her straight in the eye. "Promise me you won't tell anyone yet—not until . . ."

Until when? Until Dev was back from London or Singapore— or wherever the hell he was going? Until I could admit that it was *him* that I wanted to marry, and not another woman? The man who humiliated me? Who humiliated Nani?

"Just promise me you won't say anything yet. Please?" I took a deep breath. I would come clean and tell Nani everything. Dev would return, and we would get back together—and I would make Nani realize he was right for me.

I would make them both realize.

"Okay." Nani sighed, and her hand slid to my chin. "But Raina. Eventually, you will have to face them."

No, Nani, I thought, my stomach wrenching. *Eventually, I will have to face you.*

FOURTEEN

I worked the next five days straight to make up for my "ill-timed Christmas holiday," as Bill had called it, and then just before 5 A.M. on New Year's Eve Day I took a taxi to the airport for the first flight out to LaGuardia. Serena was already there, a coffee in her hand and a crime thriller tucked between the thighs of her skinny jeans.

I sat down beside her hesitantly. I hadn't seen her since she and Kris had broken up, but she seemed happy to see me. Slowly, the rest of the group started to trickle in—Shay's twin cousins, Nikki and Niti, who'd been a few years behind us in school, and now had jobs in brand management and social media. Then came Julien's friend from the hospital, another resident named Matt, and Julien's younger brother, Victor, who'd sworn up and down that his fake ID would work.

Finally, Shay and Julien arrived, hugging us all through fatigued smiles. I hadn't made time to see her since they got back from Quebec—and I couldn't even remember the last time we saw each other, or spoke on the phone. Lately, our only contact had been brief texts hours apart, which were always about plans for the wedding or for the trip to New York.

Shay eyed me oddly as she drew closer. I thought she was going to lean in and hug me, but then she stopped, and patted me on the arm. "You look good."

"You, too."

Did she know I was avoiding her? That I was hiding something?

"Good Christmas?" she asked.

I nodded. "You?"

She didn't reply as she looked around the terminal and, after surveying the crowd, looked back at me. "Where's Asher?"

I shrugged, and a moment later, I saw him.

"There he is," said Julien.

Asher jogged down the moving sidewalk toward us, a duffel bag swinging in his hand. He'd let some of his beard grow back, a soft scruff on his chin and cheeks, and instead of a suit or sweatpants, he was wearing loose jeans and a faded leather jacket. Along with a white T-shirt and sneakers. He slowed down as he approached us, and without looking at me, smiling broadly, he wrapped an arm around both Julien and Shay and steered them toward security.

He avoided me as we waited, and then at the front of the line, when Shay bent over and took her time unclasping the buckles on her boots, I veered in front of her, angling myself behind him.

"Hi, Asher."

Whether he heard me or not, he didn't answer.

"How was your Christmas?" I said a little louder.

He retrieved his passport from his back pocket. "Festive."

"Were you with family?"

"Sure was."

"Did you guys have fun?" I paused. "Play any basketball?"

"Guess that depends on your definition of fun." He leaned on the metal rail and slid off his shoes. "My nephews prefer *SpongeBob* over—you know, *weed*—"

"I am really sorry about that."

He tossed his wallet and keys into the plastic bin.

"Asher, come on. I said I was sorry."

But he walked away through the metal detector, and didn't turn around.

There were only a handful of others on board, and after takeoff, we spread out sideways on the seats. I blinked in and out of sleep, and it felt like only minutes passed before we started our descent into New York City. I sat up and peered outside my window, watching the clouds feathered above the Rockaways. The snow sprinkled over the city like icing sugar.

I had booked ahead for transportation, and a square black van was waiting for us outside the airport. I sat in the front seat chatting with our driver, Ramón, about the state's public school system, the newest speakeasy that just opened beneath a pho takeout in the Lower East Side, camouflaged in red and yellow string lights, and we drove down the expressway toward Manhattan. I'd been to New York often—with Shay or other friends for weekend shopping trips or music festivals. A dozen conferences with colleagues, with days at the office on East 55th, nights in the hotel bar on Lexington in a black pencil skirt, charging Gray Goose martinis to the expense account. It was one way to live. It was Dev's way. But as the chalky gray peaks of Midtown rose onto the horizon, I tried to push thoughts of Dev out of my mind. Whether he, on those countless fall trips to New York, winding around that last bend on the Long Island Expressway, had thought of me, too.

On the other side of the Queens-Midtown Tunnel, we hit traffic, and after thirty minutes of crawling, block by block, Ramón muttering about tourists and the traffic reroutes around Times Square, we reached our hotel. I'd booked us two suites at a hotel in Hell's Kitchen the week after Shay got engaged. She'd showed up to my apartment, drunk, with two butter chicken burritos, and told me I was her maid of honor, and instead of Vegas, or some cheesy night doing the limbo with a tanned stripper, she wanted her bachelorette party to be during the New Year. And she wanted to share it with Julien.

We said good-bye to the guys, dumped our things in the room, and set out for Fifth Avenue. It was still early, foot traffic in the shops and on the sidewalks sparse, and Shay was acting unlike herself. Bubbly, almost, and she couldn't stop smiling, picking up clothes and modeling them, her eyes glossed as she walked by a storefront, exclaiming at something showcased in the window, and then hustling in to buy it. She chatted ruthlessly with the girls working at Chanel and BCBG, trying everything on as she stood in front of the mirror and surveyed the room for an opinion.

"So, what do you think?" she asked us, her fingers playing with the sequins of a stiff black dress. "Is it too much?"

Everyone chimed their approval as Shay twisted and turned in front of the mirror, sucked in her stomach and elongated her arms behind her. Surprisingly, she had the perfect figure. Petite and curvy from a diet of hospital cafeteria food, from the exercise of running from patient to patient.

"You look like that new movie star," I said to the mirror. "Priyanka Chopra."

"Priyanka Chopra's not new," said Nikki. "She's been around for more than a decade."

"Who's that new one then?

"Parineeti Chopra?"

"Yeah." I nodded. "You look like *her*."

"You have to buy it, Shaylee," said Serena.

"Can't. What if Ma sees the pictures?" Shay shrugged and turned away from the mirror. "She'd hate it."

"Shay—"

"And I'm ten pounds heavier and a thousand shades darker than any girl who makes it in Bollywood." Shay unzipped the dress, and stalked back into the dressing room. "Parineeti Chopra, my ass!"

"What a nut bar," Niti whispered to the rest of us. "We're going to buy it for her anyway, right?"

We bought the dress when she wasn't looking, and when we stopped for glühwein at the German Christmas Market, Serena handed her the bag. Shay eyed us suspiciously.

"I told you guys not to get me anything."

"Just open it," I said, and when she did, she started to cry.

"You guys"—she spluttered—"I can't believe it."

"Calm down." I rolled my eyes. "It's just a dress."

"It's not just a dress," said Shay, wiping her nose with her wrist. "It might be the only thing in this whole wedding I actually pick out for myself."

"You're our Parineeti Chopra," said Serena, hugging her, and the rest of us joined, and soon all of us were clumped madly together in the middle of Union Square, shopping bags and scarves flung to the side with pigeons knocking at our feet, the tourists walking by, nodding and smiling at us like we were some interesting occurrence that made up the landscape of the city.

"Should we take a picture here?" I asked Shay.

Shay nodded, and her eyes landed on a miniature wooden lodge selling wicker crafts and discount Christmas wreaths. "Yeah. Over there in the light. Raina, do you have him?"

I nodded, tapping the side of my purse. "I have him."

Him was Draco, and as maid of honor, or, perhaps, because he didn't fit in Shay's clutch, I was in charge of lugging around the stuffed teddy bear Julien had bought for her on their first real date. Ever since, Julien and Shay had carried him around like a child, ready for every photo op: Draco perched on one of their shoulders at the CN Tower or Niagara Falls; in the operating room with a clinical white mask over his face; in sunglasses on the beach; or riding the neck of an alpaca at Machu Picchu. The last time I'd seen him was the weekend before my twenty-ninth birthday when Shay, Draco, and I went camping, and we took pictures of the three of us canoeing Lake Nipissing, then chugging beer by the campfire. By now, Shay had accumulated enough Draco photos to warrant his own slide show at the wedding, and although Auntie Sarla had originally vetoed the idea, it was the one thing Shay insisted on.

After, we caught the 4 train uptown and took more pictures with Draco at Wollman Rink in Central Park, in Christopher's shadow on the steps of Columbus Circle, and later, propped on a velvet chair at the Ritz. High tea was a surprise for the bride-to-be. We walked into the hotel on the pretense of looking around, and when I took them up to the hostess and told her we had a reservation for a "Shaylee Patel," Shay looked at me, and again started to cry.

"You remembered."

We went to New York City on an overly chaperoned class trip in high school. We snuck off to the Ritz just for a moment to take a look: the dining room was full of old men and money; the decor of another century, wine red–colored carpet, and classical music. We fantasized about the lives of the people who were allowed inside—what they ate, what they did. We promised each other that one day we would get there—wherever *there* was.

I handed Shay a Kleenex. "Of course I remembered."

After tea, we went back to the hotel to change—Shay, into her new dress—and we were still full of foie gras and lavender macarons by the time we arrived at our reservation in Chelsea: a jazz-themed seafood grill where all the waiters—like in any fine city establishment—appeared to moonlight as models. An Italian with sideswept hair flirted with Shay as he took our order, and she giggled in response, played with her hair, and ordered everyone the chef's tasting menu, and several bottles of wine.

The table was large, and we were spread out. I was at the end, Shay sitting closest to me, and as the other girls chatted, Shay and I looked at each other. I realized that neither of us knew what to say.

"Did your Ma tell you?" I finally asked. "She booked that band from Vancouver for the wedding. They'll fly in before the *sangeet*—"

"Are you seeing anybody?" she asked suddenly. "Is there anyone you haven't told me about?"

"No. Why?"

"Where have you been then?"

"I'm right here."

"No," she said. "Where have you *been*?"

I shrugged. "Busy working."

"And before?"

"And before"—I trailed off—"before, well, I've just been busy. I've been working, Shay. Same as ever."

"Is this about Asher?"

"What?"

"This morning"—she paused, and looked away from me—"it looked like something was going on with you two."

"At airport security?" I shrugged. "He walked through with change in his pockets, was subject to a frisk and search, if you know what I mean . . ."

I trailed off when she didn't crack a smile.

"It was nothing, Shay."

"Nothing."

By the way she bit her lip and dropped the subject, then promptly engaged herself in conversation with the other girls, I knew she was hurt. Whether it was the offhand comment some guy in history class had made, or how a few unwanted edamame beans got on our order from the bitch at our favorite salad bar—with us, it was never *nothing*.

I didn't know what I was supposed to say to her. Nani thinks I'm a lesbian, and—*oh yeah*—Dev sort of moved to Toronto and we might get back together, but he's still not quite sure he wants an actual relationship? Just like you would have predicted? I knew what she would say, and I didn't want a lecture. Not from a girl who could memorize an algorithm or an amino acid structure in the blink of an eye. Not from a girl who it seemed never had to work hard for anything. Shay was my best friend. She always had been. But some things she just didn't—she *couldn't*—understand.

My stomach felt queasy throughout dinner. Unsettled. And I had to keep reminding myself that I was lying to Shay for a reason. She wouldn't understand why I was waiting for Dev, and letting Nani believe I was a lesbian—so what was the point of telling her? When I poured my wine into Nikki's glass, everyone had drunk too much of their own to notice—most of all Shay. The waiter had flirted with her throughout dinner, sneaking her shots of ouzo from the back room, and I had to peel his hands off her waist as he helped her into her coat. She was practically catatonic. Outside, I ducked into a mini-mart and bought her water, and then we walked toward Hudson Street, most of her weight collapsed onto me.

The guys were waiting for us outside the club. I saw Asher first, several inches taller than everyone else, leaning against a handrail with his coat open, a charcoal gray suit beneath. Shay unfastened herself from me and stumbled straight into Julien, but somehow we managed to get her into the bar without drawing too much attention.

The hostess led us toward our reserved area at the back. We were seated in a corner section with two long plush couches facing each other, a table full of glass bottles of vodka and gin, cranberry and Coke, lined up in between. We were at the edge of the dance floor, just in front of a terrace. The doors were wide open, and each gust of wind brought in the citrusy smell of perfume, the diesel of the heat lamps. I sat at the end of the group, disengaged, at the fringe of the conversation.

Asher was sitting across from me, and I kept catching his eye. But every time I turned to face him, he looked away. Annoyed, I finally waved at him, and to my surprise, he waved back.

"How was your day?" I yelled over the music.

"What?"

"How was your day?"

"Great." He smiled. "Smoked *loads* of weed—"

"Okay. Cut it out."

He grinned. "Cut *what* out, princess?"

I leaned forward. "You know what? I said I was sorry—three times, now. And I'm done. So if you don't want to—"

"See the thing is"—he walked around the table, perched himself on the armrest beside me—"you don't even know what you're apologizing for."

"Yes, I do."

"Do you? Because you're *hilarious*, Raina. Always making jokes. And you can't offend anyone if you're kidding."

"I really didn't mean to offend you. I just thought—"

"You just *thought* I smoked weed because you smelled it on me at the engagement party—which, by the way, you were wrong about. I was outside on the phone with my sister, and some kids were smoking right next to me, so that's why I smelled like it. I haven't even touched weed since college."

"Oh."

"And you also assumed that I had drugs on me at my workplace." He grabbed his drink from the table. "I mean, I'm just some shaggy guy who hangs around on a high school basketball court, must be—"

"Look." I took a deep breath. "I knew you'd been traveling and that you'd barely been back since you left—and everyone I know like that also—"

"Well, obviously, I'm just like them."

"Yes, okay? I made an assumption. I know your type. My own mother is *your* type. I mean, who leaves their family for *ten* years?" The lights around the dance floor kept slicing me in the eyes, and I blinked hard. "But it's all fine, right? You've been 'finding' yourself. Learning about the world. Not really having to deal with how selfish you are."

"Sounds like you have me all figured out."

"Don't I?" I snapped. "And don't *you* have me all figured out?"

"All I did was try to get to know you."

"But you *did* know me, didn't you? You knew that I was twenty-nine and my best friend was getting married before me"—I coughed, my voice catching—"so obviously, I'm desperate to get married, right? I take home bartenders to feel some validation?" He had looked away, and I glared at him, shaking, until he looked back. "So go ahead. Validate me. I *really* need it."

He rubbed his lips together, and then his hands, and when he looked at me as if he might say something back, I heard Shay calling my name. I looked over. She had hoisted herself off Julien's lap and was inching toward us.

"What's going on here?" she asked, leaning down between us. She dipped down and planted a wet kiss on my cheek. She moved for the other cheek and missed, hitting my chin.

"Do you want some more water?" I asked.

She shook her head, hair falling onto her chest as she wavered in front of us. "No. It's picture time."

"Now?"

She nodded. "Group shot."

"Sure. I'll bring Draco over right away."

"Okay," she said, slurring. "Let me know when you're ready."

She stumbled toward Julien, and I grabbed my coat from the back of the couch—kicking myself because I'd forgotten Draco at the hotel.

"Are you leaving?" asked Asher.

I nodded.

"Why?"

"It's nothing."

"Who's Draco?" He followed me as I cut through the dance floor, trying to lose him, and then up the stairs toward the club entrance. Outside on the sidewalk, I stopped, trying to catch my breath. I felt him behind me, his hand on my shoulder.

"Raina, who's Draco?"

I rolled my eyes. "Oh, you know. Just another guy who won't marry me."

FIFTEEN

"Shit." I stepped back on the curb as another cab drove past me. I let my arm fall down by my side and turned around. Asher was still leaning against a lamppost, his left foot propped up, his arms folded across his chest.

"What time is it?"

He glanced at his watch. "Eleven twenty. Do you want a hand?"

"No, thanks." I raised both my arms and waved frantically at another cab as it whizzed past.

"You know," I heard Asher say, "if the light's off, it means it's taken."

"You're being a nuisance."

"That's because you're not letting me be helpful." He uncrossed his arms, and then crossed them the other way.

"Fine." I gestured to the street. "Be my guest."

Asher pushed himself off the lamppost, and as he walked toward the edge of the sidewalk, a cab pulled up. The door opened, and three girls in stilettos and long parkas filed out. Asher placed his hand on the roof of the car as he helped them out, and then looked at me smugly.

"Lucky bastard." I got into the cab, and before I realized what was happening, Asher slid in next to me and pulled the door shut.

"Thirty-eighth and Tenth, please—we're going to the hotel, right?"

"Wait, *we*?"

"No problem," said the driver, steering sharply into the traffic.

Asher reclined in his seat and drummed his fingers on his lap and, a moment later, looked over at me. He smiled. "What?"

"What are you—why are you—"

"It's eleven"—he glanced back at his watch—"twenty-two. In New York City. On New Year's Eve. I'm not letting you go alone."

"So you're being chivalrous, are you?"

"Something like that."

We made it to the hotel in good time, and Asher waited in the lobby while I ran upstairs and grabbed Draco, who was still sitting on the windowsill where I'd left him. I stuffed him into my purse and then ran back downstairs. Asher was talking to someone at the concierge desk, and as I walked up, he shook the man's hand and walked briskly toward me.

"They can call us a black car, but it will take a while to get here. Or we can walk over to Eighth Ave. and try and catch a cab there. Apparently, we won't find one around here."

I reached for his hand, and rotated his wide wrist until I could see the face of his watch. Eleven thirty-five.

"Subway?"

He shook his head, looking at his wrist where I'd touched him. "It's out of the way—walking there and then back again—we might as well just walk down."

"Well, why don't we?"

"Walk?"

"Yeah. We'll go fast." I lifted up my right boot, the flat edges covered in salt. "We might even make midnight."

We cut toward Ninth Avenue and then turned south. Our strides long and brisk, we walked silently in step, the faint smell of salt and gasoline hanging in the air. We passed delis and tapas restaurants, low-income housing and upscale condos alike; the windows light and dark like a checkerboard. The crowd thickened outside of Penn Station, and we darted through the throngs of pedestrians, delivery boys on bikes, pizza boxes and steaming white paper bags strapped over the back wheels. And after a few blocks, the sidewalks thinned out, and the silence between us once again became palpable.

I looked at him out of the corner of my eye. "Are you still—uh—mad at me?"

"Not really." He dodged to the right of a couple walking their dog, while I curved around to the left, and when we'd passed them, he said, "Are you still mad at *me*?"

I shook my head. "No."

"Good." He smiled. "Your apology is officially accepted."

"I haven't apologized . . ."

"But you're about to."

"Yes, I guess I was." I laughed, hopping over a crushed beer bottle. "I'm sorry."

"I'm sorry, too."

I sighed. "I'm sorry I misjudged you, Asher. I'm sorry I assumed you were a stoner and an irresponsible drifter. And a nuisance. And—um—implied you were a slut."

"Ouch." He raised his eyebrows. "When you say it like that, I'm not sure I have forgiven you yet."

"Oh, calm down," I teased. "You're fine."

"Raina," he said after a moment, in a tone I couldn't quite read.

"Did you really think that badly of me? I know I've led an unconventional life, but I'm just not as scandalous as some may think."

"No Thai ladyboys during your travels?"

He laughed.

"Because I hear you can never be quite sure."

"Nope," he said grinning. "And no bastard children, either."

We dashed through another intersection, the streets dirty with melted snow. I looked down at my boots. Mud had caked onto the edges, and with each step, I tried to rub some of it off.

"Did I say something wrong?"

I shook my head.

"Tell me, Raina," he said softly.

"Really, it's nothing." I shrugged, and as his pace slowed even more, so did mine. "But I guess, technically, *I* am a bastard child."

"Oh."

"It happens all the time, doesn't it? Same story. Different characters. I never knew my dad, and Mom's kind of all over the place. He had blue eyes and blond hair—and was *tall*. That's all she ever told me." I smiled. "She was too young."

I felt Asher's hand on my shoulder.

"My grandmother—my nani—was different back then. Different with my mom. She wasn't allowed to do anything, not even take swimming lessons, because a swimsuit was too revealing. She rebelled, she had me—and then when I was young, I guess she'd had enough. Mom left, and has barely been back since."

"I'm sorry."

I shrugged. "It's not your fault. It's not really hers, either, though."

"Your nani was tough, sure. But that doesn't mean your mom is allowed to blame everything on her childhood, forever, don't you think?"

"To be honest, I'm not sure *what* I think." I glanced at him. "Anyway, Mom is still finding herself. She travels, she switches

jobs when she feels like it—kind of like you did. We all find ourselves in different ways . . . although I suppose your way is far more
interesting than mine."

"Interesting—sure." Asher kicked at a loose rock. "But being
away from everything and everyone you've ever known—it's so
easy to get lost. You can lose your perspective on life, rather than
find it."

"Is that what happened to you?"

"Who knows. I've been everywhere, tried everything"—he
winked at me—"almost. And I don't regret much. Except that I
wasn't home when I was needed."

"What did you miss?"

"My sister's wedding, for one. It's taken her a long time to forgive me."

"But she forgave you."

"Of course, she's my sister. But she has kids now. I'm an *uncle*,
and a pretty great one, too. And I know that when I have kids, I
would need Anna to be around for them. So now, I want to be
around for her. It's a small family." His voice quieted. "Our parents are dead."

"Asher. I'm so sorry."

He smiled. "I was at university—my last semester, actually.
Their car slid right off the road."

"Was that why you quit school?"

"It's life, you know?"

I felt his hand brush against mine, and I squeezed. "*Life* doesn't
make living through that any easier."

His fingers stayed intertwined through mine until the light
changed. On the other side, people had started to gather on the
sidewalk in front of a yellowing sign with "Punjabi Hut" painted
on in dark blue lettering. I'd seen shops like this in New York before: twenty-four-hour Indian eateries with platters of authentic

dishes served up on plates for a five-dollar bill. Never more than three rickety tables inside, yet always full, always ready for the next wave dashing in and out for a quick taste of home.

"What's going on?" asked Asher as we walked toward them. More people were arriving, from the handful of cabs parked halfway up the curb, pouring out from the restaurant, the scent of spices and oil trickling outside as they propped open the door. Someone was setting up a speaker outside the shop, and we gathered at the edge of the growing crowd, watching everyone speaking excitedly in Hindi or Punjabi, buttoning up their coats over saris and kurta pajamas.

The speaker pulsed to a start. Bhangra. Asher smiled at me in recognition, like he'd heard the lively, low-swinging beat before. Soon, everyone around us—old and young—was dancing with their hands clapping or twisting, their hips moving as fluid as a belly dancer's. A woman who reminded me of Nani, petite and with a kind face, walked by with a Tupperware full of *laddoo*, popping the sweets into people's mouths at random. She walked up to Asher and tapped his stomach. He opened his mouth, and she plopped the whole thing in, and part of it crumbled off his lips. He caught it with a smile. "What is this?"

I wiped the crumbs off his chin. "It's a blessing."

"It's good!"

The crowd formed a circle on the sidewalk, and everyone took turns dipping in and out of the middle, bobbing their shoulders with the beat, dancing with such vigor Asher and I couldn't stop watching. On an impulse, I dragged Asher inside, and laughing, I taught him the *lehria* step, and he jerked his arms from side to side, a silly, childish grin painted onto his face. We danced and spun, and the saris swished, the smell of masala overflowed, and being there—right *there*—with Asher, I felt something I hadn't in such a long time.

Happiness.

The music swelled, and in a chaos of shouts and laughs, the countdown began. I could feel Asher looking at me. Our bodies pressed together. I was sober, but suddenly woozy, drunk on the scent of pepper and his aftershave.

"We're missing midnight."

He was inches away, and it was like the crowd was pushing us closer. My ears rang, my neck prickled, and I could feel the heat of his body as he stepped closer.

"No, we're not."

As the numbers fell away, reverberated through the street, the mass of people, I couldn't breathe. I couldn't move. My hands were so close to Asher's, and his fingers brushed against me.

"Five . . . Four . . ."

I could smell him. Pepper, earth, aftershave. Our fingers locked together, and I looked up.

"Three . . . Two . . ."

And I couldn't look away.

"One."

Then, in the middle of New York City—as I thought of nothing and no one else—he kissed me.

Asher . . . What just happened!?

SIXTEEN

I woke up alert, ready to hop out of bed and grab my sneakers. I peeled back the covers, then noticed the floor-to-ceiling window with a view of the West Side Highway, the bleach white linen, and remembered where I was. I stretched my arms far above my head, and then let them tumble back onto the pillow. I looked over. Shay's side of the bed was empty, the evidence of the rest of last night scattered around the room: our boots and coats and dresses in piles on the chairs and dresser; wine and water glasses still half full of champagne. An empty carton of Chinese takeout, its grease dripping onto the bedside table. I sat up and wiped it with a napkin, and then scrambled for my phone. I had a handful of work e-mails—from Bill, mostly, sent just after midnight about a file I hadn't finished on time. One new voice mail from Nani, and a text from Asher.

Good morning :-)

I smiled until my cheeks hurt, and rolled sideways onto the duvet. *Asher*. Who would have thought—and what was I thinking?

I wasn't thinking. I still wasn't. But, for whatever reason, I couldn't stop smiling. The rest of the night had passed by in a blur, even though I'd barely had a sip to drink. No one had even noticed Asher and I had disappeared, and after taking the photo with Draco, we spent the rest of the night partying with the group, dancing to old-school R&B. Then, after a quick hug at the end of the evening, the bride's and groom's parties had gone their separate ways.

I lay there, staring at the ceiling, wondering what to text back. A simple good morning? A mentioning of last night? But what *was* last night?

Would there be time to talk about it in New York? We were flying home that afternoon and likely wouldn't have a moment alone together until we were back in Toronto. I wondered where Asher lived, whether he'd want to see me again.

I swung my feet over the bed and pulled on a bathrobe hanging in the closet. Shay was sprawled across the futon in the main room, her morning-after hair tied in a bun at the top of her head. She had an ice pack on her forehead, her cell phone on her stomach, and Nikki and Niti were limp on the other couch, half dressed, their eyes half closed. Serena was in the kitchen pouring coffee, and she pushed a full cup toward me as I sat down at the counter.

"Coffee?"

"Sure, thanks." I took a sip, and then glanced back at Shay. She was glaring at me now, and I wondered if she'd figured out what had happened with Asher.

"How was everyone's night?" I asked to no one in particular. I took another sip, and then glanced over at the twins. "Nikki, you seemed to be having fun."

She groaned, lifting her head slightly before letting it flop back down on the pillow. "I made out with Justin Bieber."

"You made out with a guy who told you he was Justin Bieber," Niti said, "and you believed him."

"But his name *was* Justin, right?" Nikki sighed. "I hope I didn't post any pictures."

I heard Serena laugh behind me, and when I turned to look at Shay, I saw that she was still staring at me.

"Shay, you feeling okay?"

She didn't blink. "I talked to Ma this morning."

I crossed my arms. "How was her New Year's party?"

"It seems she had a nice little chat with your nani." Shay sat up slowly, curled her fingers around the edge of the futon. "Want to guess what it was about?"

I laughed. "Did your dad get drunk and sing again . . ." I caught her eye, her icy glare, and when seconds passed and still she didn't say anything, I knew. And my stomach dropped. "I—"

"Is this all some kind of elaborate *joke* from you?"

"Shay—" I stopped. I glanced at Serena, coffee cup frozen half-way to her mouth, a blank expression on her face.

"Look," I said, turning to face Shay. "I can explain. Can we go talk in private for a second?"

"In private?"

"Shay, come on—"

"What the fuck is going on, Raina?"

I hopped off the stool, walked past the twins, and started to pull her up by her wrist. "Please, let's just talk—"

"No—"

"—in private. Shay, please—"

"Get off me!"

"Shaylee? What's—"

"Stay out of this, Serena," Shay growled. The air in the room had gone flat. Nobody spoke, and I could hear my heart beating furiously.

"So," she continued after a moment. "You have an audience now. Always begging to be the center of attention—well, here you are, Raina. We all want to hear your joke now. Since when does your nani think you're a lesbian?"

I heard a shuffle behind me, and turned around. Nikki and Niti were off the couch, one behind the other, walking toward the door. Serena was already gone. A moment later, the door clicked shut, and all I could hear was the hum of the fridge, its door still slightly ajar.

"Well?"

I looked back at Shay. She was standing there, staring at me with an anger I'd never seen from her before.

"What's going on with you?"

I sat down on the couch. I couldn't breathe, and I wished that I could open the window. Everything felt trapped inside me, and I didn't know how to—I couldn't—let it out.

"Unbelievable." She threw her hands in the air. "You're going to sit there, and not even look at me? After everything we've been through—you're going to *keep* lying to me?"

I concentrated on my toes as I tried to steady my breath. But what was the truth? That I wasn't as strong as her? That I hated myself; that I hated the way Dev treated me, yet I couldn't stop it? That I was ashamed, and alone?

"Fine," I heard her say. "Lie. Let's go with that. Let's go with you being a fucking *lesbian*."

My mouth dry, I swallowed, tried to find words—*any* words.

"You—coming out to your nani." Shay's voice cracked. "*You*— a lesbian—the same girl who became a doormat for the first guy to really look at you, some guy who didn't give two shits—"

"Shut. Up."

"And now—you're telling people you've given up on men? Want to try the *ladies* for a while?" She laughed cruelly. "Good fucking luck."

I looked up at her. "I said. Shut. Up."

"You know what." She shook out her hair. "I'm not going to 'shut up,' not like I did when Dev turned you into a puddle and *I* had to deal with that mess—"

"Shay—"

"It was pathetic—and *this*"—she threw out her hand—"whatever you're doing now, is really pathetic."

"You know, I always thought that I was the judgmental one. Not you." I scratched my chin, and I heard my voice grow cold. "I wonder if Julien would still marry you if he knew what a slut you used to be."

Her mouth dropped.

"Who knows, maybe you still are."

"You know I would never cheat on Julien," whispered Shay.

I stood up. "How would I know that, *Shaylee*? Maybe I don't know you at all. After all, you didn't know I was *gay*."

"Raina, you're not gay."

"How the hell would you know?" I screamed. "You haven't been around. You've been off with the man of *your* dreams, lecturing me about my problems whenever—"

"*I'm* not around? You're the one that keeps disappearing, keeps shutting me out—"

"If one day, you and Julien were just over—*over*—would you want me to tell you to 'get over it'? Tell you to grow a pair, and be strong?"

"I never said that. I was always there—"

"You didn't even try to understand what I was going through. You lectured. You sat up on your high horse telling me what to do, telling me to *move* on, telling me I could fix it all by screwing other guys—"

"How long was I supposed to let you sulk? Look at you—how long has it been—and you're still not over that jerk—"

"He's not a jerk—"

"Your nani flew all the way to London, and he wouldn't even meet her."

"It wasn't like that. He was called to Zurich, and then he—"

"You're still defending him. Why? You need to delete that picture in your head. That guy who rolls in cash and runs the world, because guess what"—she poked me—"you already dated him. And he never had time for you. He didn't even—"

"You don't even know what you're talking about. You with your perfect family and job, perfect fiancé—you growing up with Auntie Sarla's silver spoon stuffed down your throat."

"Right, because only *your* mother was the fuckup. No one else gets to screw up their child." Shay had tears in her eyes, and she took a step backward.

"So I'm screwed up," I said softly. I was crying, too. "I'm pathetic, and screwed up, and *gay*—"

"You're not gay!"

"Maybe I *am*, maybe I—"

"You won't even tell me what's going on."

"And why do you think that is, huh?" I walked toward the bedroom door and slammed it behind me, screamed, "Because you're so *fucking* understanding."

MAY 20, 2005

The girls are spread out around the room; groups of three and four on each couch, some flopped down or cross-legged on the shag carpet, others with their knees up, their backs against the sprightly papered wall. They take turns switching their favorite CDs into Raina's portable player—Macy Gray and Destiny's Child, Missy Elliott and Creed. The coffee table is full of kettle corn and fuzzy peach candies, ketchup and salt and vinegar chips. Birthday cake. Sprite—although some of the girls have brought cans of beer, water bottles full of vodka and lemonade mix, and they drink this instead.

It's Raina's birthday and, decidedly, a girls' night. Who decided it, Raina cannot remember, but nonetheless, Nani's entertaining room is now full of them. Girls from the team. Girls with bad haircuts who play the clarinet or the trumpet. Ones who run track, or met Shay in Chemistry Club. They are all shuffled in together at random, high on sugar, on one another, and they are giggling about boys.

Boys—thinks Raina, listening to them—the only thing of any concern on a girls' night.

Shay stands on the couch cushion, and everyone watches her body wriggle as she talks about Theo. He is a senior, and after class, Shay recounts, he drove her home in his dad's Mercedes, first parking the car behind the hockey rink. Raina is anxious to hear more when she hears the door open. Shay slinks down, slides her can of beer beneath the seat, and a moment later, Nani shuffles into the room. She sets down a tray of *pakoras* and samosas, tamarind and mint chutney in adjacent clay bowls, and smiles to the girls. Everyone murmurs their thanks, and Nani hovers expectantly as they examine the food.

All the girls in the room except for Shay are white, and they follow her lead, carefully selecting one of the flaky fried chunks like a chimp with a new toy, biting off tiny pieces. Selecting the smallest of morsels to place on their tongues. It is a success. Their eyes pop, and their expressions brighten in thanks. Raina suspects most have never tried Indian food before, and they lick their fingers clean.

"Thanks, Mrs. Anand!" they cry, as Nani turns to leave.

"Please," she replies, heading back up the stairs, "call me *Nani*."

Shay waits until the door clicks shut, and then turns back to the group. She is smiling from ear to ear and, Raina knows, waiting for someone to prompt her.

"So," says the girl beside her. "What happened with Theo? Did you . . ."

Shay smiles coyly. "Did I *what*?"

"Just tell us!"

"Come on, Shaylee," says another.

"What happened?"

Shay squeals and topples off the couch, rolls back and forth on the floor. After a moment, she sits up, arcing one arm high in the air. "Okay, okay. I'll tell you." She is breathless. "We didn't do *it* . . . but he—" She smiles and, after a moment, points between her legs, and there is a chorus of gasps around the room.

"Down *there*?"

Shay nods, and another girl chants, "Shaylee, no way!"

"Did it feel good?"

She squishes her nose like she's about to sneeze. "I think so."

"You think so?"

She nods again. "He says he knew what he was doing."

"Of course Theo knew what he was doing," says one of the girls from track. "He always knows what he's doing." Two other girls laugh.

"Shay," says Raina. "You never told me that." And after Shay turns to her and shrugs, Raina asks, "Is he your boyfriend?"

Shay glares at her, as if she is irritated. "I don't care about things like that."

"Do you think you'll have *sex* with him?"

But Shay has already turned away, turned her attention to another girl, another question, and they launch into a discussion about things Raina has never done—things she can barely fathom. Shay reaches into her backpack and pulls out a *Cosmopolitan* magazine—bright yellow and pink, Sarah Michelle Gellar posed on the front cover. Everyone leans in, and as they paw over the glossy pages, shrieking, Raina slips out of the room unnoticed.

Upstairs, Nani is splayed out on the couch, her calloused feet resting on Nana's lap. And although he appears to be asleep sitting up, eyes closed, his fleshy chin pillowed onto his neck, his hands are in motion. Softly stroking Nani's feet.

"What are you doing?" asks Raina, watching them from the hallway.

Nani looks over, and Nana snorts himself awake. "Raina." His yawn lands in a wide smile. "How is the party?"

"Good." Raina walks over to them as Nani slides her feet off the couch, and Raina wedges herself between them. She sinks into the cushion. "What are you watching?"

"*Mohabbatein*," says Nana, wrapping his arm around her shoulder.

"Again?"

He nods toward the TV. "Your nani loves this one."

"Should we start it again?" asks Nani. "Your friends want to watch?"

Raina shakes her head and stares at the screen. The actors are in a market throwing colored powder into the air, dancing beneath the festive debris. It seems like the DVD has been on a loop ever since Nana brought home a pirated copy from the restaurant, and from time to time, Raina has watched it with them. The characters have just started college and are falling in love for the first time, and as Raina watches them, her stomach drops. Their lives, their experiences—it all seems like an eternity away. But Raina is now sixteen, and college is not so far off in the future.

Raina cannot imagine having to decide what to do with her life. What—or whose—path she should follow. Shay already knows she will be a doctor, but Raina is not strong like her, and she cannot see herself in a hospital, in the witness-box of death and decay. Kris studies engineering—but Raina does not know what that means. She likes math, physics—even wants to understand his job, but these days Kris rarely sleeps at home. Nani despised his Sri Lankan girlfriend, a nutritionist with buckteeth and giant breasts, but she convinced him to propose, and now talks excitedly about the wedding even though a date has yet to be set.

Her nana tells her that she would make a good lawyer, but Raina has never met one before, and other than episodes of *Law &*

Order, she has no idea what lawyers actually do. Often, she wonders if she should go to university at all. Nani didn't, and neither did Manavi. The last time her mother lived at home, instead of a degree postered above her desk, she had a map. Tea-stained and pricked with a slew of red and blue pins. All the places that Manavi had been—or wanted to go. Places that Raina knows nothing about.

"Are you okay, my sweet?" Nani brushes Raina's cheeks with both hands. "Are you having fun?"

Raina nods. "Yes, thank you. Everyone loves the food."

Nani wiggles her eyebrows. "Don't worry. I saved spicy ones for you." She grabs a plate of *pakoras* from the end table and hands them to Raina, and Raina pops two in her mouth at once. She smiles, crunches the spicy warmth between her molars.

"Now," says Nani, setting the plate back down. "Go have fun."

Raina stands to leave, but lingers by the doorway. "Hey, guys?"

They both look at her.

"Manavi had just turned sixteen." Raina looks at her socks, toes the lines in the hardwood. "She was sixteen when I was born." Her lips quiver, and inexplicably, she wants to cry.

"Raina." Nana's voice is strong and sweet. Raina feels him, both of them, as they draw near her and stand on either side of her. Nani takes Raina's hand into hers.

"Listen to me." Nani squeezes her hand. "You are such a capable girl."

"A *good* girl," adds Nana. "With such bright future ahead."

A tear drops, and Nani wipes it away. "You are *nothing* like your mother."

"Do you understand?"

Raina nods. Forces out a smile, and a moment later, she says, "I understand."

Raina rejoins the party. Her seat has been taken, and so she curls up on the floor by the coffee table. The girls have moved on from the magazine. They are sillier now, passing cans and bottles around to one another, giggling, already thinking they are drunk. A bottle of beer reaches Raina. It has gone warm, and her hand sticks to the green glass. She takes a deep breath, wraps her mouth around the lip of the bottle, and throws back her head. As she drinks, Raina cannot stop thinking about what if Nani is wrong. What if she actually is like her mother? What if Raina, too, is a disappointment?

SEVENTEEN

For the first time ever, I was grateful for the long hours and sleepless nights at the office, the distraction of the cutting-edge, thankless world of banking. Winter churned on outside my window, and I sat in my twelve-foot-square cell poring over financial statements and market data, working and reworking a balance sheet. Dissecting a cash flow problem, an economic implication. I worked without really working; I spat out what I was supposed to, and as I sat there on the phone with a client discussing pharmaceutical investments and market shares, made notes on a risk analysis, I was thankful. For the diversion. The disturbance. Thankful that I didn't really have to think. I tore through reports faster than they were assigned, and Bill warmed up to me again, happy to see that I was "back to my old self." Ironically—although, predictably so—I felt further away from myself than I'd ever been.

January and then February dragged on, and still the winds sliced brisk and sharp, the sleet and snow creeping in through the revolving doors, at the edges of frosted windowpanes. It seemed like spring would never rear its willowy horns, fill the city with light and sun. It seemed that Dev would never show up, either. He'd been temporarily assigned to a project in Jakarta now—something about an emerging market, heading up a risk analysis. These days he called often, and his texts and e-mails were flowered with *darling* and *missing you*, constant reassurances that he'd *be back in a jiff*. But even when—even *if*—he came back, I wasn't sure what I'd do or say, or how he'd fit in to the spectacular mess I'd created and, with each passing day, obstinately ignored.

I mean, it wasn't every day that someone managed to single-handedly divide a community.

After New York, I'd gone straight home and asked Nani what had happened, and she'd simply apologized and collapsed sound-lessly onto the couch. I prodded, but she couldn't remember all that much about Auntie Sarla's New Year's Eve party, except that she'd reacted when Auntie Sarla made a derogatory remark about two men kissing on television. And then, partway through the ar-gument, Nani had told Auntie Sarla—told *everyone*—what she thought to be the truth.

Nani outed me to a room full of people born in a country where homosexuality was still a crime, to a room full of people who quickly took sides. Overnight, everyone knew, half of them disgusted with Auntie Sarla, the other half disgusted by me. And in the months that followed, Nani had cut ties with at least half of her friends, despite my urgings that it wasn't necessary. She'd dis-invited herself to dinner parties and to the movie club, to any so-cial gathering organized by someone on "Team Sarla." Anyone who believed homosexuality was wrong.

"You should have *seen* her reaction, Raina. Terrible!" Nani had sobbed, clutching me in her arms. "But if you saw—you would have done the same. In front of everyone, she *screamed* at me, asking me how I could allow this"—Nani panted, exhausted from the dramatization, and then continued—"and I reply, 'What is there to allow?' Then, that *voman*, she told me to leave the party. Told me of course I would make all my girls turn strange."

My stupidity and weakness had ignited a war between Auntie Sarla, a social pillar of west Toronto's Indian community, wife of a neurosurgeon and mother to two successful children, and Suvali Anand: a blue-collar, social-climbing widow. Mother of rebels. Grandmother of, apparently, a lesbian.

Right then, I'd opened my mouth to tell her the truth: that I was straight. And this spectacular mess was actually about a *man*, a man I'd barely heard from over the holidays—a man who probably didn't even deserve me. But I'd pressed my lips together, and turned away. Because I wasn't strong like Nani, or Shay, or Zoey. Or even Mom.

I was much, much worse. I was a coward.

Now I sat in my office, my belly full of a Vietnamese noodle bowl Zoey had brought me for lunch, and I let my face fall onto my desk. My forehead stuck to the varnish as I breathed against the hard surface. I was bored and restless; it was becoming harder and harder not to think about Shay. She'd gone to India with Auntie Sarla and Julien, and had already been back for a week, Nani had told me. At yoga classes, she'd seen Auntie Sarla, who'd refused to turn around and look at her as she attempted chair pose at the front of the temple rec room.

"That woman is so inflexible—it is not *stool* pose," Nani had said cattily, waiting for me to laugh.

For the millionth time, I flicked through my phone, scrolled back to my last message from Shay. It was dated from over a month before: New Year's Eve. 11:51 P.M.

Where are you Raaaaaina?

I peeled my head off the desk and stared out the window. It was the middle of the afternoon, dark and miserable outside my office, and I missed Shay.

I missed my best friend.

I looked back at my computer screen, inundated with numbers, formulas, and I tried not to think about her. Concentrating, narrowing in on my work, there was something else I tried not to think about; *someone* else I hadn't seen since New Year's.

I'd left New York in a rush, and I was sure the rumor that I was gay had spread to Asher. No wonder he hadn't texted or called me.

Had he chalked up our kiss to a New Year's frivolity with a lesbian? Or did he think about it, too? A part of me wondered if I did call him, if he did know the truth, if anything would happen between us. The other part of me was sitting on my hands like an idiot. Screwing up my life—and worse, Nani's—while I supposedly waited for a guy I wasn't sure was coming back.

My intercom buzzed, and I hit the button. "Yes?"

"Raina, you have a—uh, visitor here."

My stomach fluttered. "Who is it?"

"A Dep-oosh Sax-ee-na?"

"Oh." I caught my breath. "All right, thanks, Emma. Send him up."

I opened my office door and waited out in the hall. A minute later, the elevator opened and Depesh appeared; fresh-faced, even taller it seemed than when I saw him the previous summer.

"How's university?" I asked. "Haven't heard from you in a while."

"Haven't heard from you, either."

As he followed me into my office, and sat down in Zoey's usual chair, I guiltily remembered that I'd never made an effort to see him.

"You're right." I sat down beside him. "I'm really sorry."

He shrugged.

"You want some coffee?"

"Hmm?"

"Coffee."

"Oh." He shrugged, and then looked down at his feet. "Nah, it's all right. I'm fine."

"Okay."

He went silent, and I watched him as he shook his foot wildly, refusing to meet my eye.

"Is everything okay?" I paused. "Is it Sharon Auntie?"

He shook his head. "Ma is fine."

"And you don't want coffee?"

He shook his head.

"Uh, tea?"

"No"—he stood up, started pacing the office—"I *don't* want tea, all right?"

"Depo?"

He stood by the door, and when he put his hand on the knob, I thought he might leave. But then he closed the door and sat back down. He paused, and then said, "I heard you're gay."

"Oh." I sank back onto the chair. "*That.*"

He glared at me. "Thanks for telling me, by the way. And what are you, like, thirty?"

I blew out air through my teeth. "Nearly."

"*Everybody* knows now, do you even know that? Like, everybody is talking about it."

"Yeah. Thanks." I scratched my head. "I am acutely aware."

"Why couldn't you just keep it a secret?" He looked at me like I'd done something wrong, like I was being ridiculous.

"Excuse me?"

"What made you come out?" He shook his head. "You hid it this long—and now—explain it to me."

"Explain what exactly?"

"You knew it would cause a scene with everyone, our whole community, and still—"

"Listen, I really don't have time for a lecture."

"Raina, please just explain it to me, okay?" His voice came out softer. Pleading. "I need you to explain because"—he paused—"I *am*, too."

"Come again?"

"I'm gay, Raina. Just like you." He slumped forward in his chest, and his head fell into his hands. "And I have no idea what to do."

We waited in the cocktail bar on the ground floor of my office building, and I sat there playing with my hands, watching Depesh drink his second whiskey and Coke in ten minutes. He'd slurped down the first in three clean sips and noisily chewed on the ice cubes until a waiter came back and asked if he wanted another. At first, I was surprised they hadn't asked for his ID—Depo, a kid in Converse sneakers and a T-shirt on Bay Street; a kid who, to me, still looked like the ten-year-old I used to babysit; who I'd seen cry after I let him watch a horror movie. Whose eyes lit up whenever I'd suggested ice cream.

But then I looked again. He had stubble on his chin and above the lip, and the baby fat had been sucked from his cheeks, exposing a chiseled jaw and brow bone, a beaky nose. He wasn't the kid I knew anymore. He was eighteen—nineteen, now—and I struggled with what to say. I could feel my heart pounding in my stomach, and I checked my watch. Zoey was on her way. Thank *goodness* Zoey was on her way.

It was the middle of the afternoon, and the bar was empty except for us; all the waitstaff were cluttered behind the bar unloading glasses and chatting about whether this year—finally—the Leafs would make it into the playoffs.

"They're not going to make it," I murmured.

"Pardon?"

"The Leafs," I said, gesturing at the waitstaff. "They're not going to make the playoffs."

"Of course not. But neither are the Devils."

"I have a New Jersey fan sitting next to me?" I scoffed. "And here I thought we could be friends."

"As long as you're not a Canucks fan . . ."

"I don't think the Canucks have fans. Just suckers."

He laughed, and just then, I saw Zoey waft through the entrance.

"There she is."

We were at a booth by the window, and she pulled up a chair to the end. She looked at Depo curiously, and then extended her hand toward him.

"I'm Zoey."

"Depesh," he said. He shook her hand, and then set his own back on his lap.

"Hi, Depesh." She glanced between us, and her eyes landed on me. "You texted this was some sort of emergency?"

"Not quite . . ." I looked at Depesh. "You're sure?"

He nodded, and I looked back at Zoey.

"Zoey, my friend Depesh wants to talk to us about something." I swallowed. "He is . . . gay."

"Also," he said, his eyes flicking between us, "Raina says you guys are, too."

"*Also* gay," repeated Zoey, her eyes still on me. I saw her press her lips together, and I could feel my cheeks flush.

What was I doing? This boy who'd been like a little brother to me was gay, and I was going to lie to him?

For a few seconds—what seemed like an eternity—nobody spoke. Depesh stared at his hands, Zoey stared at me, and all I could hear was the bartender's ignorant position on which Leafs players deserved to be in the Hall of Fame, the elevator jazz drifting from a distant speaker.

"Sorry," I heard Depesh mumble, and I looked up at him.

"What on earth are you sorry about?" I asked.

Looking as if he might cry, he shrugged his shoulders.

"No, we're sorry"—Zoey flicked her eyes at me, and then back him—"just a little stunned, is all." Smiling, she pulled her chair closer to him. "Is there anything in particular you'd like to talk about?"

He shrugged.

"Raina, do you want a drink or something?"

"I'm good."

She flagged down the waiter and ordered a small glass of chardonnay. While he walked away, lingered chattily behind the bar, and then sauntered back with the wine, none of us said a word. Zoey then lifted the glass to her lips and took a slow sip.

"Perfect." She set it back down, wiped off her lip print with her thumb. "What are you studying, Depesh?"

"Biochemistry." He shrugged. "I'm going to apply to medicine."

"That's pretty cool."

"Not really. Like, everyone wants to be a doctor."

"Well, why do you?"

He looked at me like he was expecting me to answer for him, and when I didn't, he glanced back at the table. "My mom is sick."

"I'm sorry to hear that."

"Don't be." He chewed another ice cube. "You didn't give her MS."

Zoey nodded her head slowly.

"We're close, you know? I'm the only son. The only *child*, and I gotta help out a lot. My dad has to work a lot more now, too—" He glanced at me again, like he was surprised I wasn't interrupting, offering my own version of events. "We used to live in Jersey, but her treatment got too expensive. Gotta love American health care."

"No kidding." Zoey chuckled. "How long have you been back?"

"Six months or so."

She nodded again.

"And there's treatments here, too, but"—he shrugged—"there's just not a lot *anyone* can do. It's secondary progressive, and sometimes between attacks, she's back to normal—almost—but it's a waiting game. Like, you never know who or what the trigger is going to be." His voiced quieted. "Whether *I* would be the trigger."

Zoey nodded, and as I sensed what was happening, what she was doing, I fought the urge to leap over the table and hug her. She was patient. Empathetic. She knew people, how to read them, and what they needed, and I felt an overwhelming sense of gratitude for her being there for me; being there for Depesh.

"Did Raina tell you my coming-out story, Depesh?" she said after a moment.

He shook his head.

"Well. It's a pretty standard story. I was about your age, and I'd known for a while." Zoey stared intently at her wineglass. "And because I'd figured myself out so easily, I just assumed everyone else would, too, and"—she paused—"that my parents would someday just figure it out."

He nodded.

"So I just didn't think about it. I didn't think about the fact I was always hiding, or lying, or making excuses for why I never had a boyfriend. Of course my best friends knew, and I dated—well, I *slept* with women. And then one day I met a girl, a girl who turned out to be pretty special to me. This girl was *gorgeous*, intelligent, sassy as hell. And of course she went on to break my heart, but in retrospect I swear to you, Depesh, it was still worth it."

He nodded, his eyes still down on the table.

"I told my parents about her. And they screamed and they cried—and they threw shit—"

"Did they forgive you?"

"Depesh, there was nothing to forgive. I am who I am—and they simply can't or won't accept that. Don't get me wrong, I sacrificed my relationship with them for a new relationship, but those feelings are part of who I am. They're a part of all of us. Love and heartbreak—it's everywhere, it's universal, and there's no shame in any of it."

I thought of Dev, and how my whole mess had started because I was ashamed.

As if she knew what I was thinking, Zoey reached for my hand beneath the table. I grabbed it, and it gave me strength.

"And"—I said, looking Depo in the eye—"if there's anything Zoey and I can impress upon you . . . it's that *you* have absolutely nothing to feel ashamed about."

EIGHTEEN

A young Rani Mukerji danced in a train station wearing a blue tube top, shaking her hips, lip-synching to a voice likely a full octave higher than her own. An actor I didn't recognize—wearing aviators, dressed like a sailor—appeared behind her, sang to her as he did push-ups and made the street children laugh.

I looked over at Nani. She had her feet on the coffee table, one toe bouncing along with the beat, but her eyes were glued to her tablet, her finger winding in long, slim lines across the surface.

"If you're not watching, can I put something else on?" I grabbed a pillow from the floor, and wedged it behind my back. *"Anything* else?"

Nani didn't reply. She pushed her glasses up her nose with the back of her hand, and then resumed her finger positioning at the tablet.

"What are you doing?"

"Candy Crash."

"Candy *Crush*?"

She smiled at the screen, and a moment later, let out a mild shriek. "I *von*! I beat the level." Turning to me, she winked. "Pretty good for old woman, *nah*?"

I laughed. "Good job."

"While you are here," she said shuffling over to me, "can you teach me how to download new game?"

I grabbed her tablet and clicked on the app store. "Sure, what's your password?" She didn't answer, and I looked over. "You wrote it down, right?"

"Raina, there are so many, *nah*? I don't know." She clucked her tongue. "Banking. Restaurant banking. U-*teel*-ity bill. Security code—"

"Don't you have a password manager?"

"Don't I have a granddaughter?" She winked at me, and I burst out laughing. It took about twenty minutes to find all her passwords and organize them in a way she'd remember, and by that time, the Rani Mukerji movie had ended, and a Madhuri Dixit one had begun. As Nani settled in to watch, I looked over at her face. She was smiling, her neck bobbing slightly to the melody.

Was she really watching? What was she thinking? Why was her granddaughter—supposedly successful, in the prime of her life—home with her watching Hindi movies on a Friday night?

And then I shuddered. Because as long as I could remember, Nani had never been home on a Friday night, either. She had dinner parties, temple gatherings, and pujas; was helping with festivals and volunteering.

"Why are you staring, *beta*?"

I sat up, and leaned in closer to her. "Have you spoken to Auntie Sarla recently?"

She pressed her lips together, and then after a moment, looked back at the screen.

I wanted to say something, to come clean. It felt like a wall had been built between us, and I'd never been so far away. And I knew that no matter how many evenings per week I came home to visit, no matter how many new *subjis* I learned to cook, I couldn't fix the fact that I'd ousted her from the community she'd helped build without telling her the truth.

And now Depesh thought I was gay, too. What the hell had I done? Why hadn't I realized such a lie would never be harmless?

This had all started because of Dev: I didn't want to take Nani's matchmaking seriously, because I thought he was the man of my dreams. The man I had to lie for. The man who was working half a world away, but still called once in a while, still e-mailed. Still wouldn't leave me alone.

I loved him, didn't I? And I *knew* he loved me, even if he didn't say it. But Dev coming back wouldn't fix anything anymore. I had to fix it on my own. I'd been selfish—thought only of myself—and now it was my turn to face the consequences.

I looked back at Nani, and watched the TV glow flicker across her face. "Hey, Nani?"

"Hah?" She didn't look up, and I took a deep breath. How was I even supposed to start this conversation? There'd be no good time to tell her the truth—not now. This was as good a time as any, wasn't it?

"I . . . uh—"

The phone rang, and my stomach dropped with relief, even though I knew I needed to fix things between us. Nani reached for the cordless phone and then pressed the answer button as she held the receiver to her face.

"This is Mrs. Ah-Nund. Hello, who is speaking?" She made a face into the phone, and then looked at me. "Raina, for you."

I reached for it. "Hello?"

"Raina, it's Julien."

"How did you get this number?"

"From Shaylee's phone—when she wasn't looking."

I looked over at Nani, staring at me curiously. "Work," I mouthed to her, hopping off the couch.

"You didn't try my cell phone?"

"If you saw my number, I wasn't sure you'd pick up." He paused. "And I saw your car there when I was driving home from Sarla's tonight."

"Ah." I walked into the kitchen, and the door swung closed behind me. "How was *that*?"

"All right." I heard the faint whir of a coffee machine, a few echoing voices, and I could tell he was in the doctors' lounge Shay used to call me from. "I was over there for dinner."

"I see."

"You know we went to India?"

"I heard."

"We've been home for weeks already," he said. "I was hoping you guys would have made up by now."

"Yeah, well . . . I wouldn't hold my breath." I sat down at the table, slumped my body onto its hard, cold surface. I could hear him breathing into the phone, and as I waited for him to say something, anger surged through me. She was getting her fiancé to call for her?

"Raina, listen . . ."

A moment passed. "I'm listening."

"Okay, here it goes." He sighed hard. "I wasn't going to say anything about this—but—to hell with it. Listen, Raina. I'm Catholic, so I guess I understand why some people reacted the way they did—"

"Are you really calling me to defend your mother-in-law?"

"No, of course not—that isn't even why I called."

"Why did you call?"

"Let me start over." He sighed again. "Something has happened with you and Shaylee—and I'm not even going to pretend to know what that is—or what's even going on with *you*, for that matter. You haven't exactly been there for her."

"Helping plan the wedding, organizing the trip to New York—that wasn't being there for her?"

"You know what I mean, Raina. Things have been off with you and Shaylee for a while. Well before New York . . ."

I could almost picture Julien, brow furrowed, chewing his lip, sitting there on those hideous orange couches Shay had described to me a thousand times, her hand buried beneath the cushion while she guessed how much change she would find, what gadgets she might excavate.

"Whatever happened between you two, she won't talk to me about it. She won't say a word. But I know her—and she feels terrible."

"Good. She should."

"Whosever fault it is, whatever it was that caused this—don't you think it's time to make up?" He laughed. "For Christ's sake. She still brought you home a bridesmaid outfit."

I didn't respond. In the other room, I heard the cuckoo clock start to chime, and a shiver crept down my spine.

"I don't know if I can forgive her, Julien."

"Don't you want to try? Don't tell me that you of all people haven't said anything in the heat of the moment. There's nothing you wish you could take back—something you took too far?"

I bit my lip.

"You have been best friends—you've been *sisters*—for over twenty years. You know her better than anyone in the entire world. Whatever you fought about, ask yourself, is it really worth it?"

"I'll talk to her," I said slowly. "But she has to apologize first."

"Funny. That's exactly what she said."

"Well"—I rolled my eyes—"we were best friends."

"You *are* best friends. And Shaylee needs you right now—what with the wedding coming up. And I know that Sarla is driving her crazier than usual because of—"

"All the drama I've caused?"

"You said it, not me."

I smiled, and I realized that even though they'd been together for nearly five years, this was the first time Julien and I had ever spoken on the phone. Indeed, it was the longest conversation we'd ever had.

"Will you think about talking to her?"

I nodded. "I'll think about it."

"Good. And just so you know, Raina, you may be Shaylee's best friend—but she's *my* best friend. And I know everything about her. Everything." He paused. "And I love her just the same."

I thought about it. And the more I thought about it, the more I realized how much I missed Shay, and how the last few months had felt empty without her. I wanted to know if she'd liked India this time around, and what it was like visiting her family now that she was *finally* getting married. I wanted to be filled in on the wedding plans, on her favorite patients at the hospital; find out if she ever bought that phallic-shaped figurine—of what, exactly, we never figured out—that we once saw at Urban Barn.

I wanted to know if she missed me, too.

And so the next weekend when Julien asked me to meet him, Shay, and Asher at the diner, I reluctantly agreed.

I only had an hour's notice. I showered and changed, and tried to style my hair—curled, jutting out at the back—the way Shay had once said suited me. I found my makeup bag beneath the sink, and outlined my eyes. Curled my lashes.

It was only a quick walk to the diner. On the way, I tried not to think about the fact that Asher would be there, and remained focused on Shay. What I would say. What *she* might say. And with each step, I grew more nervous, and less confident about what the hell I was doing, or what the right thing to do was. Why should I be nervous? It was Shay who owed me the apology, wasn't it?

I pushed through the front door of the diner, and saw Shay, Julien, and Asher sitting in our usual booth at the far corner, right beneath the neon Hollywood sign. Shay and Julien were both in powder blue scrubs, hoodies open over them. Asher was wearing his leather jacket again, a gray T-shirt underneath, the same color as his eyes.

I could feel my heart beating in my stomach.

Did he still think about New Year's Eve, too? Did he think about me at all? So much had happened since. In a way that night—that *kiss*—felt so far away, so surreal, I often wondered if it'd even happened.

I started to panic, and just as I was about to turn around, Asher saw me. I took a deep breath and kept walking.

Julien looked up first and, a moment later, Shay. She followed his gaze to the side, and looked up at me like she was waking up from a dream. I blinked, and a moment later, she snapped her head back toward Julien.

"I *knew* you didn't want to eat here."

"Wait," I said, dumbfounded. "She didn't know I was coming?"

Julien smiled at us sheepishly, and then he and Asher scooted out of the booth.

"I'm not staying."

"Me neither," said Shay.

"Babe. Yes, you are."

"*Her* babe—or me babe," said Shay, cuffing Julien on the arm. "Traitor."

"You're the traitor," I mumbled, just as I felt Asher's hands on my shoulder blades. His peppery soap smell clung to me as he gently guided me into the booth.

"Hey, Raina," he said without looking at me.

"Hey . . ."

"Julien, can you please tell *her* I'm not speaking to her?" I heard Shay say.

"Shay, she's right there. You need to talk to *her*."

"And since when do you tell me what to do?"

"Since now." Julien drummed the table with both of his palms. "You both are talking. Right now. This is enough."

Julien brushed a flyaway hair from Shay's forehead, and when she slapped his hand away, he laughed. "We're going to be outside guarding the door, so don't even think about leaving." He took a step backward, Asher in stride, and said, "That means you, too, Raina."

After they'd gone, Shay wouldn't look at me. Instead, she rolled her eyes, and then rolled her head back against the seat. She stuffed a french fry into her mouth, chewed it purposefully, and still, she wouldn't look at me.

"Child," I muttered.

She looked up, stuck her tongue out, and took out her phone.

"Typical *Shay*."

Another moment passed by, and then she set down her phone, dug into her purse, and retrieved a copy of *White Teeth*. My copy of *White Teeth*. She roughly flipped through the pages and lifted up the book so it blocked her face.

I slid her plate toward me—three-quarters of a chicken sandwich, a fistful of fries—and then reached to the side for a bottle of mustard and noisily opened the lid. She moved the book down an inch. I smiled as I slowly flipped over the bottle and then squeezed it as hard as I could, yellow mustard in thick swirls pooling over the entire plate.

Shay hated mustard.

"What the hell?" She tossed the book to the side. "I was eating that."

"I'm sorry." I stuffed three fries into my mouth. "Did you just speak to me?"

"You're such a child."

"Yes." I nodded. "*I* am the child."

"A child. And a liar." She reached for the plate, and I swatted her hand away. "And a brat—"

"Shay." I pulled the plate back, so hard that her butt rose off the seat. "Let go!"

"You let go!" She tugged on it, and then I tugged back, and just then, the plate flipped over and everything toppled onto the table in a big angry flop. "Look what you did!" cried Shay.

"Me?"

"Yes—*you*." Her voice was hoarse, and as we used paper-thin napkins to scoop the mashed fries back onto the plate, I looked up at her and saw that she was crying. Thick tears rolling down her cheeks. I handed her a napkin, and she roughly wiped her face.

After a moment, she stopped crying. She balled the napkin up in her palms, and then tossed it at me. It ricocheted off my shoulder and dropped into my lap. I picked it up, and then threw it back at her, hitting her square in the nose.

She smiled, and then a moment later, the happy expression on her face disappeared.

What had happened to us?

A waitress came by and glared at both of us as she grabbed the dirty plate, and then again we were left in silence. The diner was mostly empty, a few quiet tables closer to the front with children and grandparents, teenagers on day-dates. A speaker above us was playing the easy listening radio station, the tune and lyrics barely audible, but entirely familiar.

Shay stared at her hands, and I knew she was working up the courage to apologize. That face—sheepish, red, and sullen—I'd seen it a hundred times; Shay facing up to her mistakes, Shay acknowledging when she was wrong and trying to make amends.

But this time, if I were honest with myself, was it really *her* fault?

Why did it feel so awful that my best friend fell in love before me? Even after she started dating Julien, hadn't Shay always been there for me? Hadn't she always supported me whenever Mom came home, and when Nana died? And when Dev and I ended, how many times had she shown up in the middle of the night with half a caramel cheesecake and a bag of popcorn, determined to cheer me up? Belted out Coldplay until my sobs turned to laughter and the neighbors complained?

And what had I done for her?

I'd been too busy making sure my calendar matched Dev's to invite her to visit me in London. I'd pushed her away whenever she tried to help. I'd distanced myself as her wedding approached, as her residency drew to a close: whenever her life went right and, seemingly, mine went wrong. I'd lied to her, abandoned her when she needed me.

It was my fault: The fight. The lie that ballooned with each day that passed. It was all my fault.

"I'm sorry," I said finally.

Shay looked at me, a surprised look on her face. Her smile reappeared, and then she shrugged. "I'm sorry, too."

"No, *really*, I'm sorry—"

"I was such a bitch to you."

"What I said was horrible, too, Shay."

"I was just so angry, you know? I was angry, and I just didn't—

I *don't*—understand what's going on, why you're lying to everyone—"

"It's okay, Shay." I paused, and took a deep breath. "And I guess . . . I just couldn't believe you're getting married."

I looked away, embarrassed by the blunt and bitter truth: I couldn't believe Shay was getting married, and I couldn't believe it wasn't me.

Shay reached across the table and found my hand. "It's okay."

I blinked, trying to force away the tears, and she squeezed my hand until I looked her in the eye.

"Are you ready to tell me the truth now?"

Wasn't this why I came? Wasn't I ready?

"What can be so bad, Raina, that you're lying to everyone about *this*?"

I told her. Over two pieces of fresh pecan pie and cups of coffee, the whole story came out. I told her how Dev was back in my life— sort of—and I still didn't know what to do or what it meant. I told her about Nani—the dates, the pressure, the slip-of-the-tongue lie—and how annoyingly supportive she was being. I told her about Depesh, that I'd been talking to or texting him almost every day. How we'd talk about his feelings of isolation and disappointment, of having to lie about who he was to everyone he knew.

I told her about the situation snowballing, how I had no idea how to fix this without hurting him, without hurting Nani, and that I needed her help; I needed my best friend's help.

When I finally stopped talking, I was close to tears. Shay hadn't said a word the whole time, her face expressionless.

"Well?" I asked.

"Well"—she paused, pressed her lips together—"truth is, Raina, I don't know what the hell we are going to do."

Despite everything, I smiled. *We.* Shay and I were back.

"Jesus, don't *cry*," she said. She stood up from the booth, walked around the table, and sat down next to me. She wrapped an arm tightly around my shoulder, and I let my head fall onto hers. I could smell her shampoo, her soothing tang of sweat and hospital scrubs.

"You okay?"

I shook my head. "Seriously, what am I going to do?"

Abruptly, she pushed me off her, and then angled her body to face me on the seat.

"You can't go on pretending forever, but we're not going to tell anyone until we've figured out how to handle it," Shay said a moment later. "At some point, this is all going to come out. You're going to have to tell Depesh and your nani. We're just delaying the inevitable."

I looked up at her and nodded. I knew that, too.

"And your nani . . ." Shay sipped her coffee, and then set it back down. "She'll be okay, I think. She's resilient. Maybe we *should* tell your nani now. It would be hard, but she'll understand, won't she? She'd keep the secret until the time is right?"

I'd been asking myself those questions for weeks, and I still didn't have a clear answer.

"When is the right time though, Shay?"

"Down the road, after Depesh comes out? After he's more—I don't know—comfortable with himself?" Shay sighed, and wrapped her hand around her coffee cup. "At some point—whenever that is, whenever you tell him the truth—you're going to hurt him, and he may never trust you again. There's no way around that."

I'd racked my brain so many times, conjured up a million scenarios where he, my nani, didn't get hurt; but there weren't any.

"Everyone thinks I'm gay," I blurted. "How is it going to be okay? Now, how is anyone ever going to look at Nani the same after the truth comes out?" I laughed, despite myself. "How is *she* going to look at me after this? I've seen her browser history. You know, she's been *so* supportive, I think she might actually want me to marry a woman? Have children with a woman? I don't know how I let it get this far."

"You'd do anything for her, Raina. Everyone knows that." Shay shrugged. "And she'd do anything for you, even accept—"

"That her granddaughter isn't actually a lesbian?"

"Just a bit of a liar," said Shay, rolling her head backward onto the booth. "Shit, I should really go."

"Already?"

Shay nodded. "I have to train the new residents, and then go help Ma with—I don't know—*something*."

"How are the wedding plans?"

Shay groaned. "She has been such a pain. The three of us brought home *eleven* suitcases from India. Eleven. Can you believe it?" She reached for her coffee cup. It was empty, and she slammed it back down on the table. "I don't even know what's in the stupid things. It's turning into such a spectacle—ugh—and to think, Julien and his family wanted a tiny church wedding."

"And what did you want?"

She shrugged, and then in the clearest of voices, said, "I just wanted him."

I turned around in the booth and glanced out the front window. Julien and Asher were still standing on the sidewalk just outside, arms crossed, talking to each other. I looked back at Shay.

"Do they know I'm . . ."

Shay smiled. "Julien thinks whatever Ma has been telling him. I haven't said anything about this; that bozo can't keep his mouth shut. Did you know they have dinner together when I'm working late?"

"I did know, actually."

"And Asher—well, he thinks it was a *damn* good kiss for a lesbian—"

"You know about that?"

"Of course I know." She glanced at her watch, and then reached across the table for her purse. "But I have to go back to work. And you're going to call me tonight and tell me what the hell has happened between you two, okay?"

"Promise."

She stood up, fumbling with her coat and scarf. When she was all wrapped up, I got out of the booth and stood beside her. She came up to my nose.

"Shay"—I paused, struggling to find the words—"all this time, you never told anyone I was lying? Not Auntie Sarla, not Julien or Asher? . . . Why?"

"I was *mad*," she said, rolling her eyes. "But I'm still your best friend. I was never *not* going to cover your ass."

NINETEEN

After she disappeared from the diner, I took my time finishing my pie. When I finally left, I saw Asher standing across the road propped against a lamppost, waiting for me. For some reason, I wasn't surprised he was still there. I put on my sunglasses and, through their shelter, took in his broad, shadowy physique. The strong line of his jaw, upturned corners of his mouth. He smiled as I crossed the road toward him, and I found myself smiling back.

We wandered aimlessly, wrestling our way through the downtown sidewalks. It was one of those rare winter days that almost felt like spring, and the whole city felt alive; everyone seemed to be outdoors, their winter parkas tied hastily around their waists, shopping or sporting bags flung over one shoulder.

It wasn't until we'd walked past my office building that I realized that some twenty floors above, Bill and Zoey were probably waiting for me; that I'd told him I'd come in and help with the next report. I looked behind me as the skyscrapers fell away and followed Asher toward the lake, resolving not to think about it. Resolving, for now, not to care.

Cherry Beach was spotted with snow, and as we walked westward along the lake, a breeze picked up and I shivered.

"Are you cold?" he asked. "Do you want my coat?"

I shook my head. He took off his sunglasses and squinted at me for a moment, and then, smiling, he put them back on.

"Have you and Shaylee made up?"

I nodded.

"In New York, she didn't take your news well, I'm guessing."

I didn't say anything, timed my footsteps with his.

"People don't always understand what's not right in front of them." Asher's feet kicked sand up onto mine. "Not right away, at least. And how much can we really blame people for not knowing better? But then—when they do know better—I think we can blame them for not trying."

I swallowed loudly. Asher thought I was gay; he thought the fight was about me being gay.

"I think she's trying." I felt him looking at me, and after a moment, he continued. "I haven't told you about my sister, Anna, have I?"

I kicked a loose rock. "Have you?"

"About the time she swallowed everything in the bathroom cabinet and had to have her stomach pumped?"

"Asher, that's horrible."

"It was. She's okay now—thank God—but at the time, Anna was just a kid who needed help." He shrugged. "She's gay, and she didn't know how to deal with it—not even in a progressive family like ours. I can't imagine what it would have been like for someone growing up someplace less . . . tolerant."

He looked over at me expectantly, and my stomach felt as if it might tear in two.

Asher's sister was gay?

"Anyway, Anna's happily married now," he said after a moment. "Jess is great. They have two kids in the suburbs. Piano lessons, bake sales, the whole deal. But it just terrifies me to think how easily none of that could have happened. Actually"—he glanced at me—"it's one of the reasons I wanted to be a teacher. Kids should be happy, you know? I never want to see what happened to Anna happen to anyone else."

I nodded, stared furiously at my shoes as we toed our way across the sand. Asher's sister was gay, and like Depesh, it had been a struggle for her to accept it. I was making light of that. I was making a mockery of everything.

Would Asher understand? I wanted to tell him the truth, too. I barely knew him, but I already sensed that I could trust him, that despite everything he *would* understand. We stopped at a part of the sandbar that jutted out into the lake; a small peninsula of granulated rock and glass, and I stared across the water.

"I heard you're done with teacher training?"

"Yep. I've got a full-time position at your old high school. I'm teaching history, English, politics—"

"Basketball?"

He grinned. "Of course."

My stomach tightened. "Asher, look"—I breathed out—"I need to talk to you about something."

"If it's all the same to you"—he glanced away—"I'd rather not."

"But—"

"In New York, I"—he hesitated—"I got carried away. That's all."

Was that all?

"It's all behind us, for better or for worse. I've thought about you a lot since New York. And in hindsight it really does make sense."

"What does?" I whispered.

"Maybe it's growing up with Anna, or traveling and meeting so many other—I guess you could say—*lost souls*. You have that same look. Like you feel completely inadequate despite your accomplishments. Like you're struggling to fit in, searching for something else, and—"

He paused, looked me straight in the eye, and I knew this was my chance to tell him the truth. Tell him that I had lied, and dug myself into a hole so deep that I needed help getting out. That I *was* searching for something else—and even though I wasn't quite sure what it was, or how my life might ever make sense—that maybe, around him, it didn't need to make sense.

He was looking at me, his breathing deep, but I didn't know what to say—or how to say it. His gaze was too heavy. His longing—I felt it—was too much. The moment passed, and I didn't say anything.

"—and, I suppose," continued Asher, glancing back at the water, "what you were looking for . . . I just never guessed it was this."

Asher . . . What just happened!?

WAY TOO GOOD FOR ME

TWENTY

Asher invited me to go watch the Toronto Raptors game with him and a few of his friends, but I declined with an excuse about work, even though I'd already e-mailed Bill to tell him I couldn't come in. I walked Asher to a sports bar just off Queen West and continued north, but I didn't go straight home, either. And it was somewhere between Dundas Square and College that it hit me.

I had feelings for Asher. Real feelings. And the more I thought about it, the more palpable and real they felt. How was it even possible? Sure, he wasn't Indian. We'd led polar opposite lives, and I wasn't sure we had that much—if anything—in common. Then what was it about him that made me feel so stable? With Dev I'd been out of breath constantly, chasing him, always pushing for a different kind of life, but when I was with Asher, it felt like everything was exactly how and where it was supposed to be.

When I got home, I flopped down on my bed and texted Depesh, asking him if he wanted to catch up for dinner that evening, and then opened my laptop. I was staring at the home screen, trying to figure out what it was I needed to do to prepare for the week ahead, when I received a notification from Dev requesting a video chat.

I don't know why I answered. He was in Hong Kong now, and I lay faceup on my bed as Dev nattered away to me about the politics of our foreign office, even though all I wanted to do was tell him to shut up so I could be alone to eat a bag of salt and vinegar chips, and watch bad TV.

He steered his webcam around the patio of his suite, out toward the view of the harbor.

"Look what's just cropped up there—the Central Plaza, you see it?"

I nodded, and then realized he wasn't looking at me. "Yes, I can see it."

"Huge, innit?"

He turned the camera back to face him. He was wearing sunglasses and a tangerine polo with the top two buttons undone, and as his pixelated smile filled up my screen, I felt that familiar surge. The shortness of breath. That smile—the way he could wield it as both shield and sword.

"It's great, Dev. Looks like you're having a nice time."

I didn't recognize the shirt. Had a woman bought it for him? I wondered whether he even had time for women with the hours he worked—and it was me he had been calling whenever he had a spare moment, wasn't it? A part of me wanted to scream, ask who had bought him that shirt, and what we were, and why he couldn't have made up his mind to commit already.

The other part of me was just too exhausted to care anymore.

"Your work all right, darling?"

"It's okay. Busy. But okay."

"That's the beauty of it though. The business, the rush, don't you reckon?"

"Yeah, sure."

"Complacency, Raina. It doesn't suit you."

"Yeah, well . . ." I thought about what to say next: that neither does this job—after Dev and I split, had it lost its last redeemable feature? Dev glanced behind him and out onto the harbor. The image wasn't clear, but clear enough, and I could tell from his tensed chin, the square of his jaw, that his mind had already wandered off. He wasn't looking at the blues, yellows, and grays of the morning skyline, enjoying the few minutes he would spend outdoors. He was already thinking about that day's agenda; the intense session at the gym he'd fit in between client meetings, the conference call in the back seat of the 5 Series on the drive back to the office.

Dev had traveled constantly while we were together. Direct flights from Heathrow, gone for two days, or two weeks—then the fast train to Paddington, and back to the office. After each business trip abroad, I'd swing by his office with two coffees and pastries from Pret, and he'd have nothing to say about the observation deck on the Burj Khalifa or the white sands of Copacabana. Wiping the crumbs from his chin, he'd tell me about the swanky boardrooms in our Dubai office, the portfolio he'd sorted out in Rio—complaining about what went wrong, or what they had but we didn't. Dev wanted it all, to be a part of the whole world. But going that fast, I always wondered if he'd end up missing out on everything.

I heard my cell phone buzz on the end table.

"Where'd you go, love?"

"Hmm?" I said to the screen. Dev's picture had frozen—his mouth open, tongue slightly curled—and I waved my hand.

A second later, his screen unfroze. I picked up my phone. It was

Depesh, suggesting a ramen place nearby my condo, and I replied with a thumbs-up emoji.

"I have only twenty minutes, and you're going to chat with someone else?" I heard Dev say.

"Excuse me? You can run off for however many months, but I can't look at a *text*?"

"Raina, please don't."

"You call me when it's a good time for you, but did you even ask whether now is a good time for me? Did you ask me how my day was, except for *work*? Do you even know what else is happening in my life? Have you once asked me how Nani is doing? Or Shay?"

He held up a hand to the screen, and I heard him sigh. "Sorry, you're right. I don't want to fight, darling. I'm knackered. I slept like shit last night, and—"

"And it's always about you, isn't it?" I pressed my lips together. He repositioned his screen, and his face was closer now.

Was this the man I was waiting for? Was I—months later— still waiting for *him*?

"I need to know," I said, looking at my hands. "Are you coming back to Toronto?"

"Soon, Raina."

"What does *soon* mean? In a week, a few months? Maybe never—"

"Where is this coming from?"

"You're a smart guy, Dev. It's not that difficult."

"Raina, we've never played games with each other. Yes, I'll be the first admit I wasn't—I *haven't*—been great to you." He ran his hands through his hair. "But being away, bouncing around between offices . . . It's been hard for me, too."

"I'm so sorry this has been hard on *you*. Truly sorry."

"I've never led you on, darling. I've always been honest—*we've* been clear about the situation between us. You knew when I came to Toronto we weren't quite sure whether I could . . . that I was still . . ." He trailed off, and I could feel my ears burn.

He was right. I'd gone along with what he said, what *he* wanted, desperate to make him happy; convinced that it would make me so, too. But what for? When had I become this woman—weak, desperate—my everything dependent on him? I'd lied—I'd created this whole mess—because I loved him, but I was so tired of it.

All of a sudden, I was so fucking tired of him.

". . . you know how I feel about you. I just don't know what else to—"

"Dev," I said, interrupting him. "Let *me* be clear then. Crystal clear." I took a deep breath, and stared straight into his pixelated eyes. "Come back. Don't come back. It doesn't even matter anymore."

"Darling, you *can't* mean that."

Didn't I mean it, though?

"I mean it," I said, slowly. Firmly.

"Raina—"

"Because I'm done waiting for you."

I slammed the laptop shut. My bedroom was silent. Murky dark, except for the sliver of light coming in from beneath the door. I got off the bed and opened the curtains, stared out into the dark night.

And then I closed my eyes, let the tears drop; finally ready to let Dev fall away.

~~Dev . . . ?~~ Never. Again.

TWENTY-ONE

"You are inviting that woman *here*?" Nani had asked me, when I announced I'd invited Auntie Sarla and Shay over for tea.

I nodded, pulling a box of *laddoo* out of the Deepfreeze.

"And she agreed?"

"Yep."

She stared at me as I set the sweets out on a china platter, and then disappeared upstairs. Shay and I had been planning the reconciliation for weeks—an afternoon tea where we'd force Nani and Auntie Sarla to set their differences aside, and be friends again.

They'd always had an unusual relationship, one based on both rivalry and genuine affection. Auntie Sarla had been Nani's saving grace when our family had moved to Toronto. She'd helped Nani grow the restaurant, and had supported her after Mom got pregnant. Even though Auntie Sarla was everything negative about our Indian traditions incarnate, Nani had lost her friendship because of me. And while I would never truly forgive Auntie Sarla for her judgment, I wanted Nani to.

"Raina?" I heard Nani call, as she walked down the steps.

"Yes?"

"Can you give me hand?"

I went into the living room and stopped short in my tracks. She was holding up a giant rainbow flag, and it was nearly as tall as she.

She had bought a pride flag? What the hell had I done? My stomach lurched as I wrestled with whether to just spit it out: tell Nani I wasn't actually gay. Zoey and now Shay were on my case to tell her the truth, but I kept finding excuses. One week Nani had the flu, and the next I had to be in Montreal for a few days for a seminar.

"I was thinking we should put above the mantelpiece."

And in moments like these, when I did find myself face-to-face with Nani, I knew deep down that I should tell her. That I *wanted* to tell her.

But I never managed to do it.

"Amazon sent it to me." Nani moved her hands, and it sent a wave down the fabric. "Don't you think it's nice to have it out for"—she smiled sweetly—"our *guest*?"

I opened my mouth. I was ready, wasn't I?

"Nani . . ."

"Hah, my sweet?"

I hesitated, and then I shrunk back. "Do you think the flag matches the room?"

"It matches perfectly," she snapped. "It is absolutely *perfect*."

They were an hour late. Auntie Sarla opened the front door and marched in like she lived there, Shay following, rolling her eyes in my direction as she sat down on the couch opposite us. Nani turned off the television, and as Auntie Sarla stood in front of the three of us, her hand planted firmly on her hips, no one said a word. Shay and I looked at each other, trying not to laugh as Nani and Auntie Sarla stared at each other in silence. Finally, Auntie Sarla sighed, and dramatically folded herself onto the couch next to Shay.

"Sarla." Nani smiled at the ground. "Do you like our new decorations?"

Without looking up, Auntie Sarla growled. "Suvali, I am saying this once. I am here against my will. Shaylee is the one who insisted—"

"Ma, please—"

"No, no," Auntie Sarla cut her off waving a hand. "*She* should know. I am not okay with this—I am not okay with either of you, but"—Auntie Sarla cleared her throat, and glared around the room accusingly—"Shaylee *insisted* that we all get along."

"I threatened to cancel the wedding." Shay smiled at me as she reached for the bowl of cashews. "And I was serious, too."

Through gritted teeth, Nani and Auntie Sarla spent the next hour discussing preparations for the *sangeet*. The billeting of various relatives and friends flying in from Jaipur, Singapore, and Dubai; where they would stay and what they would eat. It was almost back to normal, and Nani and Auntie Sarla were bickering about something inconsequential when Shay sidled over to my couch.

"I need to tell you something," whispered Shay.

I glanced over at Nani and Auntie Sarla. They were still discussing Shay's great-uncle's dietary restrictions and weren't listening to us. I looked back at Shay. "What is it?"

"Asher is seeing someone."

I felt my heart drop.

"Thought you might want to know."

I nodded, and wondered what gave me the right to care so much. He and I were friends. I let him believe I wasn't interested in his entire sex. What else could I expect?

"She's another teacher at his school. I'm sorry . . ." Shay kissed me on the forehead. "But she's a bit of an idiot. I wouldn't worry"—her head turned—"*what*, Ma?"

I looked up, and Auntie Sarla was staring at us, her mouth frozen mid-sentence.

"What, am I not allowed to *kiss* my best friend?" Shay snapped.

Auntie Sarla growled, and then she tore her eyes away from us. "*Disgusting.*"

"Stop it." Shay's voice shook. "Raina's no different than before."

"This is true. Raina was *never* a good girl."

"Sarla," said Nani. "Do not speak about Raina like that. Not in my house."

Auntie Sarla laughed, and gestured to Nani. "But what could we expect? Another one raised by *her*."

"Ma," said Shay unsteadily. "I'm warning you. You think I'm kidding, but so help me—if you don't stop—"

"Fine, fine." Auntie Sarla smiled and reached for her tea. "It's all fine." She glanced pointedly at Nani, and then toward me. "I am sorry." She smiled, and spoke slowly. "I am very, *very* sorry."

Nani's face was bright red, and I could tell she was breathing hard. I tried to catch her eye, but she just kept staring at Auntie Sarla.

"Would you like some water?" I asked Nani. She didn't answer. "Nani?"

She was shaking, and I felt myself shaking, too. She was fighting for me, but why was I putting her through this? Whatever her reaction to my deception, it couldn't be worse than this. I needed to tell her the truth, *now*, but first I needed to get Auntie Sarla out of the house.

"Auntie, maybe we should continue the plans later—"

"Yes. Very good idea. She needs to *leave*. I am not taking this— I am not taking *her*—any longer," said Nani. She stood up and pointed at the door. "Leave, Sarla. Right now. This is not acceptable treatment. You have been an interference *too* long—"

"I am being honest. Are friends not honest?" Auntie Sarla stood up also, face-to-face with Nani. "We have been friends for more than *thirty* years, Suvali—"

"You insult us. You insult Raina. She is a wonderful girl, and I am proud of her." Nani reached for the phone. "Let's call her girlfriend. I'll *show* you, you ignorant woman—this Zoey girl is more decent than—"

"Nani, Zoey and I are just friends—"

"—some of these boys she could have married. She is more decent than your husband, than *my* husband—"

"Can Zoey give her children? No. It is *wrong*, Suvali. I am trying to help. Have I not always helped you?"

"No, you—"

But then the phone rang, a shrill, reminding pierce that silenced us all. It was Depesh.

Sharon Auntie was in hospital.

TWENTY-TWO

The waiting room was full, and I crouched down on top of a vent in the hallway opposite. It was chock-full of Indians—some I recognized, some I didn't—and I kept my eyes low. Beneath the white fluorescent lights, my hands looked ghostly pale. I picked at a piece of dirt beneath my fingernails.

Shay had used her ID badge to sneak Nani and Auntie Sarla into the ICU, past the barricade of nurses and attendants who refused to let Sharon Auntie's other friends through. I checked my phone again. Shay hadn't responded to my last text, but as I scrolled through my alerts, I saw another e-mail from Dev.

These days, his messages came often; they were verbose, but said absolutely nothing. And every time I read one, and then forced myself not to reply, I tried not to wonder what my life would have been like if I'd listened to Nani and Shay when they first told me I should cut off all contact. What my life would have been like if I'd given myself the chance to move on.

"Raina? Is that *you*?"

I looked up. An auntie was standing just in front of me, and I stood up to hug her. She smelled like old clothes and soured perfume, and I racked my brain for her name.

Poonam? Vish-*mi*? She was in one of Nani's temple community groups, but I couldn't remember which one. I smiled at her, and we made stilted brief small talk—in English, with whatever Hindi words I knew thrown in—and then she continued on her way.

I watched her as she found a free seat at the far end of the waiting room. She sat down between some other aunties I recognized, and a moment later, I saw them all turn and look in my direction.

I looked back at my hands. It was the first time I'd seen any of them since Christmas. What were they saying? Which ones cared that I was supposedly gay, and which ones didn't?

Did it matter?

I looked up and saw Shay walking toward me, and I stood up.

"How is she?"

"She's good." Shay smiled. "Completely fine. It's not a relapse. She fainted, and Depesh brought her in to be safe. They're going to keep her overnight."

"Is Depesh in there?"

"He said he was going down to the cafeteria. Ma and your nani took over the room the instant they got in there. I'm surprised the doctors are letting them stay."

"What are they doing?"

"They're coordinating a phone tree to raise money for home care, figuring out who gets to cook Depesh dinner"—Shay rolled her eyes—"arguing over whose Tupperware they should use."

"Wow."

"Yeah," said Shay. "Looks like the gruesome twosome are back together."

I nodded, and looked back down the hall.

Within the hour, the news had traveled and dozens in the community had shown up in support of Sharon Auntie. It was strange—how connected we really were. An invisible safety net that I'd never really stopped to think about. As frustrating as they could be . . . I knew that they'd be there for Nani and me, too. They always had.

"Who are you looking at?"

I shrugged.

"It's embarrassing, isn't it?" Shay said after a moment. "The way some of them are acting."

"And what are we supposed to do? Do we accept them for how they are, and blame it on their upbringing? Appreciate everything that's good"—I turned back to Shay—"and try and not focus on the bad?"

"I guess so, *yeah*"—she pushed her hair out of her eyes—"but I don't know, Raina. I don't know if I have an answer for that."

There was good and bad, light and dark—yin and yang—to everything, wasn't there? Their homophobia, their reluctance to accept what they didn't understand—wasn't that just a relic of tradition? Something bound to be trampled on over time?

I heard Shay sigh, and I glanced back at her.

"I don't know if I've ever explicitly said it to you—if I've ever said—but I'm sorry for the way my mother has treated you and your nani."

"I brought it on myself, didn't I?"

Shay crossed her arms, and I knew exactly what she was about to say. "Depesh didn't."

I found him at the farthest table in the cafeteria. His hair was greasy, and he had dark rings under his eyes. He was staring out the window—a dark sliver peeking out into the parking lot—and he didn't see me until I was right next to him.

"Mind if I join?"

He shook his head and dropped his legs off the chair. I sat down, and he leaned in, hunched over the table. His eyes and the tip of his nose were red.

"How are you doing?"

He didn't answer, smiled halfheartedly at the table.

"Your mom can go home tomorrow," I said. "Have you heard? She's completely fine."

He wouldn't meet my eye.

"Depesh, what are you thinking?" I whispered. "You can tell me."

"I don't know, Raina." He sighed—an exasperated, frustrated sigh. "My mom is in hospital, she has a disease that one day might actually kill her, I'm in the middle of writing final exams—and all I can think about right now is a guy." He shrugged. "A *guy*."

"You met someone?"

He nodded.

I smiled and poked him in the arm. He didn't look up, and I kept poking him until he smiled, too.

"Tell me about him." I leaned back in my chair. "But only if you want."

"His name is Caleb, and we met in Human Biology a while ago . . . He's one of the friends I told you about."

"So he's a friend?"

Depesh smiled, shaking his head. "Not anymore. Yesterday, we"—Depesh paused—"Raina, I'm falling for him. I want to be with him."

"Depo, you *can* be with him."

"No." He shook his head. "I can't. Not the same way everyone else is."

"What do you mean?"

"I want to hold his hand. Like, I want to show him the house I grew up in—and bring him as my date to—I don't know, Thanksgiving dinner with my family. I'll never be able to do any of that stuff."

"You don't know that . . . Remember what Zoey said?" I sat up straighter in my chair. "You have to work up to telling your parents, work *yourself* up to it. Besides Caleb, you've talked to people, right? You told me some of your new friends know now?"

Depesh nodded.

"And how was that?"

He shrugged. "It was fine. They were great about it. But my parents, Ma is sick, and—and—"

"Your mom is getting the treatment she needs. She's getting stronger overall." I leaned in closer. "There's never going to be a right time, Depesh. If you want to come out to them, then—"

"They think I'm some kind of *dream* child, Raina. They respect me and love me, and *rely* on me—how am I supposed to take that away?" Depesh shook his head. "Raina, you think Auntie Sarla is bad. You should have heard what they said about you."

I pressed my lips together.

"They are who they are, and if they can't—or *won't*—change, how are they ever going to look at me the same again?"

A strange silence passed between us, and I became conscious of the wind-like rustling in the vent along the wall; a vacuum roaring faintly in another wing of the hospital.

"When I was younger—maybe you were too young to remember—but you should have seen the way people used to look at me when I was little, before my mother moved out. You should have seen how they looked at my whole family." My breath caught. "Do you know she was sixteen when I was born?"

He shook his head.

"And do you remember Vikram Prasad's wedding, about ten years ago?"

Again, he shook his head.

"Half his family didn't show up for the wedding because he didn't marry a Hindu."

"Really?"

I nodded. "And now? I'm all grown up, and does anyone care about how I was born? Does Auntie Sarla—does anyone in our community—care that Shay is marrying a white Catholic guy?"

He shook his head. "No. They don't."

"A lot of them are behind the times. It's going to be hard for the first person to do anything different." I smiled. "But as much as Auntie Sarla—as much as everyone—talks shit, and bickers, they stick together. Yes, they're judgmental—and *yes*, it's fucking frustrating when they don't see things the way we do, but this community is a family, and it's always stuck together."

I heard him swallow.

"And whether your parents kick you out, cut you off, cry, scream, disown you—they're still your family. And they're still going to love you."

He nodded.

"If you tell them, it's going to be hard, Depesh. I'm sorry that I can't change that for you. But—but you're brave enough to be that person, okay? I know you. I know that you're the one who's supposed to do this."

"You did it, Raina—you're *doing* it now."

I swallowed hard, and the guilt tore through me.

"But, maybe you're right." He took a deep breath, and looked me right in the eye. "Maybe I can be brave, too."

TWENTY-THREE

A few days later, I found myself parked outside of Depesh's house. He was sitting on the front step, elbows on knees. The summer I babysat for him, we used to sit on the porch step of his old house and wait for his parents to come home from the hospital; we'd eat ice cream or grape Popsicles, wash our sticky hands and faces with the garden hose before going back inside. He was a kid then, and now? I got out of the car and walked toward him, hopped over the cracked cement, and realized that he wasn't a kid anymore. He was going to face the truth about himself to the people he loved; he was going to do what most adults never have the courage to do. What I didn't have the courage to do.

I sat down beside him. The block was more run-down than it had been the decade before; trees and shrubs overgrown, taking over the sidewalks and fences; graffiti trimming the lampposts and the fire hydrants.

"How did your Chemistry final go?"

"It was good." He shrugged. "Physics is tomorrow . . . Human Biology the day after that."

"That sounds heavy . . . Are you sure you're—"

"I'm ready, Raina. I'm as ready as I'll ever be."

Was this the definition of bravery? Someone who didn't make up excuses, or find reasons to put off the inevitable? A boy—no, a man—who was about to come out to his parents, and stand up for who he was—in the middle of his exams?

"It might even be better this way, right?" He laughed. "They can't come down on me too hard if I have to study tonight."

"You know, Depo . . . I'm really proud of you."

He didn't reply, and then after a moment, he whispered, "They won't be."

"No," I said. "Probably not." I turned to face him, waited until his eyes met mine. "But you'll be proud of you."

"You don't know that."

"If you respect yourself, your own choices"—I looked back out toward the road—"isn't that what matters?"

A group of kids were walking by, drowned in skipping ropes and plastic traffic cones, soccer balls and netting, giggling, stamping across the pavement in a tight pack. They were oblivious in their own happiness. In silence, we watched them pass, and I wondered how many of them would one day have to go through what Depesh was experiencing right now.

As they grew up, as they discovered life in its imperfection, weren't there greater problems to dwell on, to agonize over? Far greater than fearing the implications of one's own sexuality. The world was disturbing enough as it was; not just across the world—deserts and oceans away—but right here at home. And before anyone could grow up, grow the courage to change any of it, surely, *home* was where it had to start.

The kids disappeared around the corner, and after their high-pitched voices faded behind them, I could hear Depesh breathing hard beside me.

"I've never disappointed them before, Raina. I've never not been what they wanted me to be."

I turned to him, and steadied his hand in my own. "Who do you want to be, Depesh?"

It went exactly how one might have expected it to go. Yelling and crying. Complete and unabashed outrage. Depesh defended himself. And when Sharon Auntie didn't drop dead in front of us, and his father's yells became hoarser, Depesh suggested that I leave; told me he wanted to handle the rest of it on his own.

It was dark by the time I pulled into the driveway, next to Kris's car. I turned off the ignition, but my legs and spine were frozen to the seat as I prepared myself to go inside and face Nani. I had made light of something I had no right to joke about. Depesh had come out, and I would tell him the truth next, but first, it was finally time to face Nani honestly.

What would she say? I shook my head. It didn't matter. I had to face it—I *wanted* to face it.

It was late, but for some reason, the front door was unlocked. I stepped into the house. The hallway lights were off, the house coated in silence; no television or kettle whistling, or Nani humming or singing or snoring in the background like white noise. All I could hear was the discerning tick of the cuckoo clock as the handle tapped its way around.

I stepped out of my shoes and crept into the living room. It was empty, and as the pale light of the muted television ghosted through the room, I noticed a full mug of tea abandoned on the coffee table.

"Hello?"

I turned, drawn by a noise in the kitchen, a sliver of light beneath the doorway. And when I pushed through, the door swinging wildly open, there they all were sitting at the kitchen table. Space and time, backward and forward; my childhood playing tricks, playing out right in front of me. Nani and Kris in their usual spots, jaws tensed, shoulders slouched. And across from them, seated cross-legged on my chair, there she was.

"Hi, Raindrop." Chin resting on her palm, Mom grinned at me. "So I hear you're a lesbian."

MAY 20, 1996

Nani surprises Raina with all of her favorites: thick yogurt, mango chutney, an *aloo paratha* with extra butter. Raina sits at the kitchen table eating her breakfast, sipping her glass of apple juice from the table without touching it; her top lip curled over the glass, her greasy hands held up as if in surrender. She eats carefully, tearing a piece of the paratha off with one hand the way Nani taught her, dipping it, and then bringing it slowly to her mouth. She has covered herself with three paper napkins. It is hours until her party, but she is already wearing her new dress. Manavi reappeared with it—a belated Christmas present after a trip to Las Vegas last year—and only now has Raina grown into it. It is lavender, the same shade as the pillows on Raina's bed, and she admires herself as she chews; the white and violet frills on the cuffs, the hem that skirts around her knees.

Her feet do not touch the ground, and she swings them as she eats, kicking a ball across an imaginary field. Raina is only partway through her breakfast when the murmurs from downstairs become louder. Staccato and sharp. She slips quietly off her chair and tiptoes toward the door that leads down to the entertaining room. She slides down onto her knees and presses her ear against the door, trying to make out the sounds.

Before, Kris used to take Raina to her room, turn on the radio. If that wasn't enough, he'd press her hands over her ears and tell her to keep them like that until they stopped. But these days, Kris is rarely home, so when they yell, Raina tries to listen; she is curious to understand why everyone seems to be so angry all the time. They yell about the mess of long hair Manavi left in the bathtub drain, or the door she slammed too hard, or the boy who dropped her off. About the right way to teach Raina to tie her shoes. Raina listens hard, but this time their voices are too muffled, as if they know she might be listening.

Raina hears a thumping up the stairs, and she bolts back to her seat, reaches for her glass of juice. Manavi swings open the door, followed seconds later by Nani. Manavi crouches down beside Raina and tugs on one of her braids.

"Do you want to go to Wonderland, Raindrop?"

Raina's eyes widen. "Wonderland?" Her face breaks out into a smile. "Really?"

"Manu . . ."

But Nani stops short when Manavi snaps her head in Nani's direction.

"Yes, Raindrop." Manavi turns her head slowly back to Raina, and blows her bangs from her face. "Let's go. Get your coat."

"Now?" Raina slumps forward. She wants to go, but not today. Today is her seventh birthday, and there will be a party at the new restaurant. "But there's going to be a magic show!"

"Raina, come *on*." Manavi leans back, balancing on her heels. "I got us tickets for today—"

"Please, Manu." Nani is now standing at the kitchen sink, her hands leaning against it like she's trying to catch her breath. She turns to them, and says, "Please, not—"

"I *told* you they're only valid for today!"

"Did you even remember it was her party?" Nani's voice is strained, and Raina looks down. Her eyes start to water when she notices that, despite how careful she's been, a fat droplet of juice has found its way onto her dress.

"So, are we going?" Manavi snaps. "I don't have all day."

Raina's eyes are locked on the stain, and after a moment, she says, "Can we go tomorrow?"

"Tomorrow?"

"But today is—"

"No, we can't go tomorrow," Manavi growls. She stands up in one fluid motion. "I'll go with my friends." And with that, she grabs her leather jacket off the hook, and marches out, mumbling inaudibly until the kitchen door bangs heavily behind her.

The new restaurant is bigger than the last one, Nani says, although to Raina it looks very much the same. Raina and her friends sit around two of the long restaurant tables pushed together. Nani and Nana have decorated them with white plastic tablecloths and gold confetti, pink and purple helium balloons. They have set out supplies like it's art class—with every color of cardboard construction paper, pipe cleaners and Popsicle sticks, cotton balls and glue. The expensive Magic Markers.

Raina makes her crafts sitting next to a boy from her soccer team, and an Indian girl named Shaylee that Nani keeps inviting to the house. When the magician arrives, they are all herded toward a makeshift stage in the corner. Raina sits at the end of the row, and when the magician makes a rubber duck disappear into a hat, her friends gasp. Raina thinks she knows how he did it: the hat is wide and long, and surely, the duck is being hidden inside; in a secret pocket, perhaps. She thinks about raising her hand, or leaning over and telling Shaylee how it happened, but she doesn't want to ruin the trick. So she doesn't say anything.

Next, the magician pulls out a deck of cards, and Raina blinks hard, trying to memorize the sequence, trying to unlock the secret of this trick, too, when she thinks she hears Manavi's voice behind her. She turns around, and is excited to see that Manavi has decided to come to her birthday party. Nani is whispering to Manavi, and although Nani is smiling, flicking her eyes toward Auntie Sarla and the other adults at the back, Raina can tell that her nani is angry. After a moment, they go into the kitchen, and silently, swiftly, Raina follows.

Inside, she can hear their voices, and she ducks behind a garbage bin, carefully peers around the side.

"I don't care—"

"Shh!"

"—what the fuck—they think about me."

"Manu!"

"And don't *shhh* me." Manavi stamps her foot like a child. She is crying, and her words are slurred. Raina has never seen her like this before; at least, not in the middle of the day.

"There is party happening, *nah*? Sarla is here. You must settle down."

"Who cares about *Sarla*?" She grabs a frying pan from the stove and tosses it between her hands. For a moment, Raina thinks she might hit Nani, swing at her with it like a baseball bat, but after a few catches, Nani lunges for it. She knocks it out of her grasp, and it clambers to the floor. Nani reaches down to get it, one hand on her lower back, and then sets the pan back on the stove.

"Never could let me have a little fun, could you?"

"You've been having your fun for a while."

"It didn't start out that way. Did it, Ma?" Silence, and then a moment later, Manavi says, "I'm moving out."

"You've been saying for years. Go ahead. Move out."

"And Raina?"

"She will stay with us."

"You don't have the right—you think *you* have the fucking right to decide that about her?" Manavi laughs. "I dare you. I dare you to stop me."

"You are not taking that girl with you."

"I'll take you to court."

"Take me wherever you like"—Nani takes a deep breath—"but you will not take my Raina."

"She's *my*—"

"Boozing, men—doing God knows what. You coming, going— we never know. Raina never knows. You think you can be her mother?"

"I *am* her mother," cries Manavi, tears rolling down her face and leaving black mascara tracks. "I am her fucking mother!"

"You are not a mother. Grow up. Stop being child. Start acting like you care about Raina, like you want to *be* mother to her—"

Manavi cries harder, slams her fists against the counter.

"—always blaming others. Never your fault, *nah*? Never taking responsibility—"

"I hate—you—you self-righteous *bitch*." Her words pour out in chokes and gasps, and Nani turns her head.

Manavi inches closer to her, and by the way Manavi is leaning against the counter, sobbing, their shoulders nearly touching, Raina has the feeling that if only her nani would turn around, there wouldn't be so much yelling.

But she doesn't turn around, and after a moment, Manavi stops crying. She grabs a roll of paper towels, uses the whole of it to dry her face. Nani is motionless, still facing away. Manavi inches toward her—and then, she retreats.

"You want her?" Manavi stares at Nani's back and, a moment later, whips the roll at her head. "You can *fucking* have her."

TWENTY-FOUR

How long did it take a freaking kettle to boil? I tapped my socks against the linoleum floor as I waited for the water to heat up, crushing cloves, cardamom, and fennel into Nani's favorite teapot. I couldn't find the cinnamon sticks.

"Sugar?" I asked the wall.

No one answered. In fact, no one had said another word since I walked in, and it made me wonder what I'd interrupted. I snuck a look behind me. Kris was pouring himself a glass of whiskey, Mom was looking at something on her phone, and Nani—well, something was wrong. Nani always froze up whenever Mom turned up unannounced, but this time it was different. Worse. Nani's chest was moving up and down too rapidly. And she was sitting down; how could she be out of breath?

When the kettle finally boiled, I poured the water over the tea bags and spices, and then set the teapot on the table next to a carton of milk, Nani's polka-dot sugar bowl, and a few teaspoons.

"Are you not forgetting milk jug?" Mom asked, mocking Nani's accent. "One must never pour guests chai from milk carton, *nah*?"

Nani didn't even flinch. Rolling my eyes, I went into the dining room to fetch the milk jug, and set it down on the table. Mom just laughed, and turned back to her phone.

I sat down fuming. What the hell was she doing here? Had she dumped her latest boyfriend and needed a place to crash? Run out of money again? Around nineteen, I'd stopped wondering when she'd call or visit, and stopped caring when she did.

It was the days after she left that were the hardest. Days when I'd come home and find Nani sitting alone somewhere, her eyes puffy and red, just staring at her hands. Days when I could do absolutely nothing to help.

"No one's talking?" Manavi asked, reaching for the teapot. "What, am I boring y'all?"

Y'all? Was she trying to be funny, or had she really been living in America *that* long?

Nani stood up abruptly from the table, and when Mom looked at her accusingly, Nani just shrugged her shoulders. "I am cold. I am getting something warmer to wear. Do I need your permission?"

The moment Nani stepped out of the kitchen, Mom let out a huge yawn. "Well, this is boring. You, me, and Kris—we should go out after she goes to bed."

I glanced at my watch. It was nearly 8 P.M. I hadn't eaten, and I could feel the beginnings of a headache.

"Why don't we go to a gay bar . . ."

"Hilarious."

"Google tells me there are *six* in a three-kilometer radius. Since when did this neighborhood become cool?"

"Since Drake," Kris said. "I heard somebody in his entourage lives nearby."

"Drake. *Really?*"

"Guys, I'm not going out."

"Don't be such a party pooper, Raindrop."

"Can you *not* call me that?"

Mom's eyes widened as she reached for the teapot. She poured out the cups and then pushed one toward me.

"Thanks."

"Look, Raina . . . I'm sorry I didn't know." I heard her sigh, and I looked back toward her. "You know I'm not in touch with anyone here. If I knew you were going through something like that, I would have called more. I would have come home sooner."

I snorted.

"I'm serious." She nodded earnestly. "Kris called me the other day. He's been having a tough time since Serena broke up with him"—she shrugged—"anyways, he told me you're gay. And I thought . . . I thought that maybe I should come home."

Her voice trailed off, and I didn't respond. She'd come home to make sure I was okay? This time, had she shown up out of the blue for *me*? And not because she needed something? I glanced at Kris. He was staring at his phone, but eventually I caught his eye.

How was it that I had no idea Kris was having a difficult year, or that he had emotions at all? Sometimes I forgot she was his sister, and that they'd grown up side by side. The same parents and upbringing, and the same lethal mix of genes: Nana's nose and Nani's mouth. Big, wide eyes that, when shone right at you, almost hurt.

"I want you to know I'm proud of you," I heard Mom say. "This is really cool."

My cheeks burned. "It's not *cool*."

"Of course it is."

"No, it isn't, I'm . . ." I shut my mouth as Nani walked back into the kitchen, wrapped in the woolly shawl I'd bought her for her sixtieth birthday.

"Hi, Nani."

"Hi, my sweet."

"Should I cook us some dinner?"

"Finally, yes," Mom said, slapping her hands on her thighs. "I'm starving. Anyone else starving?"

"You must be," Nani said, sliding into her chair. "In your condition."

I turned to face Mom, and her pale brown skin looked to have reddened. "What condition?"

The air in the room seemed to have lost its oxygen. Everyone was just staring at me.

"What's going on?"

"Thanks, Ma. I was going to tell her on my own time."

"Wait, what?" I searched Nani's face, then Kris's, but they weren't giving anything away. Mom had leaned forward on the table onto her elbows, and she was rocking side to side. Then, as she stood up, it hit me. Her fuller cheeks, arms, and thighs. The dark circles beneath the eyes. The slight curve of her belly.

"You're . . ."

"Having a baby, yes."

I was frozen to the seat, and only my hands were moving. Shaking.

"You're going to have a baby sister, Raina."

She smiled. Was it a smile?

"Are you going to say anything?"

"I . . ." What was there even to say? "You're forty-*six*."

"So—"

"Are you out of your fucking mind?"

"Hey, now. I have a good doctor—"

"Was it an accident? You just forgot to use a condom, *again*?"

She didn't reply. She leaned toward the counter and grabbed a bag of popcorn, ripping it open.

"You planned it."

"IVF." She nodded, shoveling the popcorn into her mouth. "First try, too. You see, Roger doesn't have kids. We're planning to stay put in Philadelphia. Roger's got a sister there, and his dad's in a nursing home. It'll be good." She paused, sitting down again. "And you know it's only a quick flight from here, an hour and a half. You could do it in a weekend—"

"Why the hell would I visit you?" I was livid, seething, and I didn't recognize my own voice. "I haven't even *met* Roger. And how many times have you come home to see me? How many—"

"Raina, seriously. *Calm* down—"

"I'm *your* daughter!"

"What am I supposed to say, huh? That this is how I thought *my* life would turn out? That I got what I wanted out of life? No. Not even close. But, like I said, Roger never had any kids, and . . ."

And *what*, Mom?

You didn't really come home to make sure I was okay, but to tell your old family you'd started another one?

You actually weren't that different from us "good Indian girls," and you wanted a marriage and children all along?

You just didn't want me?

"Get out."

"Excuse me?"

"This is not your house." I grabbed the milk jug and slid it hard toward her. "Drink from the jug, Manavi. You're only a fucking guest here."

"Can you calm down—"

"A guest no one wants!"

"*She* didn't want me."

"Quit blaming Nani. All the time—"

"Hah," Nani said, standing up. "Manu, you have no responsibility, no shame, no—"

"And *you* were so perfect, Ma?" Mom folded her arms across her chest, and she stood up to meet her. "It's not like this house was a fucking prison!"

Suddenly, it was like I was six years old, powerless, as Mom and Nani stood over me screaming at each other. Kris looked at me blankly, and all I could do was stare back. I half expected him to grab my hand and lead me to the other room, distract me by letting me play with his Lego sets or Game Boy. And between the shouts, couldn't I make out the sounds of Nana shuffling back and forth in his bedroom upstairs? Ignoring everyone? Waiting for it to end.

But would it ever end?

Tears running down my face, I stood up and held my arms out.

How many times had we been here? How many times had I done nothing—just waited, watched, avoided.

But I wasn't a child anymore. I wasn't just helpless Raina.

"Both of you need to stop." I wiped my face, steadied my voice. "It's enough."

Surprisingly, they stopped. Or maybe they were tired of it, too.

I leaned my weight forward onto the table, and stared hard at the surface. "Mom, you're selfish and careless, and even though I know you love us, it wouldn't hurt for you to fucking show it sometimes."

She didn't respond, and I couldn't look up. I couldn't face them.

"Nani, you wanted Mom and me to be perfect daughters . . . find the *perfect* husband." I laughed through my tears. "You think we don't remember how it used to be? How you took care of us, and Saffron, and Nana—and he didn't even lift a finger for you? After watching that, why the hell would we *want* a husband?"

"Do not speak ill of your nana—"

"Did you even love him?" I reached down into my handbag, and pulled out the list. It was crumpled into a ball, and I flattened it before I set it firmly on the table. "Did you even care if I was happy?"

"Raina, my sweet." Was she crying, too? "All I wanted was your happine—"

"No, Nani. You cared about what people at temple thought about *her*, about *me*. And what good is there *possibly* to say about an unmarried Indian girl?"

"My sweet—"

"Why am I not good enough on my own? First I needed a husband, then Zoey, or *someone* else to complete me as a woman?"

I was gasping for air. Was this it? The moment of truth.

"What's the *point* of having a brain, or dreams, or even a heart, if this is all we'll ever be good for, huh?"

She was sobbing into the table now, but I couldn't look at her. I couldn't look at any of them.

"I'm not gay, Nani." I sat back down in the chair. "I was just *sick* of buying into this bullshit."

May 20, 1990

"Make a wish, my sweet."

Raina sits on her nani's lap, her chubby legs dangling. One of her socks falls off, and Nani reaches down to retrieve it.

"I can do it, Ma." Manavi lunges for the sock, and her head bangs against Nani's with a loud thud.

"*Oy!*" Nani turns to Manavi as she sits back up, plucks the sock from her hand. "Clumsy girl." Nani massages her head with the back of her palm, shifts Raina on her lap.

Raina giggles as her nana brings out a pan of brownies. He slowly cuts them into squares, and the chocolate drizzle drips onto the kitchen table as he sets a thick slice on a small white plate.

"Mine!" Kris licks his lips as he eyes the brownie. He reaches out and digs his finger into the icing, and Nani swats it away.

"First the birthday girl," Nana says, gently scolding. He cuts more slices and passes them around. A cassette of Ravi Shankar plays in the background as they sit and chew the warm cake, as Raina squirms in delight, her pudgy cheeks dropping like jowls. She is still teething and smacks her lips together often, dark brown crumbs falling out of her mouth, and after each bite, her nani licks a napkin, dabs the stains from her chin.

"Just leave it until she's done," says Manavi. "Babies get dirty." But it's as if no one has heard her, because nobody answers.

Raina no longer likes eating baby food. She likes unspiced *aloo gobi*, rice and dal mashed together, spoon-fed by Nani's fingers. She drinks apple juice and mango juice, bottles of fresh whole milk. She knows only the scent of a heated home and a warm bath, the beige and wood paneled walls insulating her existence. She knows only love and security. Abundance and affection.

Raina's skin is lighter than the rest of her family's; and this seems to be something that excites her nani. Her hair sticks out in two short pigtails above her ears, and saliva bubbles out of her lips as she tries to blow out a candle.

Nana focuses the lens of the Pentax. "Say cheese!"

Everyone else is smiling, and so Raina smiles, too.

"Good girl!" Nana sticks out his tongue, and Raina giggles. She claps her hands together as if the performance is just for her.

"Can I hold her now, Ma?"

"Manu, clear the dishes."

"Ma, I want to—"

"Dishes." Nani shifts Raina to her other knee. "*Now*."

Manavi gets up from the table, a load of dishes piled on her forearm. She turns back to Nani, and whispers, "May I at least put her to sleep tonight?"

"Did you finish schoolwork?"

Manavi breathes hard, sharp, and then she turns back to the sink.

Raina has chocolate frosting all over her face, in her hair, and on her clothes. Nana and Nani carry her upstairs to the bathroom, where they fill a warm bath with strawberry bubbles. Later, they carry her to bed, envelop her in a baby blue sleep suit, and tuck her into her crib.

"How fair she is, *nah*?"

"A beautiful girl," the deeper voice says. "She will have no trouble finding husband."

"It is Manu that will cause trouble. What boy from good family will take her knowing she has mother like this?"

Raina is drifting, her eyelashes batting.

"There are options, Su. We will explain . . ."

Raina's in a dreamlike state, full of chocolate and love and laughter. Nearly asleep, she hears the door shut, then open again. Light cuts into the room. She opens her eyes and, startled, sits up in the crib. Manavi is in the room, and Raina squints as she watches her tiptoe across the carpet, sit down on the floor beside her. Manavi reaches her hand through the rails and strokes her hair, brushes her fingers along her face.

"Say MA-MA."

Raina whimpers.

"MA-MA?" And when Raina says nothing, no noises come to her lips, Manavi stands up, lifts Raina out of the crib. She squeezes her tight, presses their cheeks together. Raina struggles to pull free. She squirms, tries to unfasten her body from Manavi's grip, and when she is unable to, Raina starts to cry.

"Oh, baby. Please don't cry," begs Manavi. She rocks Raina back and forth, pats her on the back lightly the way Nani does. But Raina keeps crying, marble-size tears rolling down her cheeks, and she presses her tiny fists against Manavi. Pounds them—trying to push her away.

"My Raindrop, please—"

"Manu!" The light flicks on, and Nani sweeps into the room. She pulls Raina into her arms and cradles her. "Manu, look what *you* did."

Raina is quickly soothed. She is basked in a warm light and the soft touch of her nani. Comforted, firm in her nani's grasp, she stops crying; and the sharp voices around her fading, she drifts safely toward sleep.

TWENTY-FIVE

"The Tonight Show?"

I shook my head. Kris set down his whiskey glass, and then reached for the remote control.

"What about *The Daily Show?*"

"Nah."

"You don't like Trevor Noah?"

"No, I do." I shrugged, pulling the blanket tighter around me. "I'm just not in the mood . . ."

I heard him sigh, and then the television flashed to another channel. Then another. When it stopped on a Katherine Heigl movie, Mom let out a soft grunt of approval. Kris sighed again, and set down the remote.

I couldn't remember the name of the movie, but I'm sure I'd seen it a half dozen times before. Mom, propped up against a pillow on the floor in front of me, moved her head to the side, obscuring my view.

She was pregnant. Again.

She was starting a *family*.

This time she'd get it right; she'd order baby furniture from IKEA and paint the room sunshine yellow, eat her vitamins and rub oil on her belly so she didn't get stretch marks. She'd do things the right way—with *Roger*—with her new perfect daughter.

My whole life, it had taken so much energy to feel *anything* for her—love or hate, apathy or just plain amusement. Now, the feelings came all at once. Jealousy. Rage. Resentment.

Confusion.

After what just happened, here we were watching a movie about bridesmaid dresses, like nothing had happened at all.

Halfway through the movie, a car horn honked outside. Mom pulled herself off the ground. "I guess that's me."

"You don't have to leave," Kris said. He gave me a look, like he wanted me to say it, too.

"I think I do." She let out a short laugh. "Sounds like there's enough going on here without me."

Kris grabbed her duffel bag and headed outside, but Mom just hovered over me. Eventually, I stood up. She was shorter than I remembered; closer in height to Nani than to me.

"I'll come back soon?"

She phrased it like a question, as if she needed my permission. Like I had a say in her decision about the kind of mother she wanted to be. Or could be.

"And you'll think about visiting?"

My stomach clenched, but I nodded. What was there to think about? As hard as it had been, of course I wanted a real relationship with her. I'd always wanted that. She hugged me good-bye, and as she brushed a stray hair off my cheek, I still didn't know if she really wanted that, too.

I sipped whiskey with Kris well into the night, and we fell asleep watching late-night television. In the morning, Kris still sound asleep on the sofa opposite me, I stole into the kitchen and made two cups of tea, then quietly trekked up the stairs.

Both Kris and Mom had suggested I give her space, and so I'd let Nani retreat upstairs—crying, and alone. It was hard, but I'd known all along it would be. I took a deep breath before pushing open the door, but she wasn't in her bedroom. I checked my room, the bathroom, and even Kris's old bedroom, but they were all empty. I took a deep breath, crossed the hall toward the last un-opened door. Slowly, I turned the handle and pushed my way through.

Nani was sitting cross-legged in the middle of the bed. Her pastel pink pantsuit stood out against the beigeness of the room. Our family photo album was open on her lap, and her palms were resting on the open page. She looked up at me, blinking, and then snapped the album shut.

What had Nani and Nana expected out of their lives when they left everything behind, and moved across the world? Did they really love each other? Or had their culture, their obligations, and children bound them together?

What had happened in this house before I was born? Or when I was young—too young to remember?

Mom once told me that she wasn't allowed to decorate her room. Nani had torn down all her posters of movie stars and boy bands, and refused to cook breakfast until Mom had folded the stiff white sheets perfectly in all four corners, aligned every pillow.

But I remembered how Mom's wardrobe poured out of her bedroom door like a waterfall, down the stairs, her handmade jewelry and shoes flooding the closets, scarves washing up on the end tables. She was different from everyone I'd ever known. She was beautiful and interesting and oddly insightful. But Nani had never seen that side of her; she hadn't wanted to see it.

Was that why Mom left? I couldn't really remember, and every time I tried, all I could picture was the room spinning around me. I was sitting waist deep in a pile of her clothes as she slowly plucked them one by one from around me, and stuffed them into garbage bags. Nani was holding her tea, looking in from the doorway, where I was standing now.

Was she crying?

I closed my eyes, clutched the scalding mugs in my hands. Still, I couldn't remember. It was sunny that day, and the window was open. It smelled like lawn and pollen. It must have been summer, but I wasn't sure. All I knew was it was the only day they hadn't fought. The only day I hadn't fallen asleep with my pillow over my head, praying it would all stop.

Nani cleared her throat, and I opened my eyes.

How had we gotten here? How had I gotten us here?

I took a deep breath. I sat down beside her on the bed, set the mugs on the nightstand.

"Manu has gone?"

I nodded.

Nani let out a deep breath. A sigh of relief? Of exhaustion? Disappointment?

How easy it would be to blame the mess I'd made on Mom, on Nani's high expectations of us. But I didn't want what was easy. Finally, I wanted to do what was right.

"I'm sorry I yelled at you. And I'm sorry I lied to you."

Nani's lips pressed together, and then she shook her head.

"I have no excuses, Nani. I made a terrible mistake." Why wouldn't she look at me? "I'm sorr—"

"You are sorry." Her voice trembled. "*Sorry?* Was I not worthy of truth? Am I not strong, have I not shown you love?"

"Nani—"

"Encouraged you? Protected you?"

"Always."

"Then? What is the truth? I want all of the truth. Right now."

All of the truth. I trembled, looked down at my feet.

"I was tired of you telling me I should get married. Of hearing that I needed someone to be happy. But the *truth* is . . . that's what I thought I needed, too."

Out of the corner of my eye, I could see her blinking at me, her face unchanged. She was waiting for me to continue.

"I was scared. And alone, and then Dev moved to Toronto—"

"*Dev?*"

I nodded. "He moved here, and I wanted to"—I hesitated—"I *thought* I wanted to—"

"Reconcile," said Nani.

"But we didn't. And we're not going to." I sighed. "I was so ashamed that I still wanted him, Nani. Ashamed of myself. I just—just didn't know how to tell you the truth about him. That's why I let you believe I was gay." Tears again welled in my eyes, and I wiped my face. "I just wanted you to be proud of me, respect my decisions. I didn't"—I swallowed—"want to be another disappointment."

Nani's lips were squeezed together. She didn't say anything, and I inched closer toward her. I could smell the talcum she used, and overwhelmingly, I wanted her back. I wanted my nani—her sweet strength, her imperfections—back in my life.

Tentatively, I reached out and placed my hand on her shoulder. I could feel the weight of her collapse slightly onto me. "I am very sorry."

Her eyes were glued to the floor; she wouldn't look at me. She was barely moving.

"Nani, please say something."

"After Manu . . ." she said finally, "I vowed that this time—with *you*—I would be better. I would, this time, not be like my own mother. But perhaps, this is all of our destinies. I was just as hard on you as with Manu. I must have been too hard on you if you could not tell me this truth."

"You were wonderful, Nani—"

"*Nah*"—tears formed in her eyes—"I failed many, *many* times."

"You did your best. That's all we can do."

"You thought I would blame you for still being in love, Raina. You thought I would *judge*, disapprove." She smiled at me, a fading, distant smile. "Love is never easy, Raina. This I know very well. With your nana"—she sighed—"it was love, but it was not easy."

"I wanted to tell you. I was just so . . . embarrassed."

"There is no shame in love. We make choices, and then, we try and move on the best we can. We try and live with those choices."

I thought about my choices; how many wrong ones I'd made in the last year. I thought about Dev and Asher.

I thought about Depesh.

"Raina, my sweet. Don't cry."

"I wanted to tell you, Nani. But Depesh confided in me that he is gay and . . ."

"Ah." Nani nodded, cutting me off. "I am seeing now what happened. You wanted to help him, *nah*?"

"But I'm not sure it worked."

"What is it you just said to me?" she asked, her eyes twinkling. "You did your best? That is all we can do."

Kris and I both called in sick to work that day. We stayed with Nani, helped her cook and clean the house, and in the afternoon, sat next to her while she watched her silly Hindi soaps. None of us spoke much, and even though Nani accepted my apology, I knew I had yet to earn real forgiveness. I felt lighter, slightly, but my chest was weighed down knowing Depesh still didn't know the truth.

That evening I called Zoey and Shay and told them everything. Zoey was swamped with work and couldn't stay on the phone long, although she was relieved that I was going to come clean as soon as Depesh finished his exams. But Shay sounded strange, and when I called her out on it, she played dumb.

"I'm okay, honestly!" I could feel her smiling at me through the phone, but it was one of her fake smiles. "I'm just . . . stressed."

"Talk to me, Shay. What is it?"

"Nothing, really. I'm just so happy your drama is coming to an end." She laughed. "Now it's time for *wedding* drama . . ."

"Is there anything I can do?"

"Loads. I'm about to add you and Serena to the spreadsheet. Do you know how to use filters?"

I rolled my eyes. "Yes."

"Good, because I don't. And by the way, you're still coming to Julien's birthday party tomorrow night, right? Can you come to the bar early and help me save a few tables?"

"No problem." I paused. "Is—"

"Yes, Asher's girlfriend will be there."

I swallowed hard, nodding at the phone.

"And I don't mean to be harsh," she said softly, "but you're just going to have to deal with it, Raina."

TWENTY-SIX

I stayed the night again. The next morning, I didn't want to leave Nani alone, but she insisted that she was fine and that I go back downtown. That she usually spent the whole of Saturdays at Saffron anyway.

Was she fine? I wanted it to be more than "fine" between us, but that would take time.

Back at my apartment, I spent the afternoon on my balcony—sunglasses, a wool sweater for the wind. I didn't even look at my work e-mails. I tried reading a book that had been sitting untouched on my bedside table for months, but every few pages I found myself distracted, staring at the blank margins as a nervous feeling rose in my stomach.

Eventually, I gave up on the book. I showered and found a charcoal-colored dress that I'd bought in New York and still hadn't worn. I curled my hair, and put on makeup. Staring at myself in the mirror, I took a wet cloth and wiped most of it off.

I was restless, and I fell back onto my bed to keep myself from pacing. I could feel my heart beating in my stomach, and I took a deep breath trying to calm myself down. Why was I so nervous? I was the one that screwed it up, and Asher had moved on. Shay was right. I just had to *deal* with it.

My phone buzzed, and I lunged for it. I thought it might be Depesh, but it was an e-mail from Dev. I pressed delete without reading it, pushing past the curiosity, past that fractional part of me still desperate to know what he was thinking and where he was. Instead, I texted Depesh.

> *Everything OK at home? How did your last exam go? Celebrate hard—you deserve it.* ☺

I took a deep breath, and then sent him another text.

> *I'm aware you may be hungover tomorrow, but can we meet for lunch? Need to talk x*

Shay was doubly right. I had to deal with this, too.

Alice was out of town, and so I took Zoey as my date to Julien's party. The lounge was typically urban: chic decor and angular couches, a DJ in the far corner playing classics from the eighties and nineties. We perched by the back tables to hold the area while Shay and Julien fluttered from guest to guest as each person arrived. Just as Zoey went to the bar with Serena to buy another round, I spotted Asher at the entrance.

His jeans and faded leather jacket had been replaced by khaki trousers and a white button-down shirt, like he'd been dressed by the brunette beside him: petite and rail thin, wearing a white silky dress that stopped right below the crotch. They stood in the entranceway talking to each other, her hand on the base of his spine, and as she leaned up and whispered something in his ear, he caught my eye. He smiled at me, and I waved in return. He started to walk toward me, and the girl grabbed his hand and trotted along next to him.

I tried not to look at her too much as he introduced us; how she constantly flicked her bangs around, the way her glittery eye shadow made her look stupidly young.

As her eyes skirted around the room, I wondered how old she was.

"Rebekah is also a teacher," said Asher, as if he knew I had my doubts. "A middle school teacher."

"I teach music," she said, rifling through her purse. She pulled out a fat tube of lip gloss and began to smear it onto her pout. "Orchestra band, jazz band"—she smacked her lips—"and what else, sweetie?"

I winced.

"Choir, *right*. I run the choir."

I nodded. "That's great."

"She's also a musician," said Asher.

"And do you play basketball, too?"

She shook her head. "Too short. Always been more into singing."

I smiled, trying to look earnest. "Good for you. I sing terribly."

"So do my students." She laughed, and then tugged twice on her ponytail. "So"—she turned to Asher—"why don't we go buy me a drink?"

"Sure." Asher glanced at me. "Raina, would you like something?"

"Mine's coming, thanks," I said to them both, although Rebekah had already started to walk away, tugging at Asher's sleeve behind her.

They disappeared into the thick queue of bodies around the edge of the bar, and I watched Asher's head, a foot taller than most, bob above the crowd. It was dark, and for the next few minutes, I tried to make out whether he was smiling, and to whom he was talking.

"Who's that?"

I hadn't noticed Zoey reappear, and she pressed a drink into my hand. I took a long sip through the straw, just as Asher disappeared out of sight. "*That* is Asher."

The night passed painfully slowly, and I only had the chance to speak with Shay again briefly as she darted between Julien's cousins, friends, and coworkers, all of whom were pawing at them like they were a scratching post. Zoey and I chatted with the groups we met—friends of Julien's from the hospital, rec leagues—and then a whole crew from Quebec who'd rented a bus and drove in that day and, now drunk, indulged me as I tried out my remedial French. But I kept seeing Asher and Rebekah everywhere; standing in line again at the bar as she played on her phone; and then later at the edge of the dance floor, Rebekah bobbing her head up and down as Asher and Victor talked, it seemed, about the Raptors playoff game.

What did he see in her? Maybe Rebekah was the kind of girl Asher briefly thought I was. One who was passionate and talented and followed her dreams; one who could stand in a crowded room and not care what anyone else thought; because she knew exactly who she was, and didn't give a damn who cared or judged her for it.

I left Zoey at a table with two chatty residents Julien worked with, and got in line for the restroom. Half a dozen girls were lined up on the far wall—texting, applying lipstick, whispering—while the other wall, leading toward the men's room, was empty.

I took my place at the back, and a second later, I saw Asher appear in the far doorway. He smiled, and gave me a big, goofy wave as he walked toward me.

"So she's a teacher," I said, the words coming up uncontrollably.

"Yeah." He nodded. He seemed almost embarrassed. "She's a teacher."

"She seems nice."

"Rebekah can come across a bit—I don't know." He shrugged. "But she's really good with the kids. Even if she isn't exactly *passionate* about the job."

"I see."

"I think so many people end up teaching because they don't know what else to do."

I shrugged. "It happens, doesn't it? I'm not passionate about my job; not sure I ever was."

"What are you passionate about then, Raina?"

The way he said it made me stop short, and I wished I had an answer. I wished I knew what I was passionate about.

"I don't think I've ever felt about anything the way you feel about teaching."

"What did you want to be when you were little? Astronaut? Fashion designer?" He grinned. "National basketball player?"

I slapped him lightly on the shoulder. "Hey. I *could* have been in the pros."

"Yeah?"

I was about to joke back, but then I shook my head. "No, I couldn't have. It would have been too risky."

"Risky how?"

"My grandparents were really poor. They were immigrants. They worked hard, and after my mom never amounted to anything in their eyes, there was so much pressure on my uncle Kris, and then on me, to really . . . become something. To get jobs that were—I don't know—impressive. Stable. That earned a lot of money."

"So you always wanted to be an investment analyst," he said softly.

"I never knew what I wanted to be." I shrugged. "I suppose I never had a chance to figure it out."

"It's not too late," he said after a moment. Then he winked. "You're not that old."

"I'll be thirty next week."

His mouth dropped, and I fake shoved him again. I loved the creases around his mouth when he smiled.

"What does your gut tell you?"

I drew back. "About what?"

"About your passions. About what—and who—you want to be." He ran a hand through his hair. "Although, look at me. It took me years to figure out that my first instinct was right. I really did want to teach."

"My gut instinct on what to do has never been that helpful," I said, suddenly thinking about Dev and Depesh. "It's been misleading, actually."

"That's not your gut you were listening to. That was your fear. You see, you have to listen harder, go further down." He palmed his stomach. "And then you'll hear it."

Was he right? Was it just fear that had led me? An ex-boyfriend I was too afraid to let go of? A grandmother I was too afraid to disappoint?

A man I was afraid to let myself love.

My body was trembling, and my arms—crossed and shivering—recoiled away from him. "I need to tell you something."

"Yeah?"

I made myself look at him. What was stopping me? I took a deep breath. "Asher, I'm not—"

"*There* you are."

I dropped my arms and turned toward the voice. Rebekah wobbled toward us, a scowl on her face. She walked up to Asher, and put an arm around his waist.

"Hi, Becka."

"What are you guys talking about?" she asked him, not looking at me.

"The wedding," Asher said quickly. "Raina's also in the wedding party."

"Is she?"

"We have to be there early for the ceremony"—he turned to me, talking quickly—"don't we? What time again?"

"The ceremony starts at ten—so five A.M., maybe six?"

"That's *early*," said Rebekah.

"It's customary for us to get married in the morning."

"Well, can I come, too?" she said to Asher.

"It's only for family and close friends. I'll be with Julien and his dad and brother"—Asher glanced at me—"and all the women will be helping Shaylee get ready."

"I like Indian clothes," she said.

I pressed my lips together.

"I'll talk to Julien," he said after a moment.

She folded her arm through his. "Thank you, *baby*."

I winced, and then as quickly as I could, I excused myself and went back into the party.

Asher . . . What just happened!?

WAY TOO GOOD FOR ME

Off the market.

TWENTY-SEVEN

Shay and Zoey found me hiding in the cloakroom. They made an effort to console me and boost my spirits, but when that didn't work, Shay insisted I go home so I didn't have to watch Asher and Rebekah together. Jokingly, Shay said she didn't want a miserable *middle-aged* woman ruining her party anyway. Zoey offered to drive me, but I refused. I could tell she was having a good time. They hugged me good-bye, and a few minutes later, I found myself walking home alone along College Street.

With Dev, I'd been jealous of anyone who got to spend time with him—his colleagues, his housekeeper, even his own mother—but this felt different, and just thinking about Rebekah made my lungs burn.

Asher was so different from anyone I knew, so unlike Dev. If he didn't have a girlfriend, if he knew the truth, could I even have had a future with him? And what about Dev? He still called, and every time, a fraction of me was tempted to answer. Didn't that mean a part of me still believed in *him*? As unrealistic as that fantasy was, didn't part of me hope he'd show up with a bouquet of flowers, get down on one knee, and tell me he'd changed?

I tripped over a crack in the sidewalk, and caught myself before I fell. My head was spinning, and I leaned against a lamppost and let my chin fall to my chest. My eyes closed, I could hear the cars whiz past, the sounds of pedestrians—high heels and leather soles clacking, the slow thud of music from a nearby bar.

I felt a low vibration coming out of the pole, through my leg and body, and it took me a moment to realize it was my phone. I found it in my coat pocket, and picked up when I saw it was Depo.

I held the receiver to my ear. "Hello?"

"Raina!" I heard him laugh, and a chorus of voices laughed in the background.

"Hey, what's up? How—"

"It was good!" He laughed again, and then shouted into the phone, "All my exams went *really* well."

"You smarty-pants. Amazing!" I stopped walking and smiled into the phone. "You're out celebrating?"

"Packing, actually. We're going to London, baby! Caleb's brother used to live in Brixton, is that good? Should we go there?"

"Wait, you're going to London? When?"

"Tonight!"

My stomach dropped.

"We booked a last-minute flight just this afternoon. Heading straight to London, then Berlin maybe? Who the hell knows. But I'm doing it. Exams are done, and I'm going to Europe. Like, me and Caleb, and a few other guys. We're going!"

"But—"

"My summer job starts in a few weeks, but maybe I won't do it. Maybe I'll just stay in London and take a year off—"

"A *year*?"

"—before doing the whole medicine thing. Caleb is thinking about taking a gap year."

I could feel the panic rising. "Please, slow down."

"I've always done the right thing. I've always been the good boy—but maybe I don't want to be that boy anymore. Maybe I want to be like Caleb. He's free. He does whatever the hell he wants. He's his own person, you know?"

"Following Caleb is not being your own person . . ."

He didn't hear me. He was talking rapidly, excitedly—and he wouldn't let me speak. He was following a boy he barely knew across the world? He was leaving with him for a year?

"Raina, like, thank you *so* much—for, you know, everything." He came up for air. "I couldn't have done it without you."

"Wait a sec. I need to tell you—"

"Can we talk later? The flight leaves in a few hours—"

"Please, just think about this—"

"—but text me, okay?"

Before I could say another word, he clicked off.

Mid-step, I was frozen in my tracks. The sidewalk was giving way beneath me. The street was spinning. I couldn't do this. There was no more delaying, no more waiting for the right time. No more being a coward. Depo was leaving, and he deserved to know the truth.

It took me less than a minute to find a taxi, and within forty-five minutes I was at the airport. I waited near security in the international terminal. After an hour of checking and rechecking the flight board, wondering whether I'd missed him, finally, he appeared.

I watched him from afar as he checked in for his flight at the kiosk, laughing with three other boys his age, small backpacks swung over their shoulders. And by the way he was looking at one of the boys—rosy cheeks, black glasses, platinum blond hair—I could tell which one was Caleb.

Depo looked so happy, with a lightness to him that I hadn't seen since he was kid. When he saw me, he gave me a big smile and waved. He walked toward me, dropped his bag by my feet, and enveloped me in a hug.

Tensely, I hugged him back. My heart pounded, and I could feel sweat forming on my face.

"You didn't have to come see me off." He pulled away grinning, and then looked toward security. "Sorry, I told them to go through. I should have introduced you to Caleb—should I go get him?"

I shook my head. "Another time. I need to—"

"That sounds good. Like, when we get back—or if we stay awhile, maybe you can come visit? Do you ever go to Europe for work?"

I shook my head.

"You're all dressed up." He smiled. "You look really pretty."

"Thanks," I whispered. "I was at a birthday party. Shay's fiancé."

"Ma's pissed I may not be home for her wedding." He laughed. "Despite everything, she still wants to show me off—tell everyone how good at school I am."

"Of course she does, Depo. Your parents are proud of you."

He shrugged, and looked at his feet. "They're barely speaking to me. Tonight, they didn't even hug me good-bye."

"Depo, your courage . . ." I put my hand on his arm. "I'm so proud of you. I really am, and"—I hesitated—"I also . . ."

"What is it?"

"There's something you need to know. Before you leave."

"Yeah?"

I looked him in the eye. I could feel myself shaking. "Depo, I'm straight."

He didn't respond. His face didn't move.

"I needed you to know before you left." I shook my head. "I'm not gay. I didn't mean to trick you. If it was something I could take back, I would. I promise you. If I could go back to last fall, I would handle things differently."

He still didn't move.

"I'd do a lot of things differently. I'd try and be a better person, a *stronger* person—I don't know. But one thing I don't regret is our friendship. I'm so happy we got to know each other this year, and I—I don't regret that. I really don't. I wanted to be there for you. I still do. And this stuff with Caleb—it's happening so quickly, and I get it. I get how you're feeling right now, and if you want to talk about—"

"*Talk?*"

I watched his face, his muscles perfectly tense, unflinching. But then he blinked.

"You. Bitch."

TWENTY-EIGHT

The next morning, I opened the e-mail Zoey had warned me was coming: Bill was concerned about my performance, and about my commitment to the team. An e-mail like this would have terrified me the year before. Hadn't I cared my whole life what people thought about me, and measured my happiness on how well I was doing in school or at work? Suddenly, my job didn't seem to matter so much anymore.

Instead of a suit, I changed into jeans and my high school basket-ball hoodie, and walked south along Yonge Street through the low light. The streets were empty, except for a few stragglers stumbling home from their Saturday night out. How many mornings had I walked this path, oblivious to why or where I was going? Stopping at the same coffee shop, with its smiley baristas and too-strong coffee that I didn't even like. Turning right at King Street, never waiting for the pedestrian walk light, rushing in as fast as I could go.

Bill was already at the office when I arrived. It was Sunday morning, and as I watched him bent over his desk scratching at his salt-and-pepper scruff, I thought about how his kids were probably having breakfast that morning with their stepfather. How even though I'd worked for Bill most of my adult life, he'd never even told me their names.

"Raina? Didn't know you were coming in . . ."

He stopped short when he saw my face, and then his hands went limp on the keyboard. We sat side by side on the couch in his office—and as I stared out the window, watching the first pink touches of light hitting the lake, he asked me if there was anything he could do to change my mind.

I could have made it more dramatic, but there was no point. I handed him my letter of resignation, and simply said my priorities in life had changed.

But they hadn't changed. Not really. Family. Friendship. Love. These were the things that had always mattered. These were the things I'd let slip, and I'd failed at each of them for the sake of a life I'm not sure I ever wanted. And eight years after first accepting a passionless job that was only ever meant to fill in the gaps, I was finally ready to leave. I was tired of letting down my family and friends, making up excuses for my own happiness. It turned out I wasn't the woman they thought I was. But that didn't mean I couldn't change.

That night, I cooked Alice and Zoey dinner—a recipe for a vegetarian jambalaya I'd once found in a magazine and had never had the time to try. After, I helped Shay with her wedding checklist, reorganized the spreadsheet filters in a way that made sense. Then, I wrote Depesh a long e-mail—one that didn't ask for forgiveness, or qualify my decisions over the past year in any way. It just spelled out how much I cared for him and how much I regretted misleading him, and I sent it knowing full well I might never get a response.

TWENTY-NINE

"Maybe I should work for you."

"As chef?"

I laughed. "I'm not that good. But I could manage the dinner shift, and then your days wouldn't be so long."

Nani flicked on the ventilation fan above the stove as the cumin, garlic, and chili started to sizzle in the pan. I reached over her for the bowl of tomatoes, tossing them in as she stirred it all around with a wooden spoon.

"Is that a maybe?"

"Raina, no more rash decisions, *nah*?" She glanced at me sideways. "You know, if you need money—of course. But this will be temporary solution until you *really* know what is next."

I nodded. I suppose I agreed. It would be too easy to get stuck working with her at Saffron, taking over for her entirely as she grew older. I could see myself managing the restaurant, or even going to culinary school—but at this point, everything felt so wide open, I could see myself anywhere. Applying my skills in banking in the public sector. Launching a girls' and women's athletics program.

Renting out my condo, and trekking my way through Southeast Asia.

I'd spent the previous two weeks working out my two weeks' notice, in the evenings cooking or watching TV with Nani, or running last-minute wedding errands with Shay. One evening, Zoey had surprised me by organizing farewell drinks for me at a bar near work, and I was surprised that Bill turned up. That I felt emotional saying good-bye to everyone. On the other hand, I felt ready for what was next—even though I had yet to figure out what that meant.

"You are quiet?"

I shook my head, shifting toward the fridge to grab the coriander. "Just thinking."

"About?"

"About . . . starting over." I turned to face her. "A new job. A new life . . . Maybe . . . a new guy . . ."

"Hah?"

Nani looked so alarmed I was tempted to laugh. Hell, I wanted to laugh myself. My community still thought I was gay, and I still hadn't figured out a way to handle that without overshadowing Shay's fast-approaching wedding. I'd broken the trust of my family, friends, and the man that I cared about. But I had to start over somewhere, didn't I?

"I've been thinking I should start dating again."

She sat down, keeping her eyes fastened on me as she rested her chin on her palm. The table was cluttered with magazines and random papers, and poking out from the bottom was a familiar crumpled one.

"*Beta*," I heard Nani say. "There is no need. I am not upset. We are okay, *nah*? We have made the amends."

I sat down next to her. "I know we have, but—"

"I don't need you to have husband." She moved her left hand to my cheek. "You are perfect, my Raina. Just as you are."

I clutched her hand, nodding. Finally believing her.

"It's not for you, Nani. It's for me. I'm ready to . . . try."

She sighed, and reclined back in her chair.

"Do you know anybody? Is there anyone I should meet?"

"Raina, I am out of touch now. I do not know of any boys these days."

Tentatively, I reached below the pile of papers and pulled out the list.

"It is here? You have kept all this time?" Nani laughed, and I watched her face as she read the notes I'd written in the margins.

"Maybe you should be comedian, my silly Raina." She winked. "Who is this Josh, *hot* like my chicken vindaloo?"

I blushed, lunged for the list. "Oh, nobody. We went on a date once . . ."

"And this Asher character—"

"Nope." My face reddened even more. "We need a *new* list. I don't know why I still have this. There's nobody on here . . ."

But something caught my eye. A noticeably blank space halfway down the page. I pushed the paper toward her, tapping on the only name I hadn't crossed out the year before.

"So what do you think?"

Nani looked at me curiously, and then shrugged. "What do *you* think?"

Jayesh—Sharon's cousin, science professor at university . . .

divorced!!!

Date #6

He was surprised when I called him out of the blue—nearly one year after we had first texted. Through awkward small talk, I learned that Jayesh was still a general sciences professor at York University, still divorced—still unattached.

"What made you call after all this time?" he asked.

I paused, thinking back to the last time we'd messaged each other. After months of me being coy and postponing our first date—and right before that disastrous date with Rahul the vegan—Jayesh was the one who'd stopped texting me. Told me that if I wasn't ready or didn't want to meet, then he wasn't going to force my hand.

"I'm ready to meet," I said finally. "That is, if you still want to."

He chose a sports bar near his condo in the Distillery District, and I gave myself ten minutes—and not a second longer—to explain myself. Jayesh's eyes bulged at some parts of the story (lying to Depesh, my profile on IndianSingles.com) and laughed at others (the gay porn links on Nani's browser history). It felt good to come clean, lay it all out there for someone who never knew the old me. So much had happened since Nani first gave me that list. My life had changed. I'd changed. And as we pushed past the small talk, I realized that what I wanted in life had changed, too.

Jayesh was an open book, liked to laugh, and as I sipped on the dregs of my pint, I realized I might actually like him. I felt my stomach growl, and I set down my empty glass.

"Are you hungry?"

We'd only committed to a quick drink, and he smiled at me, as if he was surprised I was making an effort.

"After all this time," I said, "I can at least buy you dinner."

"I suppose you can . . ."

"Do you like tacos?"

"Do you know anyone who *doesn't* like tacos?"

I grinned. "Great. I know this place off King West."

We took the streetcar, and Jayesh told me about the PhD he'd recently defended on energetics—which he explained was the study of energy as it transformed between forms.

"Energy can be stored, which is potential energy. Or it can be kinetic, thermal, elastic, nuclear—but it's always there. It cannot be destroyed or created. It always balances out—kind of like the Force."

I stared at him curiously, before breaking out into a grin.

"Sorry, that was a dumb joke. I meant—"

"*Star Wars*." My hand bumped against his on the handrail, and I let it stay there. "I get it. I love *Star Wars*."

It was warm enough to sit on the restaurant's patio, and we shared a pitcher of margaritas, a big bowl of guac and chips, and then ordered a sharing plate of baja fish and buttermilk chicken tacos.

"You know," Jayesh said, pouring hot sauce onto his plate. "Come to think of it, I've been here before."

"Oh yeah?"

"Yeah." He set the bottle down. "My ex-wife works just around the corner."

I nodded slowly, trying to figure out what to say.

"Too early to bring up the ex?"

"After what I unloaded on you earlier, not at all." I paused. "How long has it been?"

"We've been divorced three years now. In retrospect, we married way too young. Turns out, she cared more about the wedding than me."

"I'm sorry." I wiped my hands on a napkin. "The same thing happened to my uncle Kris, too. But you seem to be handling it a lot better than he is."

"I have good days and bad days still." He smiled. "On the bad days I dwell on the fact that a lot of people in the community have drawn a black mark over me. Labeled me as damaged, somehow."

"And the good days?"

"The good days, I think about the future." He shrugged. "I eat tacos with cute girls . . ."

He was smiling at me now, and I couldn't help but return one.

"And on your good days," I said, reaching for the dessert menu. "Do you eat ice cream?"

"Lots."

"Chocolate?"

"*Duh.*"

Jayesh—*Sharon's cousin, science professor at university . . .*

divorced!!!

Intriguing . . . taco tour round

#2 TBD after Shay's wedding!

THIRTY

Shay's wedding week arrived in a flurry. Serena, the twins, and I were recruited for countless errands: picking up and dropping off relatives, lugging decorations and marigold garlands to and from the venues, helping Shay manage Auntie Sarla's demands. There were dinner parties with relatives, with family friends who had traveled to Toronto, and then the Ganesh puja: a religious ceremony performed to remove obstacles and ensure the successful completion of the wedding.

I sat down near the back of the temple with Serena, and looked around the room. Up at the front, Nani and Auntie Sarla were assisting the priest as he carried out the ceremony. Shay and Julien were seated cross-legged with their eyes closed, and as the priest resumed chanting, I closed mine, too.

I'd never really tried to understand Hinduism. For most, it conjured the image of Ganesh's trunk and bright colors, bronze statues and bathing in the Ganges, and my knowledge—my understanding of it—only went a tad further.

Its belief system was supple. Its rituals and traditions were blended and nuanced over thousands of years, from one region to another. But surely, at its core, there was nothing about it that decreed its believers to be intolerant. The *Kama Sutra* encouraged homosexual relations, and so did the holy book the *Rigveda*. Shay had mentioned that there were even transgender characters in the *Mahabharata*.

But then why did so many traditional Hindus, like Depesh's parents, like Auntie Sarla, vehemently disapprove? When had it all started; why had we been taught to fear, taught to discredit everything but our own perspective?

Whatever the belief system, we were all in charge of our own values. Depesh had been brave to challenge them, to stand up to his own family and community. And now—for a while, at least—he was gone. As much as it hurt, as much as I didn't want to let him go, I knew that he would be all right.

When the puja was over, I went into the dining hall and found that Nani had slipped out ahead of me, and was now bustling around in the kitchen with a dozen other women.

"What can I do?" I asked, tying an apron around my sari.

"Your Auntie Sarla has rented extra plates, but I cannot find!"

"Where should I look?"

She fished out a ring of keys from her bra and pressed it into my hand. "I think her car."

"Do you need a hand?"

The voice startled me, and it took me a while to realize it belonged to Asher.

"Hah, she will," I heard Nani say to him. "It is very heavy."

"No problem," he said. "I'm Asher, by the way. You must be Auntie Suvali?"

"So *you* are Asher . . ." Nani beamed at him. "Yes, I am Auntie Suvali—but *you* can call me Nani."

"Oh, uh—"

"She says that to everybody." I shook my head, and Asher grinned. "She wasn't *implying*—"

"Nice to meet you, Nani," he said, ignoring me completely.

"Nice to meet *you*."

We took the back stairs up to the main level and found Auntie Sarla's flashy red car in the parking lot. I was at a loss for words, and I could tell Asher felt awkward around me, too. Was Rebekah lurking somewhere?

"I didn't see you upstairs," I ventured, as we unloaded boxes from the trunk.

"I was sitting behind you a bit—on the men's side." He paused, shutting the trunk. "Why is there a men's side and women's side at the temple, by the way?"

"It beats me."

"Tradition?"

"I guess."

"Traditions change. It takes a while, but they do . . . Or, they can."

I stared hard at the concrete beneath my feet, focusing on a crack jutting out from my left big toe. "How long are we expected to wait, Asher?"

He was breathing heavily, and I felt his hand brush against my forearm. "There are a few girls from South Asian families in my class this year," I heard him say. "In some ways, they're teaching me more than I'm teaching them."

I followed the crack with my eyes farther and farther, until it disappeared into the bushes.

"I've come to realize that as much as I'd like to, there are some things I'll just never be able to understand."

Did Asher realize that, by just saying those words, he *did* understand? That even though our backgrounds were worlds apart, his empathy, his outlook on life, brought him closer to my heart than any man had been before?

"It was a beautiful ceremony today. Wasn't it, Raina?"

But what right did I have to ask him anything? What right did I have to say all those words on the tip of my tongue, weighing down my chest?

To interfere in a life he had with another woman.

"Where's Rebekah?"

My eyes still on the ground, I saw his hands shift from his side to his pockets.

Was that a sigh?

"She's at school."

By the time we got the last of the dishes into the kitchen, everyone had started to leave the main hall and was queuing up for lunch. I figured Asher would run off to find Julien's other friends, but he didn't. He found another apron beneath the sink, and after rolling up the sleeves of his white collared shirt, he took up the post next to me. It was an assembly line. I put one naan on everybody's plate, Asher spooned the rice, and a battalion of aunties next to him dished out the *subjiis*, dal, chutney, sweets. When Asher started chatting to the aunties next to him, I tried not to eavesdrop. But I couldn't help but notice their laughter, how smitten they all seemed to be by him. I was relieved when Nani tapped him on the shoulder and asked him to fetch her a heavy Crock-Pot from a high shelf, and someone else took over serving the rice.

I could hear Asher and Nani behind me as they worked away on something. I didn't dare look. I kept my eyes on the naan, on the hungry people in front of me. My stomach hurt, but I knew it wasn't from hunger.

"Asher is *very* tall," I heard Nani say to me.

I tried not to smile. Nani, who was probably too short to go on the adult rides at amusement parks, tended to use the word "tall" when she meant handsome.

"And very sweet." She sidled in closer to me, and I could just make out her profile with my peripheral vision. "So heavy those dishes, and helping us while everyone else is eating . . ." As she trailed off, I knew exactly what she was thinking: how out of the dozens of people helping serve and prepare lunch, Asher was one of the few men. How Nana, no matter how much he had loved her, had not once helped her in the kitchen.

"Is Asher . . ." Nani shook her head. "*Hah.* Never mind. I will not again be interference." She mimed zipping her lips shut, and a beat later, I mimed reopening them.

"He has a girlfriend, Nani, if that's what you're asking."

"So Asher is just *friend*?"

I nodded, leaning in close to whisper, "He also thinks I'm gay."

Nani laughed. "A man cannot be in love with supposedly gay woman?"

"Nani, shhhh!"

"His girlfriend cannot be so pretty the way he is looking at you—"

"Nani!"

"*Kya?* It is merely observation—"

"Can we go back to you not interfering in my life?"

"No," she said, grinning. "Now I am stuck. I am in *the mix*!"

I stepped aside from my post, and took Nani off to the side of the kitchen. She was smiling so much I had to fight the urge to wipe it right off.

"Please don't go getting your hopes up, okay?"

"But why? Is it not obvious—"

"Nani, I've messed up a lot this year. You know that." After she didn't disagree, I continued. "Asher's dating someone. It might even be serious, and I'm not going to insert myself in that. I'm not going to . . . mess that up, too."

She crossed her arms, and I couldn't quite tell if she was yawning or sighing.

"And besides. I'm seeing Jayesh again."

"Really?"

"Yep." I smiled. "We had a nice time. He's very sweet. He knows Shay's wedding is this week, and so he told me to call him after, when I'm free."

"And you plan to?"

I nodded. "We're going to have tacos."

"Taco?"

"You've had tacos, Nani." I rolled my eyes. "It's like a roti, and inside there's meat and salsa and—"

"Hah, hah. I like taco." She pursed her lips together. "They are very messy, *nah*?"

I laughed. "I suppose so."

"You know," she said, resting her palm on my cheek. Her eyes beamed. "Life can be messy, too."

Another day, another ceremony. Shay and Julien had disappeared immediately after the Ganesh puja was over—to where, I wasn't sure—and so I didn't see her until the following evening's *mehndi*—a ladies-only ceremony held to decorate the bride with henna. The entire evening, Shay was stuck in the middle of Auntie Sarla's living room as two artists painted her hands, wrists, and feet with the black ink. She seemed snappy, ill-tempered, and I wanted to ask how she was coping with the wedding stress (clearly not well), but someone always seemed to be within earshot. When I saw her slip into the kitchen, I followed her and found her standing in front of the sink limply scraping off the dried henna into the sink.

"Are you okay?"

She didn't reply, and in silence, I watched as she rubbed her hands together. Her eyes were fixated on the black paste as it crumbled down the drain, and left a sprawl of bright orange on her palm.

"Here." I reached for a platter of samosas. "You must be hungry."

"No, not hungry," she said quietly. Suddenly, she looked up through the glass in the kitchen door. "Shit."

A moment later, Auntie Sarla burst in, glaring at Shay. "I *told* you—you must leave that on all evening." Auntie Sarla lunged for Shay's hands. "*Aacha?* It is all ruined! The color will be gone by ceremony!"

"Ma, it doesn't matter."

Auntie Sarla whipped toward me. "And Raina has taken hers off, too. Of course. Follow *her* example."

"I needed to call Julien. I can't dial the phone with this stuff on my hands—"

Auntie Sarla launched into a tirade in Rajasthani. I kept trying to interrupt, but Auntie Sarla ignored me, and after a few moments, even Shay told me I should leave. I wasn't going to abandon her, but I felt my phone vibrate, and when I pulled it from beneath the strap of my bra, my heart stopped. It was Depesh.

I nearly tripped over my sari as I raced into a quiet room at the back of Shay's house. Deliberately, I clicked answer, and held the phone up to my ear.

"Depo?"

I heard heavy breathing, faint music thumping in the background. I checked my watch. It was the middle of the night in London.

For almost a minute, he didn't speak, and I listened to him breathing, and I tried to work up the courage to say something.

"Where are you?" I finally asked.

"I'm in Hack-*ney*."

I nodded into the phone. He sounded drunk, his words slurring, and with every ounce of me, I prayed that he was safe.

"Are you okay—"

"So this was all about that fucking British guy."

I pressed my hand over my face. "You read my e-mail . . ."

"A *guy*? An ex-boyfriend?"

"It started out that way. I know it doesn't make any sense. I have no excuse—"

"I came out—I fucking came out to my parents—because, because of *you*, because I thought you, but—" He cut off, and I could hear a garble through the phone.

"Depesh, I don't expect forgiveness."

"Good."

"But, I'm always going to be here for you," I said slowly. "You can hate me, but I'm here."

"God. I'm not—not some baby bird that needs taking care of, okay? I don't need you."

"Depo . . ."

"And you don't need me, either, Raina." He laughed. "Apparently all you need is a *boyfriend*."

My ears burned.

"Sorry," he said after a minute. "Sorry, I'm *drunk*."

"No, it's okay. I deserved that."

The music started getting louder through the phone, and I heard shouting behind him.

"I should go."

"Depo, you're being safe? Do your parents know—"

"Yeah, okay? They know where I am—" He paused, and I heard a voice beside him. "I have to go."

"Wait, please. Just one thing."

"What?"

"I know you don't need me. I know you're hurt. But just—just know you can call me anytime. I'm here for you."

He didn't respond.

"Tell me you know I'm still here, Depo." My voice cracked. "Please."

A moment passed. And right before he clicked off, he said, "I know."

THIRTY—ONE

Shay had disappeared by the time I went back into Auntie Sarla's kitchen, so I spent the rest of the *mehndi* with Serena and the other bridesmaids chatting with the aunties, helping to tidy up. Afterward, I found my way back downtown and lay down fully dressed on the bed—but I didn't sleep a wink. I didn't deserve it. I kept my phone plugged in and with the volume turned up next to me the whole night, but it didn't ring. At 4 A.M. I caved and texted Depesh, but there was no answer.

The following night was Shay's final pre-wedding celebration and the eve before the big day: the *sangeet*, or music party, which came well stocked with dinner and dancing, live music and an open bar.

Serena picked me up in her car, and we dropped off our armory of saris, jewelry, and makeup at the hotel. Our room was next door to Nikki and Niti's, and a few floors below Shay's suite—where we'd all get ready together the next morning.

We changed quickly and then made our way into the main ballroom downstairs. Dozens of waiters in uniform bustled around the room fussing with chair covers and centerpieces, sprinkling rose petals and pouring wine. In the corner, Auntie Sarla, clipboard in hand, was instructing a group of waiters.

The guests started to arrive, and Serena and I took up posts at the entrance and handed out programs. Afterward, I tried to find Shay—but she kept disappearing, offering vague and unconvincing excuses. In fact, she had acted strange all evening—all week, really. Watching her at the head table wedged between Auntie Sarla and Julien, a fake smile on her face, I could tell something was wrong. It was more than stress; she looked miserable, even though she should have been the happiest woman in the room. The moment dinner was over, she pushed back her chair and raced out of the hall, and I was right on her heels.

I followed her to the bank of elevators that went up to the guest rooms. "Shay?"

She looked back over her shoulder, just as the elevator door opened.

"What's wrong?"

Her face crumpled, and she stepped into the elevator. "I just need a minute."

"What is it?" I blocked the door with my arm, but she shook her head as I moved to step inside.

"I need a minute—"

"Shay, you're crying. What—"

"Please?" she whispered.

What was going on with Shay? She'd been dealing with overbearing Auntie Sarla for nearly thirty years; this wasn't just wedding stress. It couldn't be.

"Seriously," she sobbed. "Haven't you ever just needed a minute?"

Reluctantly, I pulled back my arm. "You have one minute. Then I'm coming up."

She nodded as the doors closed, and I went back into the hall. I scanned the crowd for Julien, but I couldn't see him. Half of the guests had abandoned their seats for the dance floor, and the live bhangra was in full swing. From across the dance floor I spotted Asher for the first time that evening, his head visible above the crowd. I felt my stomach flutter. He caught my eye and waved. I waved back, and tried not to wonder where Rebekah was. The band was loud, and it seemed like everyone was bouncing along as the female lead singer belted out Punjabi lyrics.

I motioned to Asher to check his phone, and then I texted him.

Where's Julien? It's urgent.

A moment later, he replied.

I don't know. Want me to help you look?

I texted back.

Sure. Let me know when you find him. I'll be in Shay's room.

I put my phone back in my purse and turned around. The crowd was thick around me, and I pushed my way back into the foyer. I reached forward to press the button, and as I was waiting, I felt a hand on my waist.

"Darling."

I whipped around.

"You look *gorgeous*." Dev pulled me in for a hug. "I've been looking for you everywhere."

I couldn't breathe. What was *he* doing here? At Shay's wedding? Back in Toronto?

I suddenly remembered that it was Friday by the colored tie he was wearing. His hair—light black and bristly, a few whisks of gray—was typically parted and in place.

"Took me ages to track you down, and *wow*. And to think—I've never even seen you in a sari."

I was speechless. He tried to reach for me, and I pushed him away. He dropped his arms, studying me as if suddenly I'd become a complex graph; a banking equation it was his mission to solve.

"What happened? I flew in yesterday, and Bill said you—"

"Quit." I crossed my arms. "Yes, I quit."

He sighed, putting his hand around my waist. "Tell me this isn't about us."

"Us? There isn't an 'us.' We haven't spoken in months." I tried to shrug off his hand, but then he wrapped the other one around me, too. "The thing is, Dev, this is the first thing I've done in a while that has nothing to do with *us*—or my nani, or anyone but me."

"Raina, it's been a stressful time for me, and on top of that, you stopped speaking to me, and it *threw* me. It's thrown me right out—"

"I don't want to hear it."

"But I'm staying put at the minute. Don't you see? Don't you see what that means for us? I'll travel still. But I'm based here. Near *you*. Properly now." He smiled and leaned in closer. "Really, love. You didn't have to quit."

"Were you even listening to me?"

"You and I were happy together, weren't we? I love you—"

My head swam, and when he leaned to kiss me, I tried to pull away.

"—I always have."

I felt my cheek against his chin, his hands on the back of my neck, my waist.

"Raina, I *think* I'm ready—"

His lips pressed against mine, and I winced. I was breathing hard when he pulled away. I opened my eyes, my vision blurred, and my lashes stuck together. Finally, everything became clear. But I didn't see Dev. I saw Asher.

"Asher . . ."

Dev spun around. Asher was standing just behind him.

"Sorry, mate. Didn't see you." He extended his hand. "I'm Dev."

Asher's hands didn't move; his eyes didn't leave me.

"You a friend of Raina's?"

I could feel Dev shift beside me, and when he tried to put his arm around me, I flung it away. Asher's face was motionless.

My mind raced. This was wrong. It all felt so wrong. I wanted Asher to hold me, *Asher* to kiss me—the way he had in New York.

"Asher, I—"

He turned on his heels, started walking toward the door, and I followed.

"Raina, where are you going?" I heard Dev cry out, but I kept running after Asher, nearly tripping on the hem of my sari as I tore through the revolving door behind him.

"Asher, wait." I caught up to him, tugged on his shoulder until he turned around. "Please, don't go."

I looked into his eyes, pleading with him. Would he forgive me? Could I say anything—*do* anything—to make it right between us? Take us back to New York, back to midnight.

"Look at me," I whispered. "Please."

A gust of wind tore in from the parking lot—sharp, sandy— and I wrapped the tail of my sari around my arms.

"I know what that looked like. I know what you must think of me, but let me ex—"

"You have no idea what I think about you."

"Please, let me explain. My heart was in the right place, I swear—"

"You're in love with that guy?"

I looked at his hands. They were shaking, and I wanted to reach for them.

"I used to be," I whispered.

"And now?"

"And now . . . I'm falling in love with you." I stepped toward him, but he drew back. One step, and then another.

"I didn't mean it to go this far, I swear. It got out of hand, and I didn't know *what* I was doing." I paused, willing him to look at me. "You asked me once, what I was looking for. What if it's you, Asher? What if we can find it together?"

"I don't know what you want me to say right now."

"I'm not a bad person, it's—"

"I know you're a good person," he said slowly. He wouldn't meet my eye. "I wouldn't have cared for you if you weren't."

"So you do care?" I asked, hoping. Pleading. "You still . . . you *could* still care about me?"

"I'm a simple guy. This—*you*—it's too . . . complicated. I can't." He breathed out, and his voice caught. "I can't do this right now."

"I'm sorry, Asher. Please—"

But he wouldn't look at me, and he kept walking away. "I'm sorry, too."

I didn't want to let him go. But I did. He disappeared behind the hotel, and after ten minutes, I forced myself to realize he wasn't coming back.

Dev was still in the lobby, reclined on a sofa, his legs crossed. Right ankle over left knee, his BlackBerry in hand. He looked up as I approached, and tucked the phone into his pocket. He shifted over on the couch, and I sat down next to him. For a moment neither of us spoke.

"Why did you do that?" I asked him finally.

"Do what?" He moved closer to me. "Darling, who was that?"

"Dev, I'm not your darling. Stop calling me that." He tried to brush a piece of hair behind my ear, and I pressed his hand down. "I want you to just . . . stop."

"Raina . . . what's happening?" I didn't answer, and he intertwined his fingers through mine.

Had it really taken me this long to get here?

"Weren't we happy?" he whispered.

Maybe he really was ready this time, or maybe he wasn't. But finally, I was ready, and I knew I could never go back.

"We *were* happy. But, being with you . . . it's not enough for me." I dropped his hand. "I was just too in love to realize it."

THIRTY—TWO

Shay duped me. She wasn't in her room, and I couldn't find Julien, either. They had disappeared from the *sangeet* without a trace, and the entire night their cell phones kept going straight to voice mail. Serena, the twins, and I searched the lobby, the back rooms, and even drove over to their condo downtown, but we couldn't find them anywhere. Asher had disappeared, and when we asked the other groomsmen, none of them knew where they'd gone, either.

"Maybe they're doing it," Nikki said around 2 A.M., when we ordered room service to refuel. "Maybe they're in the next room, right now, having really raunchy sex."

"You're so immature," Niti said, as she stripped the meat off a chicken wing with her teeth. "They probably just eloped."

Eloped?

"Whatever they're doing, I hope they're okay," Serena said, and I nodded in agreement.

Why had I let her run off? Disappearing like that was so out of character, I feared the worst. Had she not passed her final pediatrics exams? Had someone *died*?

What was she hiding from me?

We decided to try and get a few hours of sleep before the wedding, and it was only as my eyes were fluttering shut that I realized it was my birthday.

That I was thirty.

I drifted in and out of sleep for a few hours until my alarm woke me up. Serena was snoring in the bed next to me, and I reached over and hit the alarm, and then threw pillows at her until she woke up. A few moments later, we crawled out of the room, knocked on Nikki and Niti's door, and the four of us—gowned in hotel slippers and robes, our matching bridesmaids' saris draped over our arms—took the elevator up to the top floor. It was exactly 5 A.M., when we were all supposed to meet to get ready. We arrived at the suite, but when Nikki knocked, no one answered.

"I know she's coming," I said. "I just know it."

"And what if she's not?" Niti asked.

I was thinking of a way to answer that when the elevator bell rang from down the hall, and a moment later Shay emerged. She still had her full hair and makeup from the previous night, and she was wearing a pair of blue-checked pajama pants and the blouse of her sari. She turned her head, and then sulked toward us. Her eyes were red, her long-wear mascara bleeding at the corners.

"Have you been up all night?"

She didn't answer and fished a key card out of her clutch. She jabbed it into the slot. She tried to swing the door behind her, but I caught it and pushed through just in time to see her collapse facedown onto one of the couches.

"Shay?" I sat down beside her.

She turned around slowly, wiping her face with the back of her hand.

"What is it?"

She swallowed loudly, and tears welling in her eyes, she said, "I think the wedding is off."

For twenty minutes Shay just lay there, facedown on the couch, her arms splayed out behind her; I couldn't tell if she was asleep or awake, crying or even breathing.

"Are you ready to talk yet?"

Shay groaned, and shook her head into the pillow. I'd instructed everyone else to start getting ready without us, thinking surely Shay would snap out of it quickly, but I was getting worried.

What had happened? Surely, the wedding wasn't really canceled?

"Shay, tell me—"

"I don't want to talk about it—"

"You know what?" I grabbed her by the waist and yanked her up from the couch. "I don't care. We're talking about it."

Somehow, I managed to get Shay into the bathroom. I locked the door behind us, and when I turned back around, she had seated herself cross-legged on the counter. I stood with my back against the door, waiting for her to speak, but she just looked at her hands.

"Did you and Julien have a fight?"

I saw the tears pooling in her eyes, and then a fat droplet rolled down her cheek. I wiped it away, and her body trembled as I put an arm around her.

"Where is he?"

"I don't know." She wiped her face with the back of her hands.

"Do you want me to call him?"

"He won't answer." She shook her head. "He's *so* mad at me."

"What *happened*?"

She hopped off the counter and started pacing in front of me, her hands on her hips.

"Shay?"

"Don't be mad. Okay? You were so mad at your mom for getting pregnant"—she paused—"and, *well*, so am I."

"Mad?"

"No. Jesus, I'm *pregnant*."

"Oh my God." Tears welled in my eyes. "Shay, you're going to be a mom?"

She shrugged.

I lunged for her, hugged her, squeezed her until she pushed me off. "This is amazing, Shay. Why the hell are you guys fighting?"

"Because I didn't want it to happen yet, Raina! I *just* finished residency. *Just* got some semblance of independence. And then there was my freaking circus wedding to deal with. Finally, I was about to get some pressure off of me."

"These things are unexpected—"

"I'm a doctor. I'm on the pill, Raina! This wasn't supposed to happen yet. I'm not ready."

"You're going to have to be ready."

"That's what Julien said." Shay frowned. "And I got mad and said I wanted an abortion."

"You *do*?"

"Of course I don't want an abortion. I want a baby with him—I just don't want one *now*. And I was angry at Julien because he was *so* excited, but he doesn't have to get stretch marks. He doesn't have to push out a baby." She grabbed a wad of toilet paper and wiped her nose. "We've been fighting all week because he wanted us to go to confession before the wedding, ask for *forgiveness* from his priest—and get married right then in the church. And last night we almost did go. We were practically in the car, and I was so mad—I don't know, hormones—and I know how his whole raging Catholic family feels about it, and I just . . . told him I wanted an abortion."

"And you didn't mean it."

She sniffed. "No."

"Then apologize, Shay. It's simple. Tell him the truth, and apologize."

Was it really that simple? Could every mistake be fixed this way? Falling to one's knees, begging those who you've hurt to forgive you?

Shay knocked over the toilet seat lid and sat down. I handed her more toilet paper; she blew her nose, and handed it back to me. I stuffed it into the pocket of my robe and crouched down next to her.

"Do you remember the night you introduced him to me?"

Shay looked up, nodded slowly.

"I was going to save this for your toast tonight, but, to hell with it. Do you know what he said to me the next morning? He came out of your room and I was in the kitchen making coffee, and he wanted to make you breakfast—do you remember that?"

"He was the first guy to ever make me breakfast."

I nodded, and grabbed her hand. "And I was showing him where the toaster was, the sugar, the milk, and then he stopped and looked at me, and said, 'Raina, I'm going to marry that girl.'"

Shay's face crumpled.

"Almost six years later, and you two are *happy*, Shay. You're a family."

"And what's our family going to be like, huh?" Shay sniffled. "Am I going to turn into my mean, manipulative mother"—she gestured around the room—"and host lavish parties just so everyone knows how *rich* we are?"

"First of all, you are nothing like Auntie Sarla." I smiled. "Secondly, the thing about starting a family, Shay, is you get to choose what it's going to be like." I fished my phone out of my robe pocket and handed it to her. "You and Julien get to be whoever the hell you want to be."

At eight thirty, Auntie Sarla and a flock of her friends and relatives started arriving, wedging themselves into the love seats and onto the room's surfaces. The makeup artist finished with me and moved onto Serena, and a second later, a hairstylist named Claire appeared, grunted hello, and started to roughly comb my hair. She angled my chair into the room's corner—so she could more easily reach her curling iron—and I couldn't see anybody.

I heard noises escalating behind me, more and more aunties arriving. Every time I tried to turn my head to see whether Nani had arrived yet, Claire sharply yanked my head back.

A few aunties came by and said their hellos, offered me tea or juice, and then quickly disappeared again. I could hear everyone fussing over Shay on the opposite end of the room, her fake placating voice agreeing to every suggestion as they tied her sari, ensured every curl was perfectly pinned onto her head. I laughed to myself, and wished Claire would hurry up. I reached up and felt my hair, but only half of it was curled and pinned back—the other half still in a limp mess by my shoulders.

"Is there a problem?" Claire snapped.

"Just wondering how much longer." I smiled. "I still have to put on my sari."

She rolled her eyes. "Well, next time tell the bride not to make the wedding so goddamn early."

"It wasn't her choice," I said softly, although Claire had already stopped listening.

I could feel the room filling up even more; it was becoming fiercely hot, and I regretted not changing out of my flannel pajamas and bathrobe before everyone arrived.

"Could someone open a window?" I said to no one in particular. The air-conditioning was on, but the room felt like a sauna. "Please?"

An auntie appeared beside me. "Already open—we have called for fan."

I thanked her, and she disappeared from my peripheral vision.

I was becoming more restless with each passing minute. I wanted to help Shay get ready, make sure she was still okay, but the progress of my updo had stalled. Claire dropped her hands from my head to grab her coffee, and I took the opportunity to turn around.

Shay's relatives surrounded her. Her makeup and hair seemed to be done, and she was sitting at the foot of the bed half dressed in her petticoat and blouse. Auntie Sarla was standing over her, and they seemed to be whispering loudly at each other in Rajasthani. Shay looked like she was about to cry again, and it was as if the aunties around them—steaming her bridal sari, lazily primping her hair—hadn't even noticed.

I stood up and walked toward them, ignoring the hairdresser's protests.

"What's going on?"

Auntie Sarla's eyes flicked toward me as she continued yelling at Shay. Then she stopped, and glaring at me, said, "*Nothing*, Raina."

Shay stood up. "Don't speak to her like that."

"Auntie, did I do something?"

"What haven't you done?"

"Ma!"

"Auntie, please tell me—"

"It's fine," Shay said. "I handled it."

"Handled what?" The rest of the room seemed to have quieted. They were listening to us.

"Some of my more *conservative* relatives from India"—Shay said evenly—"didn't come this morning to help me get ready, and—"

"Because of *you*, Raina," snapped Auntie Sarla. "You are ruining Shaylee's wedding—"

"Shut it, Ma—"

"Yes, *shut it*, Sarla."

Nani had appeared in the doorway. For a woman so small, it was as if she was suddenly taking up the whole room. She smiled at me, and then Shay, and then her eyes pivoted back toward Sarla.

"Are you really going to start again with this now?" Nani asked Sarla.

"Your Raina is ruining—"

Shay groaned. "Raina is not ruining my wedding, *you* are, Ma!"

"Me?" Auntie Sarla cackled. "You have me to thank for this whole wedding—"

"I didn't want this! You think I wanted some hyper-religious ceremony where I'm not even allowed to kiss the groom?" Shay's eyes filled up again, and her voice had grown hoarse. "I did this for you, for Dad—and you know that—"

Auntie Sarla snapped an interjection, and her arms flailed wildly.

"English *please*," I said.

Shay rolled her eyes. "Oh, she's just mad the attention isn't on *her*—"

"Ungrateful child," spat Auntie Sarla.

"I'm ungrateful?" Shay exclaimed. "I did *everything* you and Dad ever asked of me. I was perfect, I'm having your *perfect* wedding—and still, this isn't enough. You want the attention on me? You got it. Julien and I almost eloped last night. How's that for attention?"

"Elopement," repeated Auntie Sarla. "But *vhy*?"

"Because this goddamn thing is a nightmare! Because we already *live* together! Because we wanted a small wedding and I'm . . . I'm *fucking* pregnant!"

Auntie Sarla gasped, and echoes followed behind her. She collapsed onto the bed, and an auntie started to fan her with a magazine. She started mumbling something in Rajasthani incoherently, and Shay rolled her eyes.

"Ma. Are you okay?"

Auntie Sarla didn't reply, and Shay squatted down beside her.

"Ma? I'm sorry, I—"

"*Pregnant*. Shaylee!" She sat up slowly, unsteadily, her plump face flushed like a plum. "How did this happen?"

"I sat on a dirty toilet seat."

I snorted out a laugh. Shay started laughing, too. Auntie Sarla stood up, and pinned her glare onto me.

"This is *your* doing?"

"Huh?"

"You and your nani. And that dirty Manavi—whole family *always* causing trouble—"

"Ma, you're going to be a *nani*—"

"*You* were bad influence on my Shaylee—"

"Don't blame Raina for Shaylee's actions," said Nani.

"This is all Raina's doing—ever since she decided to be lesbian, nothing but hassle, difficulty for everyone. And I hear now Sharon's boy is gay, too? What did you do to him?"

"Hush, Sarla! This is not right. This is your daughter's wedding, *nah*?"

"When is the time then?" spat Auntie Sarla. "When all the kids have turned gay? When Raina marries another girl? When there are two bridal saris to tie? I will not be there to help, Suvali. No one will be there!"

As the yelling around me escalated, billowed, the dullness in the pit of my stomach mushroomed, and I just couldn't take it. I had to stop it.

"Everyone, be quiet!"

In a moment, the room was silent. Still. And everyone was staring at me. I could feel the sweat that had started to run down the base of my spine. I glanced at Shay. She smiled at me. Nodded. I took a breath, and finally I said it.

"I'm not . . . gay."

My fists were clenched tightly, and I loosened them. My vision blurred, refocused. Still, the room was silent.

"*What?*" cried Auntie Sarla.

"You're not?" said Serena.

I shook my head, and turned to face Nani. Her eyes were on the floor, and she had pressed her hands into the doorway on either side of her, but she was smiling.

"Why would you lie about something like this?" asked an auntie nearby; my ears were ringing, and I couldn't tell which one it was.

"I just wanted everyone to stop telling me to get married, and setting me up on dates." My voice trembled, and I pressed on. "It wasn't supposed to go this far. And then, I just wanted people to know that it shouldn't have mattered. I didn't want it to matter."

"But you're not," said Serena.

I shook my head.

"Well," said Auntie Sarla. She was smiling. "This is good news. *Some* good news."

"Ma," Shay said. "That's not the point. The point is that it shouldn't matter even if she was gay."

"But she's not!"

"Yes, Ma. I know. But why does it matter one way or the other?"

"Of *course* it matters."

"Are you kidding me? Wake up, *Mother*, it's the twenty-first century. People screw before—"

"Shaylee!"

"—they get married. People are straight, others are gay. What concern is it to you?"

"She's right, Sarla," said another auntie. "My nephew in Winnipeg is of the gay now."

"Ma, don't you see how backward you are? That you're . . ."

The room again became a commotion: silence replaced with horrified and bemused looks; Auntie Sarla's intermittent sobs and screams, and shouts from back and forth across the room. It was mayhem, and I looked down at Nani in disbelief. The vivacious glimmer was back in her eyes.

"It is good these people are hassled sometimes, *nah*?" I heard Nani say to me as I walked over to her. She slipped her hand into mine. "It was good for me, too. To think about things—think about *these* things."

I gave Nani's hand a squeeze while we watched the commotion unfold before us.

"Sarla is a loud woman. But she is screaming for a reason." Nani looked up at me, as if she knew that I was thinking about Depesh. Wondering how he was faring in London at that very moment, and how much he would have hated all of this. "Sarla knows she is losing. Our people are growing, changing—and that *silly* woman will soon be the only one left to resist. You *have* helped, my Raina."

But had I helped more than I'd hurt? I could only hope that was true.

"Raina," Nani said, after a moment had passed. "Are you expecting . . . *guest*?

"What do you mean?"

"Well," she said slyly. "When I arrived, there was a *very* tall young man waiting just outside the door."

My heart leaped.

"It *may* have been that Asher character . . ."

I tried not to give anything away, but I couldn't help it.

"*Jao*." Nani winked. "I will handle Sarla."

I slipped outside the room. Asher was just down the hallway, pacing back and forth in front of the bank of elevators. He stopped short as I walked toward him. It was my first time seeing him in a kurta pajama. Jet black with red and gold embroidery along the chest and cuffs. A crimson scarf hooked loosely around his neck. He looked so handsome, and when he caught my eye, it was all I could do not to buckle in front of him.

Draco sat in his arms, and he looked down at it. "Julien wanted me to give this to Shaylee."

I nodded, taking it from him. Behind me, Sarla let out another wail.

"What's going on in there?"

"I'm not sure you want to know. It's pretty . . . complicated." I shrugged. "And you said you were a simple guy . . ."

He grinned, and stuffed his hands into his pockets. "I did say that, didn't I?"

"Last night—" I bit my lip, and looked down. He didn't want to hear about my past, my excuses—and I realized that I didn't want to tell him. I wanted to move on. I wanted to make the most of the mess I'd created, and help clean it up—help those I'd hurt—in any way they'd let me.

And I wanted Asher. It had taken me too long to realize it, to recognize the simplicity of happiness when it was standing right in front of me. With Asher, I was ready to push past who I'd become, the mistakes I had made. I was ready—really ready to be the woman I knew I could be. A granddaughter, a daughter, a true friend; roles I'd often neglected in the past.

With Asher, I could be the woman who didn't lose herself to love.

"Would you like to have coffee with me sometime?"

A look of surprise washed over his face, and then he smiled.

"I know you're with someone—"

"I'm not with anyone."

I pressed my lips together, trying to keep from smiling.

"Rebekah and I broke up."

"I'm sorry to hear that."

"You don't look that sorry . . ."

I grinned. "Will you have coffee with me or not?"

His eyes moved up my face. "Are you going to wear your hair like that?"

I touched my head. My hair was still half done—part curled and pinned, the rest of it hanging straight over my ear.

"It's how the kids wear it these days."

"And those pajamas, wow." He nodded. "Sexy as hell."

"I like to keep up with the trends."

He grinned. "Is that so."

I nodded. "I'll take you to this trendy, hipster café I know. You'll love it."

"You know me so well." He smiled, and crossed his arms. "On the other hand, I'm not sure I know you as well as I thought."

"You probably know me better than I know myself."

"I'll have to teach you all about *Raina Anand*, will I?"

"Sure. I hear you're a good teacher. Although not so good at basketball."

"And where did you hear that?" He stepped toward me. "If you're not nice, you'll have to buy me two coffees. Three, even."

"I have to buy them? I don't know, Asher, I'm currently unemployed."

"So now who's the drifter?"

"How about . . . I'll buy you *one* coffee, and dessert? I won't even shove you into them."

"Really? Dessert, too?" He was right in front of me, inches away.

"Anything you want."

He licked his lips, moved in closer. "Anything?"

I could feel the heat of his body against mine. Pepper. Earth. Aftershave. I couldn't move. Slowly, he put his hands on my hips, started to lean in.

"So coffee sometime?" I was breathing hard. "It's a . . . date?"

"A date . . ."

I closed my eyes, and I felt his breath on my ear. My cheek. My lips.

"I'll have to check my schedule."

I opened my eyes. He was grinning at me.

"You're terrible."

"I'm a very busy man, Raina."

"You're going to make me pay for this, aren't you?"

The elevator bell rang, and a moment later, the doors opened. He got in, slowly turned around, and smiled at me. "Would you expect any less?"

I had to force myself not to jump in after him. Not to rush this. I knew I had a long way to go. With Asher—with everyone in my life. But right now, as I stood face-to-face with the man that I loved, I knew that I would be just fine.

May 20, 2019

Shay's bridal sari weighs nearly twenty pounds. She is made up like a Rajasthani doll, perspiring through the thick garment of a deep red *bandhani* design. The aunties adorn her with garlands and gold jewelry; shower her with praise, religious tokens, and blessings. While the hotel room is crowded and sickeningly hot, Nani has regained control, subdued Auntie Sarla's sobbing. No one mentions the pregnancy.

At the end of the preparations, Shay looks like a bride—one that could be plastered on the front cover of a Hindi magazine, or play the leading lady in a Bollywood movie. Raina squeezes her hand as Shay takes one last look in the mirror. Shay looks nothing like herself—her style bent to the will of her mother, her face made up to a point of artificial beauty. Any other day, Shay and Raina would have laughed at the image, ridiculed the excess and extravagance of it all, but today they decide against it.

The ceremony takes place in the lavish hotel hall, the bride, groom, and their families seated on a crisp white altar at the front of the room. Shay and Julien are perched on the carpeted surface on either side of the priest, who is performing the rituals in Sanskrit before a small sacred fire.

With few exceptions, this is the way Raina has always seen marriage—couples binding themselves to each other with the exchange of dark red and ivory flower garlands, measured laps around the flames. Raina watches attentively, with renewed interest, as the couple carries out the rituals. They pour water over a rock, then make offerings of rice to the flames. The priest ties Shay's *chunni* to the end of the thick, amber-red scarf draped over Julien's shoulders, a pledge of their love for each other. A literal nuptial knot.

Then, he instructs them to stand up and take seven symbolic steps. Food, strength, prosperity, wisdom. Progeny. Health. And then the seventh step: friendship. After, Julien dips his thumb into a small clay bowl and dabs red powder—the *sindoor*—above Shay's brow, marking her as a married woman.

Raina's face crumples. Shay and Julien are married, and she is deeply happy for them.

The couple moves to the front of the altar. The flower girls have passed around wicker baskets brimmed with rose petals, and the guests—all one thousand of them—line up to shower the happy couple with blessings. It is a more communal ending to a wedding ceremony than a kiss, but it is tradition, and the guests come forward to toss the petals as Shay and Julien hold hands: plastic figurines on a wedding cake. The last wave of guests makes their way to the front, and the steady stream of petals dies down. Shay and Julien look at each other, as if unsure what comes next. But then in one swift motion, Shay's eyes twinkling, she kisses him.

For a moment, the hall is soundless. Someone gasps, and then giggles emerge from the back of the hall. Raina's eyes flicker toward Auntie Sarla, who appears to be in physical pain, both of her hands folded over her mouth. Raina looks back at the couple. They are still kissing—passionately, eagerly—and without hesitation, Raina starts to clap. She cheers, lets out a whooping roar, causing some of the guests to turn and stare. But Raina doesn't stop. She hears Asher's voice join in, and in quick succession, cheering comes from the rest of the groomsmen, plus Serena, Zoey, and Alice. Others follow, and then more, until at least half of the guests are thundering with applause. Julien grabs Shay by the waist, dips her in front of the entire room as he kisses her.

And just like that, they have created a ripple. More fodder for their guests' gossip, morphing a tradition and making it their own.

A light lunch, and then the wedding party is herded into limos, shuttled from one photo shoot location to another. Shay and Julien in front of St. Basil's Church, a family photo on the college grounds, and then another in the shade of Falconer Hall. Julien and his groomsmen posed beneath arches, atop rail tracks at Union Station. The last shot of the day: Shay and the bridesmaids perched on benches at Toronto Music Gardens. After, as she's about to stand up, Raina feels two large, warm hands cover her eyes, and instinctively, she leans back against his stomach, breathes him in. A moment later, Asher peels away his hands, and a small chocolate birthday cake—stabbed through with fistfuls of thin pink candles—has appeared on her lap.

"It's your favorite," says Shay, smiling down at her. "But I'm a pregnant woman, so you have to share."

Raina stands up to hug her, setting the cake down on the bench. "Thank you."

"For the cake?" Shay pulls away smiling, and then flicks her eyes toward Asher. "Or for introducing you to him?"

Startled, Raina remembers that Shay had tried to set them up from the very beginning. That Shay had known the kind of man Raina had wanted, even before she realized it for herself.

"For both," Raina says eventually. "And for being my best friend."

The evening reception has already begun by the time they return to the hall. The hours blur together: food, drinking, music, and dancing. Raina is quickly immersed, but her mind, her heart, are not fully present. She notices her nani circling the room, obscured behind a fake smile, hiding how much she misses her daughter. She sees Auntie Sarla seated beside Shay at the head table, staring at her hands, as if the perfect wedding she's created is still not enough. She sees Depesh's parents avoiding everyone's glances, rushing through their meal and then leaving the reception early.

Raina also sees the gossip. It's hard not to. The rumors have already spread, and everyone knows Depesh is gay, and that Raina is not. Amid the cocktails, the perspiration steaming off the dance floor, the samosas and *papdi chaat* are the whispers. The lingering stares. Emboldened by alcohol, many have even confronted Raina. "What were you thinking?" they ask her, and Raina responds with the truth. She has nothing left to hide.

Some in her community are insulted, furious—while others roll their eyes and laugh. Raina tackles the questions they throw at her while standing in line at the bar, eating dinner, or on her way to the ladies' restroom. She finds that most aren't disgusted like Auntie Sarla—but neither are they as modern or as accepting as her nani. Rather, they treat the news like the latest plot twist in one of their Bollywood movies, gossip that will be forgotten in time for the next episode. Like her nani said, the community is changing—reluctantly, sluggishly—but they are changing.

The party is exhausting. Raina excuses herself from the table, and wanders outside onto the terrace encircling the hotel. The sky is clear, the wind cool yet soft. She walks, timing her breath with her step. She turns a corner, and is surprised to see she's not alone.

Depesh has his chin in his hands, and his elbows rest against the railing. He is staring out at the view—a parking lot, a building construction site. He's wearing jeans, a checked shirt, and his travel backpack sits at his feet. Her heart quickens as she steps toward him.

"You're back."

The slightest sound escapes his lips, and then he shakes his head. Raina studies his face, but he keeps looking ahead. She leans on the railing next to him.

"How was your trip?"

Still, he doesn't reply. He drops his arms from the railing and crosses them.

She knew it wouldn't be easy; she knew facing him again would be hard on both of them.

"Should I leave you alone?"

After a moment, he shakes his head. "Have you seen my parents?" he asks softly.

"I'm sorry . . . I saw them leave early."

He laughs. "Of course they did. Perfect." He picks up his bag. "There's no point for me to stick around—"

"I'm sure Shay and Julien would love to say hello," she says. "They'll be really happy you came."

He hesitates, slowly slides his bag over his shoulder. "You want me to go in there?"

"I think you should. But what do I know?"

"Everyone knows?"

Raina nods. "Everyone knows—about you. And about me."

"Well, a congratulations is in order for you, too, hey?" says Depesh, his voice edged. "You're straight again. I'm sure someone inside has a good match for you with a good Indian boy."

She presses her lips together. Raina knows he's angry, hurt—and he has the right to be. She doesn't know what to say, so she doesn't respond.

After a moment, Depesh drops his bag. "I'm sorry. I'm being a jerk."

Raina shrugs. "It's okay."

"Caleb and I are over." He turns away from her, pushes himself against the railing. "We broke up this morning."

Hesitantly, she reaches out for him. When he doesn't flinch, she rests her hand on his shoulder. "Are you okay?"

Again, he laughs.

"You didn't want to stay and have a gap year?"

"That's what Caleb wanted."

"And you?"

His mouth quivers. "He's just a boy, right? It's not the end of the world, it's . . . it's for the best"—Depesh nods earnestly, as if convincing himself—"and who knows, maybe we'll get back together down the road. When we're older. When I've figured things out."

"You're strong, Depesh. Stronger than I ever was."

He shrugs.

"I'm really proud of you."

"You keep saying that, but I don't even know why. I study hard because I care about my future. I was with Caleb because I love him." He grimaced. "I came back because I love my parents. I'm just living. I'm just doing what I want to do. It's simple. So what's there to be proud of, huh?"

"Gay. Straight. Indian. *Not* Indian." She moves closer to him. "Not everyone is brave enough to be themselves."

He doesn't answer.

"There's a lot to be proud of."

They stand there, leaning against the balcony, eyes searching the jagged skyline. Bhangra music pulses louder behind them. From the noise, Raina discerns the joyous cries of Shay and Julien celebrating to the music; the children dancing, playing; aunties and uncles chattering.

It is the sound of their community, of their family.

"What's it like in there?" Depesh asks after a moment.

"Auntie Sarla's inside," Raina answers. "But so is my nani. So is everyone else." She tries to catch his eye, wills him to understand.

Slowly, he reaches down for his backpack, and looks over.

"Are you ready?"

After a moment, he nods, and together they go back inside.

Raina's To-Do List

~~Pick up dry cleaning~~ DONE

~~Book our flights to Philadelphia~~ Leaving YYZ
7:30 a.m. October 16-23

Buy eggplant, 3 onions (white), and XL bag basmati for
Sunday cooking lessons ☺

Make reservation for Sunday (tacos??)
us + Asher + Depesh and parents

Attend university career fair (and keep your
chin up)

Pick out baby shower invites for Shay
"that aren't lame"

Organize double date w/Serena & Jayesh—
now who's the matchmaker? heh, heh

Make veg-friendly appies for Zoey/Alice's
housewarming

~~Finally beat Asher at basketball . . .~~

You'll never beat me, babe

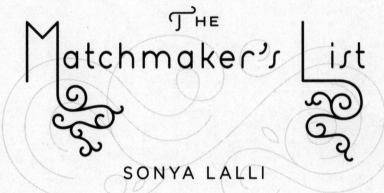

SONYA LALLI

DISCUSSION QUESTIONS

1. Why do you think Raina agrees to let her nani play matchmaker? If you were in Raina's situation, would you let your grandmother (or another family member) set you up?

2. In chapter one, Raina thinks "a man unmarried in his thirties was fine—but for me, it wouldn't be." Have you ever experienced a similar double standard in your own life?

3. Raina's first matchmaking date is with Vishal, who agrees to meet her because he is afraid to stand up to his mother about his relationship with a non-Indian woman. Do you think this sort of thing happens a lot?

4. What date was your favorite? Why?

5. Raina is under so much pressure to get married, she lets her nani believe she is gay to avoid having to go on more dates. Do you sympathize with her in any way, or do you think she is wrong to lie to her grandmother?

6. Why do you think Shaylee is so upset that Raina has been drifting from her, especially when she learns that Raina has been lying about her sexuality to others? Would you ever resort to such behavior with your best friend to avoid confronting the problems between you?

7. Although hurt, Depesh ultimately forgives Raina for lying to him. Do you think she deserves to be forgiven?

8. Raina has a very close relationship with her nani. What in their family history has made them this way?

9. Why do you think Raina holds on to Dev for so long and is so resistant to considering a non-Indian man like Asher? Do you think Raina and Asher are a good match?

10. Do you think it is a good idea for Raina to quit her job before she knows what she wants to do next? Why do you think she works so hard as an investment analyst, even though her heart is never in it?

11. Why do you think Auntie Sarla and others in Raina's community are slow to understand and support homosexuality? Are there similar divides in social attitudes and awareness within your community?

Sonya Lalli is a Canadian writer of Indian heritage. She studied law in her hometown of Saskatoon and at Columbia University in New York, and later completed an MA in Creative Writing and Publishing at City, University of London. Sonya has a black belt in Tae Kwon Do and loves travel, yoga, and cocktail bartending. She lives in Toronto with her husband.

Ready to find
your next great read?

Let us help.

Visit prh.com/nextread

Penguin
Random
House